No Guarantees

S. Easley

Writers Club Press
San Jose New York Lincoln Shanghai

No Guarantees

Published by Writers Club Press
an imprint of iUniverse.com, Inc.

For information address:
iUniverse.com, Inc.
620 North 48th Street
Suite 201
Lincoln, NE 68504-3467
www.iuniverse.com

ISBN: 0-595-00962-X

Printed in the United States of America

Also by S. Easley, *The Shake*

Acknowledgements

I would like to thank my sister for inspiring me to write. I would like to thank my mother and father for being wonderful, loving parents who have always supported everything I have done. I wouldn't be the person I am today without them. I would like to thank my wonderful wife for inspiring me everyday. I love you sweetie. I would like to thank my fraternity brother Shawn and Dr. Reginald Martin for helping me edit this novel. Finally I would like to send a shout out to all of my friends that I have kicked it with over the years: Stefan, Phil, Spears, Chill-Will, Terrance, Kevin G., Vincent, K-Mac, Cameroon, Fadale, Eric, Brent, Randall, Steve, Marcus, Cha-Ron, Goldie, Mac. G., Virgil, Corey, Phillip H., Ike, Marcus, Fry, D. Miles, El, Frank D., Beavie, Spraggs, Cedric, D. Brown and all of my Alpha Brothers. A-PHI !!

Chapter One

Damn! Another thing to worry about. I swear I got more problems. I am only 21, and I promise you if things don't change, I will have an ulcer before I turn 22.

My name is Raymond Horne, and everybody calls me Horne. I am a young black man from the suburbs. Some people think that only people from the hood have problems, but I am living proof that people from the suburbs have problems too. My problems may be a little different, but still the same, enough to drive me crazy.

It all started in elementary school. Nah...let's skip through the pre-liminaries and get right down to it. It really started two summers ago. I was attending college in Memphis, Tennessee, and I was home for summer break. I had finally convinced Shirl to go out on a 'real' date with me. You see, Shirl and I had become real close friends our first two years in college. Shirl was about 5'3, lightly complected, and had very long hair. She was very cute, and she had a real nice frame.

I had been trying to get with Shirl for about three months and she was always tripping. Talking about we were too good of friends, and that it would mess up our friendship if we were to date. I said forget that because I didn't care about messing up our friendship. I had too many friends and not enough lovers. I couldn't remember the last time that I had got me some.

Well anyway, this was the night. The night I was going to impress the
hell out of Shirl and I went all out. I bought me a new black outfit, and
I bought her a dozen roses. It was going to be on.

Eight o'clock rolled around and it was time for me to pick her up. She
lived about twenty minutes from my house. I was nervous as hell
because I really wanted this to be a great night, and maybe I would even
get lucky. I arrived at Shill's crib at 8:25. There were three cars already
there. This was odd because her family only had two cars. I figured that
her parents were probably having company. I got out of the car and
walked toward the door. I was feeling confident. I had my smooth
threads on, a little dab of cologne behind my ears, a fresh haircut, a
dozen roses in my hand, money in my pocket, and a spearmint Cert in
my mouth. I was ready!

I knocked on the door and waited for someone to answer it. After a
minute or so, Shirl came to the door, and she was looking good! She had
on a pink sundress and was smelling good as hell. I could tell that this
was going to be a good night.

"Hey, Shirl, you look so pretty," I said, as I stared into her eyes. "These
roses are for you." I gave the roses to her and she had the biggest smile
on her face. Before I could blink, she had leaned over and gave me a hug
and a kiss on the cheek. My heart was beating so fast I thought I was
going to fall out.

"Horne. Hey, Horne, are you all right? Thanks for the roses."

"You're more than welcome, Shirl. You ready to go?"

"Horne, I need to tell you something. My uncle and aunt came in
town today and my cousin came along with them."

So her cousin was here. What was she trying to say, that she couldn't
go? If she couldn't go, I was going to be pissed because I had the whole
evening planned. I bought these damn roses, a new outfit, and some
new cologne. The two of us were going out alone and that was all to it.

"Oh, so your cousin came. Well, I'd like to meet your cousin before
we leave."

"Horne, we have a little problem."

"What's wrong?"

"I can't go and leave my cousin here by herself," she said, and I thought about how all my plans were about to be ruined.

"Shirl, you mean we're not going to be able to go?" I said very excitedly, and Shirl stood there looking around for a minute as if she was trying to think of something to say. While she stood there, I couldn't help but check her out. She was so damn sexy, and I wanted her so bad. I know we were good friends, but it was time to take it to the next level. Hopefully, that was going to happen tonight. Why did she have to have any cousins anyway?

"Horne, maybe she could come too. We could show her around town."

"I was hoping to make this night special."

"You were? Well, maybe you can call one of your friends to keep my cousin company," she said, and I didn't want to, but I really didn't want her to cancel the entire date either.

"I'll try to call somebody," I said, and I hated having to say those words.

"OK. Come on in and use the phone. Horne, I'm really sorry. I didn't know my cousin was coming, and you know I couldn't just leave her here."

"Yeah, you're right. Let me call one of my friends."

"OK, I'll be back. I'm going to get my cousin," she said, and I hoped her cousin looked good, so whoever I called wouldn't be tripping. If she looked anything like Shirl, she was a total fox. I decided to call my friend Stevall. He was cool, nice, and was probably the safest bet because all my other friends were sort of foolish. In fact, Stevall was a virgin. He was twenty years old and still a virgin. This was a rarity in this day and age. I called him and he was with it. Soon thereafter, Shirl came back in the room.

"You call a friend?"

"Yeah, Stevall said he would go."

"That's good. Belinda, come on out here," Shirl said, and the next thing I knew, this gigantic girl came out the back. I mean she was very big and very tall. She had to be about 6'0 tall and weighed about 230. She looked like a big ass weight lifter. Oh Lord, what have I gotten Stevall into, I thought to myself.

"This is my cousin, Belinda. Belinda, this is Horne." Shirl said, and she and her cousin both had grins on their faces.

"Hey, Belinda, how are you?" I said, still amazed by how damn big she was. Stevall wasn't going to be too happy with me once he saw Big Belinda.

Chapter Two

I had to change my plans some since Belinda and Stevall were going with us, and the more I looked at Belinda, the better she looked. She was big, but she wasn't really fat. She was just very thick. Maybe Stevall would like her. Hell, he was desperate as hell to finally get some anyway, and she wasn't all that ugly.

We decided to go to a club and everybody was old enough except Stevall. He was only twenty, but he had a fake ID. Stevall was supposed to meet us at the club, and hopefully his fake ID would work.

When we arrived at Club Ralph's, the place was packed. "Horne," Shirl said, "is Stevall here yet? I'm tired of waiting."

"Nah, but he should be here in a few minutes," I said, and Stevall was taking a little long. The ladies were getting impatient and Belinda kept staring at me. It was sort of making me nervous.

"So, you're Horne. I heard a lot about you," Belinda said, breaking her silent stare.

"I hope you heard good things," I said, not really knowing what to say.

"Yes, they were good things, and by looking at you, I can tell they were true," Belinda said, and looked at me as if she wanted to jump my bones. I was really tripping because Big Belinda was coming on to me, and her cousin couldn't even pick up on what she was doing. Meanwhile, Stevall had finally arrived.

"What's up, everybody?"

"What's up, Stevall?"

Stevall looked around and spoke to Shirl, and then looked up and said "Hi" to Belinda. Stevall was 5'9 and real skinny, so Belinda looked like a linebacker next to him.

Stevall looked at me and said, "Let me holler at you for a second."

"What's up?"

"Man, she is big as hell!"

"Stevall, she ain't that bad, and I think she may be a freak. Maybe you will get you some."

"That's all you think about, Horne. When I do have sex, I don't want it to be with a big ass girl I hardly know," Stevall said, and I could tell already I was going to have to put some peer pressure on him. Stevall was a sucker for peer pressure.

"Man, come on. You won't never get any at this rate."

"Maybe I don't want any."

"Oh, so you like men now?"

"Hell naw!"

"Come on, Stevall, and go out with this girl!"

"I don't know."

"I promise you she will look better after a few drinks anyway."

"Okay, but your ass is going to owe me big time."

After I convinced Stevall, we got Shirl and Belinda and went to the door. Club Ralph's was a very nice club. It was a club that both blacks and whites went to, and a few white girls were at the door. They looked about 17 or 18, and they didn't even get carded, so I wasn't worried about Stevall getting in. As soon as we got to the door, two big security guards asked us for ID. This was messed up because they had just let those young looking girls in, but they carded us and we looked a hell of a lot older than them. Anyway, we all took our ID's out, including Stevall's fake. When Stevall gave the man his ID, he stared at it for about five minutes. I was nervous because I really wanted to get into the club so I could make a move on Shirl. "I'm sorry, we can't accept this," the man at the front door said.

I couldn't believe it. The fake didn't work. They had just let those two young ass girls in. Why didn't they card them? I was really getting mad. "Excuse me, why didn't those girls get carded?" I asked, and the security guards all looked at me like I was crazy.

"Come on, Horne, let's go," Stevall said.

"Naw, man, this is some bullshit. I want to know why we got carded and those young ass girls didn't," I said, and the men at the door were still looking at me crazy, and then one of them spoke.

"You need to get your friend and go before I call the police," he said, and when he said that, Stevall and Shirl both grabbed me and told me to come on. I was ready to go, but I wasn't quite finished telling the security guards how I felt.

"Hell naw! This is bullshit!" I said, and the man at the door picked up the phone and started dialing. At this point, I knew it was time to go. I cursed a couple more times, and then we left. Shirl and Stevall were both mad at me for acting a fool, but big Belinda thought it was funny.

My night had been messed up from the beginning. I hadn't even had a chance to mack up on Shirl. I had one bad habit, and it was time to indulge in it. Drinking. After arguing about the club incident, we decided to get some beer and go to the lake.

The night wasn't going that well for me so far, but I wasn't going to give up yet. When we arrived at the lake, I grabbed a few beers and asked Shirl if she wanted to walk up to the picnic area with me. She said yes, so we left Belinda and Stevall there alone. Stevall didn't seem too thrilled about this, but I was thrilled because Shirl and I were finally going to be alone. I couldn't stop looking at her. She was perfect.

"Horne, I just want to tell you again that I am really sorry that I messed up all of your plans. I really didn't know my cousin was coming."

"That's okay. At least we are alone now."

The moon was out, and Shirl looked like a super star under its light. I had been waiting for this moment for a very long time, and I was determined to take advantage of it.

"Shirl, you are so damn sexy," I said, and she looked at me in a weird way.

"What? What did you say?" she asked, and I looked into her eyes. I was nervous, scared and excited, but I knew that I wanted to be with her.

"I said, Damn, you look so sexy," I said, and she started smiling and looked at the ground. "I know we are good friends, but I'm ready to take it to the next level."

"I'm not ready, Horne. I'm still in love with Eric." Eric was Shirl's ex-boyfriend. They had been together for two years, but they had broke up two months ago. I couldn't stand that fool because he used to dog Shirl out.

"Forget that punk, Shirl. He ain't no good. You got to move on."

"I know, but…"

"But nothing, Shirl. He ain't no good and I am! Besides, I know you have some feelings for me."

"I care a lot about you, Horne, but I'm still not ready."

It got real quiet. I had already drunk about three beers, and Shirl had drunk one. I liked the fact that she liked beer and she knew about sports. You didn't meet too many women like that. We just sat there drinking beers and not talking. I drank two more beers, and she drank one more. I was starting to get a buzz, and I knew she was.

"Shirl, I'm sorry I said those things about Eric. Here, have another beer," I said, breaking the silence. I was hoping that I could get her really buzzed and maybe she would get a little loose. I knew that this was wrong, but I was getting desperate.

Shirl took the beer and started guzzling it and I could tell that she was buzzed. Three beers was about all her small frame could handle, and it was time for me to make my second move. I moved a little closer to her and started rubbing my hand through her hair. She didn't say anything about my hand. She just started talking about a lot of different things. I sat there continuing to rub my hand through her hair while I listened to her talk and watched her drink another beer.

"Yeah, Horne, and then Angela told him…," she said, just rambling about everything.

"Shirl, Shirl. Sssh, slow down. You're talking too much," I said, and she started laughing, and I started kissing her all over her face. Small, soft kisses.

"Horne, what are you doing?"

"I'm just trying to make you feel good."

"Horne," she said softly, and I just kept kissing her and caressing her back. Shirl wasn't saying anything now. She started rubbing the back of my neck. Before I knew it, we were kissing. Not only were we kissing, but we were tonguing. I couldn't believe it. I had been wanting to do this for so long. It was like I was dreaming and she could really kiss. I was really getting into it when all of a sudden, Shirl moved back.

"What are we doing?"

"Something that we should have done a long time ago."

"Horne, I don't know."

"Shirl, relax," I said, and started kissing her neck. I was so excited. She seemed to be enjoying it, so I moved down to her breast. I started unbuttoning her shirt and with every button I got more excited. I couldn't believe what was happening. It was great.

"Horne, stop," she said and I heard her, but I kept on because she didn't sound too serious.

"STOP!" she said again, and this time I jumped back because she sounded very serious.

"I'm ready to go, Horne."

"I'm sorry, Shirl. I just want you so bad."

"Let's just go," she said, and I didn't understand what was going on. Everything had been going just great at first, but now Shirl was straight tripping. However, I was still happy. The kiss had to mean something.

Three weeks passed, and I still hadn't talked to Shirl. Every time I called, she was either gone or sleep, and when I went over there, I got the same thing, "She's not here" or "Baby, she's sleep."

I had been happy and excited three weeks ago, but now I felt like shit. I thought I was in love with this girl, and she was obviously avoiding me.

It seems Stevall had some luck. He was talking all that stuff and it turned out he and Big Belinda hit it off. She had gone back home, but they had been writing and calling each other.

Chapter Three

"You can keep your car. I don't care. You always got to be right." I was arguing with my dad about the car. It had messed up a few days ago, and he was trying to blame it on me. I was just driving the car and it started smoking. The mechanic told him I must have had it in the wrong gear, but I didn't. I really didn't, but, oh no, he wouldn't listen to me. Every time we disagreed, since the car I drove was his, he would threaten to take it away from me.

"Boy, if you keep talking crazy to me, your ass will be out on the streets."

Forget this. I got up and just left. He was still yelling as I was walking out the door. "You bring your ass back in here!" I was ignoring him. I started running up the street so he wouldn't follow me.

My dad wasn't that bad. He just always had to be right. As long as I lived under his roof, everything he said was the law. Forget that. I was ready to be on my own anyway.

School started in a week, and I couldn't wait. My family was really getting on my nerves. I was going to be a junior, and I was determined to make good grades. My first two years, I bullshitted a lot. I chased after girls and got drunk all of the time, and the bad thing about it is I got dissed most of the time by the women anyway. Hell, it was time for me to stop chasing girls and get my ass serious about school. The sooner I graduated, the sooner I could be on my own.

After I got around the corner, I stopped running and walked over my friend Vince's crib. He wasn't doing nothing, so we decided to go get some brews. He drove since my dad was being difficult about the car.

I had known Vince all my life. He was wild as hell and always doing something foolish. We picked up two of my other friends, Brandon and Stewart, and then we broke camp.

"Fuck you, Brandon. That's why your mama looks like a beat up shoe," I said to Brandon, and everybody started laughing. I got him that time.

"Hell naw, Horne, you big, big snow cone eating motherfucker," Brandon said, and everybody stopped laughing and looked at him. He was always saying some dumb shit that wasn't funny.

"What the hell was that?" I asked him, and he just smiled because he knew that shit was corny. We continued drinking and checking for about two more hours. I was straight up drunk.

By the time I got home, it was one o'clock and everybody was sleep except my little sister. I had two sisters, 15 and 24. My older sister, Rachael, had her own place in Atlanta. I was so drunk I had forgotten all about the fight I had with my dad until then. Man, I hoped he wouldn't wake up.

"Hey, ugly, where you been?"

"Out."

"Horne, I said where you been," my sister said, and she always tried to act like she could tell me what to do.

"I've been licking a titty."

"Horne!"

I started laughing and walked to my room. I turned the TV on and started watching some movie on HBO. There was this fine woman on TV getting ready to get boned. I was all in the TV and then I heard somebody knocking on my door. I sure hoped it wasn't my dad. "Yeah, come in."

"Where you been?" my little sister asked me.

"Girl, what do you want?"

"I heard you and Dad got into a fight."

"Yeah."

"Well, what was it about?"

I really didn't feel like talking about it, but I knew I wouldn't get any peace until I did. "About the car."

"What about the car?"

"You know when the car messed up a few days ago…"

We talked about the car for several minutes and then she started rambling on about some boy she liked at school. I was getting sleepy, so I really didn't pay her much attention. "Renee, I'm fixing to go to sleep."

"All right, all right. Oh, yeah, Shirl called."

Shirl called? I couldn't believe it. Maybe she had changed her mind. It was a little after one, and it was too late to call, but I was going to call her tomorrow for sure.

All night I thought about Shirl. She had actually called. Maybe I heard my sister wrong. Nah. She said Shirl called. I was so excited. She must have finally realized we were made for each other. Horne and Shirl sitting in a tree. K-I-S-S-I-N-G.

I started back looking at the movie. They were showing another nasty scene. Damn, the movie was good. I started imagining that the couple on the television was me and Shirl. I would love to have slow, sweet sex with her.

I must have fallen asleep, because when I woke up and looked at the clock, it was 5:30am and the TV was still on. I had just had the best dream of my life. Shirl and I were getting busy on a school bus, doing it doggy style. It was wild. A little too wild because I had just discovered that my underwear was wet. I had just had a wet dream. I must have it bad for Shirl because this was the first time I had experienced this in four years.

Even though no one knew, I felt ashamed. I jumped up and went to the bathroom to clean up. While I was in the bathroom, I kept thinking about how real that dream felt. After I finished cleaning up, I hit the sack.

When I finally woke up, all I could think about was Shirl. I was nervous about calling her since she had been avoiding me for three weeks. I heard a knock at my door, and I was wondering who was this knocking at my door. I suddenly remembered my dad and the big argument. I sure hoped it wasn't him. "Come in." It was him, and he didn't look too happy.

"Horne, I didn't appreciate that running out shit you did last night. And just for that, you won't be taking the car back to school."

What? No car! I was mad as hell, but I didn't say anything. Not a word.

"Well, now I guess you'll start taking me more seriously. Hell, I don't play that shit, Horne, and you know it."

I was so mad, but then again, I wanted it to seem like I really didn't care. I just sat there looking at the floor.

"I'm your dad, Horne, and what I say goes."

Ain't that some shit? No car!

Chapter Four

The day had finally come to go to school. I was happy and sad all at the same time. I was happy that I was getting the hell out of the crib, but sad that I wasn't going to have the car. My parents were driving my old ass to school. How embarrassing. I was a junior and my parents were still driving me to school. Just because I had an argument with my dad. Ain't that some shit?

Well, I was hoping to see Shirl. Evidently, she had already left for school. I had tried to call her, but her mom said she left a little early to find an apartment. She probably was staying with her cousin until she found something.

We had finally arrived, and it was hot as hell. The sun was definitely not playing. My parents helped me unpack, fussed at me some, and then broke camp. I was happy I was finally at school. The hell with a car. I was there to study anyway.

My roommate hadn't arrived yet, so I finished unpacking, took a shower, and got ready to scout out the honeys. I put on a spiffy outfit, styled the hair just right, threw on some cologne, and I was off. I decided to go chill in the lobby of my dorm. I stayed in a co-ed dorm, and that's where everybody hung out. Man, there were girls everywhere. A lot of them I already knew, but there were some new honeys too.

I sat there awhile and talked to some friends and checked out the honeys. I saw a few girls that had dissed me before. Melissa. She was fine, but she had dissed me because she said I was too immature. Maybe so. Then there was Rolonda. She dissed me for some football player. And Angela. She had the prettiest ass you would ever see, but she wanted money and I didn't have any, so she dissed me. Forget those stupid girls. I didn't need them anyway, because I was at school to study. I kept telling myself that same shit hoping that maybe I would actually start believing it.

The longer I looked at the girls in the lobby, the hornier I got. I needed a woman. Bad! I should have gone and hollered at one, but I didn't feel like getting dissed.

"Horne! Hey, Horne!"

I turned around to see who was yelling my name. It was my roommate, Tim. Tim was about my height, 6'4, but he was a lot thinner than me and very conceited. He thought he was the biggest mack this side of Texas.

"Horne, what's up, pimpin'?" he said, and I almost started laughing. Tim didn't have one muscle on his body, but he was wearing some tights and a tank top. He looked a damn mess! The bad thing about it was that he really thought he was looking good.

"What's up, Tim?"

"Shit. I just got in, man."

"You put your things in the room yet?"

"Yeah. I just threw them in. I'm going to go and unpack later. Let's go get some beer."

"You'll have to drive because I didn't bring my car back."

"Why?"

"My dad was tripping."

"Shit, that's messed up. Come on. We'll talk about it in the car."

We got in Tim's car and went to the store. I told him about the car and also about Shirl. He didn't say much except that maybe I'll finally get to bone her. That was all Tim thought about. Sex.

Tim and I sat up in the room and drank a couple of beers until about seven o'clock. There was supposed to be a Black Student Association mixer at eight o'clock. This meant free food and honeys, so we started getting ready.

At about 7:15, our boys, Corey and Fred came down to the room. They were going to the mixer with us. Corey was about 6'0 and all the girls liked him. They all said he looked like that singer Christopher Williams, and he was real cool. Fred was totally opposite of Corey. He was 5'5, fat, goofy, and very loud.

"What's up? Y'all ready to go get some honeys?" Fred bellowed.

"I know I'm ready. Is your fat ass ready?" Tim said sarcastically.

"I may be fat, but I bet I get some tonight."

"Shit! Your ass ain't seen pussy since the invention of the refrigerator."

"Ask Corey! Corey will tell you!"

"Well, he told me he had sex with two girls over the summer," Corey said.

"Did you see them?" Tim asked.

"I saw one of them," Corey said. Corey and Fred were both from Chicago, and Corey was always looking out for Fred. Tim, on the other hand, was always making fun of Fred.

"Now tell the truth. Was she fat and ugly?"

Corey looked at Fred and started smiling. "Nah, she was straight," he said, still smiling.

"See, I told you! I told you!" Fred said loud as hell.

"Corey is lying. Look at him," Tim said laughing. Corey was laughing, which meant he probably was lying. "Man, your fat ass probably made all that shit up, and Corey was just going along with it."

It was time to go, and Tim and Fred were still arguing.

"Come on, y'all, it's time to break," I said, trying to hurry them up. When we finally got to the mixer, there were honeys everywhere. We had barely got in the door when some fine girl walked up and gave Corey a kiss. This was normal for him. It was probably one of his ex-girlfriends. He stayed there talking to her while me, Tim, and Fred walked around the room.

"Man, look at all these honeys," Fred said.

"Yeah, it is a lot of them here," I replied.

"Yeah, just how I like it," Fred said, and he eyed some girl's booty.

"Fred, will you shut your fat ass up?" Tim said, and he eyed the same girl's booty.

"Man, I'm ignoring you. I'm going to go check out these refreshments and then holler at some of these honeys."

"Yeah, you go do that," Tim replied. Then Tim and I found us some good seats facing the middle of the floor so we could scope out the honeys. We hadn't been sitting down two minutes when Tim started hollering at some babes. "Excuse me. Excuse me." The girl kept walking. "Well, forget you then. I didn't want to talk to your big nosed, big hip looking ass anyway." Tim had a bad habit of saying anything to young ladies, especially when they dissed him.

Another girl walked by. "Hey, girl, you look delicious." I couldn't believe what he was saying. It was so corny, but the girl walked over toward him. "Hey, sweet thing, what's your name?" Tim talked to this girl for a few minutes and then got up and walked outside with her. This left me sitting there alone.

I was horny, but I wasn't trying to holler at anybody because I felt I couldn't offer anything to these ladies. Don't get me wrong. I thought I looked all right, but if you didn't have a car or money, the majority of these girls wouldn't give you the time of day. I sat there, feeling sorry for myself and thinking about Shirl. I couldn't wait until I saw her again.

"Horne. You want a tuna fish sandwich or some cookies?" Fred said, and was standing in front of me with two plates in his hands, one full of tuna fish and the other cookies. He looked like he had gotten all the food.

"Nah, I'm straight. I'll probably go get something later."

"Yeah, they got some good stuff up there, and look at all these honeys. I don't know about you, but I'm going to get me a couple of numbers."

Forget this. If Fred was really going to holler at some honeys, I was too. I scoped out the scene. There were so many girls. I kept looking until I spotted this girl across the room standing by herself. She was short and real cute. For some reason, I always liked short girls. Since she was standing by herself, I decided to make my move. I put a cinnamon Tic Tac in my mouth and walked across the room. I wasn't really nervous because I had been drinking earlier and I had a pretty good buzz going on. "Hi. What's your name?" I asked. The girl looked at me and smiled.

"Sheila," she said, in an uninterested tone.

"My name is Horne," I said, and she didn't say anything. She just kept looking around the room, so I said my name again. "My name is Horne."

"Oh, hi," she said.

I could tell already that she wasn't interested, but my dumb ass kept trying to holler anyway. "Well, tell me, are you a freshman?"

"Nah, I'm a transfer student from UTK."

"Oh, you didn't like it there or something?"

"Nah," she murmured.

We talked, or better yet, I talked to her for a few more minutes. By this time Corey and Tim were over there by Fred. I really didn't want to, but I felt pressured to ask this girl for her phone number. I didn't want to leave the mixer without a phone number. I would have to listen to Tim all night. "Well, can I have your phone number."

"Well, I don't know."

"Come on. Maybe we can go out sometime."

"All right."

Yeah, I got the digits. I was relieved. I wasn't sure how in the hell I was going to take her out, though, with no car. I walked back across the room where the fellas were standing.

"Did you get her number?" Tim asked.

I decided to be a show off even though I knew this girl was probably going to diss me later. "What's my name? H-O-R-N-E. Hell, yeah, I got that honey's number."

"I hear you, man. I'm supposed to hook up with that honey I hollered at later on," Tim said.

We stood there and talked for a while, mingled a little, and then left. We decided to go back to Tim's and my room. It was about eleven o'clock, and I was getting tired. It had been a long day.

"What y'all want to do now?" Fred asked.

"I'm tired," I said.

"I'm not. I'm going to call this girl to see if we can hook up later," Tim said

"I'm about to get into some skins, myself," Corey said.

"You are, Corey? Who?" Fred asked.

"You know that girl you saw me at the mixer with?"

"You were with about six of them."

"Well, the first one."

"Man, you get all the luck."

"Will you shut your fat ass up? How many girls did you talk to?" Tim asked Fred. Then Tim and Fred started arguing, and it lasted for about ten minutes. When they finished, Tim made a phone call, and he and Corey left. Unfortunately, Fred was still there. He just started talking about some honey he supposedly used to talk to.

"Yeah, man, Renetha was a trip. She acted like she didn't want to give it up at first, but all it took was a little macking. Yeah, that's right."

I sat there and listened to Fred lie for about an half hour before I decided to kick him out. "Fred, man, I'm tired."

"Well, let me tell you about this honey..."

"Nah, Fred, I'm tired and getting ready to go to sleep."

"All right, man, I'll holler at you tomorrow."

Fred finally left, and it was bedtime. Tim was still gone, and he probably wouldn't be back until real late. I said my prayers. I prayed every night because I knew I did wrong. I wished that one day I would stop drinking and cursing, but for the time being, I knew I wasn't ready. I felt there was too much in store for me. I was still young and ready for all wild experiences. After I got through praying, I went to bed.

I tried to go to sleep. I was tired as hell, but for some reason, I couldn't sleep. I decided to call that girl I met earlier at the BSA mixer. I wanted to call Shirl, but I didn't know how to get in contact with her. Maybe Sheila would surprise me and turn out to be straight.

I got up and looked around for her number. It was still in my pants pocket. 678-6317. Yeah, I was about to mack, but the phone was busy. I called back a couple more times and the phone was still busy. Finally, on my fourth try, I got through. "Hello."

"May I speak to Sheila."

"Who?"

"Sheila."

"I'm sorry, you have the wrong number."

I hung up. I was mad as hell. That damn girl had given me the wrong number.

Chapter Five

A few weeks had passed, and school was going fairly decent. I was taking 15 hours, and all my classes were mostly made up of white professors and white students. My school was majority white, but we did have about 5,000 blacks enrolled.

I had been studying real hard. I was trying to straighten up my act because my parents had been on me about my grades. Also, I was ready to graduate and hopefully get a job because I was tired of being broke. I had cut down on my drinking and wasn't talking to any honeys, so my full concentration was on the books. Well, maybe I'm lying a little bit. I had been thinking about Shirl as usual. I had been up here all this time and still hadn't seen her.

I was really trying to study hard, but I was so damn horny. Every time I would really get going in the books, I would start daydreaming about me and Shirl knocking the boots. I had to do something. I decided to call Martha. I used to be crazy about this girl my freshman year, but she wouldn't give me the time of day. Since then, things had changed. Martha was now on my jock. Ordinarily, this would be good, but since my freshman year, Martha had gained about sixty pounds. Before, she was thick anyway, but now she was straight up fat. I didn't care, though. I was horny, and she had been calling me a lot lately, talking about sex. I was going to call her later to see what was up.

It was Friday, and since I didn't have a date as usual, I was going to kick it with the fellas. We were supposed to go to some sorority party.

We were excited because people had been talking about this party all week. It was supposed to be all the way live.

We got ready for the party by doing the usual drinking. We had beer, whiskey, and champagne. It was on.

"Man, I'm ready. I can feel it. I know I'm meeting a girl tonight," Fred said.

"Good luck, man. I hope you do," I said to him.

We were in me and Tim's room. Tim was in the bathroom and Corey was on the phone. "Yeah, baby. You going to get me those shoes?" Corey said to the girl on the phone. I admired Corey. He would straight up juice the honeys. When Corey got through with a girl, she was broke. It's not that I wanted to juice the girls. It was just that girls always tried to run games on guys by trying to take their money. To me it felt good to see a guy doing it to them.

"Oh, you don't have any money," Corey continued, and he looked around the room like he was frustrated. "Well let me call you back," he said, and hung up the phone.

"What's up with her, Corey?" asked Fred.

"I don't know. This is the third time that ho said she didn't have any money."

"Well, Corey, if she doesn't have any money, then she just doesn't have any money," I said to him.

"And I'm fixing to quit fucking the bitch too. She ain't got no money. I can't do nothing for her. She gets none of the d-i-c-k." Corey said, and I thought to myself damn Corey was raw.

Tim finally came out of the bathroom. He was dripping wet and trying to rap. He looked like he was drunk. He was supposedly in love with that girl he met at the Black Student Association mixer. Her name was Mellani, and they had been seeing each other every day since school started, but today they had gotten into some argument, so he decided to kick it with the fellas. She seemed to be good for Tim. He had been going to class and actually doing his homework. This was good for him because he was on the verge of flunking out. I was hoping that they would make up because without her he would probably fall back into his bad school habits.

After Tim put his clothes on, we headed to the party. It was on campus at the University Center, so we walked.

"Man, my feet hurt. I knew I should have drove," Fred said.

"Come on. We're almost there."

"I'm driving next time. Man, my feet hurt."

"Will you shut up?" Tim said, spitting everywhere.

"Man, Tim is drunk!" Fred said, and grabbed his own feet. Tim could barely talk without slobbering, and he couldn't even walk straight. We tried to leave him at the dorm, but he wouldn't listen. He said he was okay. I hated it when he was like this because he usually ended up acting an asshole.

When we got to the party, the place was packed. They were playing some cool ass mix, and I was ready to get on the floor. I scoped out the room to see who I was going to ask to dance, and that's when it happened. I saw Shirl. She was sitting with a couple of her friends. My heart started beating fast as hell. I was so happy, but I was also nervous. What was I going to say, or better yet, what was I going to do? Should I go over there and speak to her, or should I act like I don't see her and walk by her to see if she says anything? I decided to play it cool for now. Find me somebody to dance with and maybe she would see me on the floor and come and talk to me later.

I continued scooping until I saw a girl who looked like she wanted to dance. She was standing by herself next to the dance floor. She was dancing to the music a little, so I figured she would probably want to dance. She didn't look too good, but she would have to do for now. I asked her to dance, and she said yes. It was time to cut a rug.

When we got on the floor, I started showing off. I was all over the floor, doing every dance I could think of. I was half drunk myself, and I was also trying to draw attention to myself, hoping Shirl would see me. I thought I was really jamming, but the girl I was dancing with seemed to be moving farther and farther back. Forget her. She was ugly anyway. As long as she stood close enough so I didn't' look like I was dancing by myself, I would be all right. I kept looking around to see if I saw Shirl, but I didn't.

"Horne, Horne!" I heard somebody say. It was Tim. "Horne, guess who's here," he said, talking loud as hell. When I turned around to look, he had his arm around Shirl as if she was holding him up. "Look, Horne, it's your girlfriend Shirl."

Man, I couldn't believe he said that shit. I could have hit his ass.

"You ain't going to speak to your girlfriend?" Tim said, and I wanted to curse him out, but I figured it was best to ignore him. He was drunk, and if I cursed him out, he would probably make a scene.

Shirl was looking great. She had a smooth silk outfit on, and her hair was pulled up on her head. She looked like a princess.

"Hi, Shirl."

"Hi, Horne."

I had just stopped dancing with that ugly girl without saying anything to her. I had just walked off the dance floor. It was like when I was around Shirl, nothing mattered but her. "Well, you look pretty."

"Thanks," she said, and she wasn't really looking at me. It was like she was scared to look in my eyes.

"Long time no talk," I said.

"Yeah," she replied.

"I'm going to leave you two lovebirds alone," Tim said, and staggered off. I was glad to see him leave.

"You'll have to excuse him. He's a little drunk."

"I can tell. You seem a little tipsy too."

"Nah. I'm straight."

Since she thought I was tipsy, I decided to just open up with my feelings, and if something went wrong, I could always say I was drunk. Shirl seemed real nervous, and this really felt awkward. I didn't know what to say first. "Well, uh…"

"Horne, I'm sorry."

"You're sorry?"

"Yeah. I know I've been acting funny."

"Why didn't you return my phone calls. I mean, I called you. I came over your house. The least you could have done was call and tell me something. Anything!" I said, and I was starting to get upset. This girl that I was supposedly in love with, better yet, this girl who I thought was one of my closest friends, avoided me for weeks, and all she could say was that she's sorry. "Shirl, I like you a lot. You know this. You could have at least told me that you didn't want to talk to me. You could have at least given me an explanation for that kiss and why you went crazy afterwards."

I was hot. I had started getting loud, and people were starting to stare. Shirl was just standing there not saying a damn thing. "Hello, hello. Are you still there?"

"Horne, okay, I owe you an explanation, but let's go outside and talk, okay?"

I didn't say anything. I just started walking toward the door. Shirl followed me. When we got outside, I sat on some bricks and waited for Shirl to talk.

"Horne, I know it doesn't help, but I am really sorry. That night we went out, I didn't think you were really serious until you kissed me, and when you did that, I was so shocked I didn't know what to think or what to do. It all happened so fast."

"You didn't know I was serious? Shirl, I had been telling you how I felt for the longest. I gave you roses and everything."

"Well, I just didn't know," she said, and I looked at her like she was crazy.

"Now you know, Shirl. Now you know. You've had weeks to think about what happened. We kissed! I kissed you, and you sure as hell kissed me back." I looked deep into Shirl's eyes and continued. "So what happens next?"

Shirl didn't say anything for about a minute. She just stared at me. I sat there trying to look as sexy as possible. I kept moving until I hit a pose that I thought might persuade her a little toward me.

"Horne, like I told you before, I'm not ready. Why can't we be friends like we were before?" Oh, hell, the friend line. I had heard this so many times through the years that I had begun to hate to hear it. "You were one of my best friends. You are one of my best friends. I have really missed talking to you."

"Hell, you sure have a funny way of showing it."

"Horne, I want my friend back. That's what I need now, Horne. My friend back. The one I used to tell everything to. The one I used to laugh with. Horne, I want you back in my life, but as my best friend because that is what you were, Horne. You were my best friend."

All that shit was flattering, but that is all it was, and it wasn't going to fly. "Shirl, if I was your best friend, that should be one more reason why you should give us a try."

Shirl sat down next to me and looked into my eyes. "Horne, I'm still in love with Eric."

When I heard this I got mad. I stood up and started walking around. Shirl was so stupid. Eric was cool, but he was also a dog, and I wasn't just saying this because I liked her. It was the truth. "Forget Eric! Do you have any feelings for me?" I asked, and she just sat there. "DO YOU?!" I said again, but louder.

"Yeah. As a friend."

"And that's how you kiss a friend." I went over and grabbed her arms with just a little force, and then continued, "Is that how you kiss a friend?" Shirl looked at me like she was scared. "WELL IS IT?!!"

"Horne, don't do this. Calm down."

I let her go and walked away. I was so upset. I felt like crying, but I had promised myself to never cry over a girl. I walked back into the party. I felt lousy. I kept looking back, hoping that Shirl would run in and apologize and tell me she wanted to be with me, but naturally, that didn't happen.

I stood there and looked around. It seemed like everybody was with somebody. In fact, even Fred was on the floor slow dragging with some girl, and she was actually cute. I was really depressed. If I couldn't have Shirl, I might as well drop out of school. That's how I really felt at that moment. I was at an all time low.

Chapter Six

"Hi! Is your name Raymond Horne?"

I was walking to class, and some girl had just walked up to me. "Yeah," I said. She was about 5'9, dark complected, short hair, cute, and had a body like a brick house. Ordinarily, I would have been straight up trying to jock her, but Shirl had really messed me up. I had come to the conclusion that all girls were stank hoes and were only good for two things—sex and sex.

"My name is Tina Thompson," she said, grinning.

"Hi," I said, not grinning. I looked at her again. Damn! She was flat out fine, but I kept walking and she was walking beside me.

"Don't you want to know how I know your name?"

"Yeah," I said casually.

"I saw you the other night at the party, and you looked so cute, I asked one of my friends did she know you."

"Are you new here or something?"

"Yeah. I went to a junior college up in California, and I decided to come down here to finish up." Mmm, California. I could tell she was from somewhere besides here by the way she talked. "Was that your girlfriend you were outside with at the party?"

"Nah."

"Oh. Well, that's good."

"It is? Why?"

"Well, I don't want to seem too aggressive, but you seem like the type of person I would like to go out with."

This girl was straight forward. I sort of liked it though. "Well, let me give you my phone number."

"Okay. Is it all right if I call you tonight?"

"Yeah," I said, and I gave her my phone number. We talked a couple more minutes, and then I went on to class. I was feeling a little better about myself. Tina wasn't Shirl, but at least somebody cute was interested in me. Maybe she's easy. I would love to get up in that.

I spent the entire morning in class. It was hard for me to concentrate. I was still thinking about Shirl.

That night, I was real tired, so I went to bed early. Tim had gone over to see his girlfriend, and I was looking forward to a good night's sleep. I was in the bed thinking about how wrong Shirl did me when I heard the phone ring. Who in the hell could this be? I thought to myself. It was probably that girl I met today. She did say she was going to call me tonight.

"Hello," I said.

"Hey," the girl on the other end said.

"Yeah, who do you want to talk to?" I said, not recognizing the voice.

"Horne. Stop tripping. You know who I want to talk to," the girl said.

Man, it was Martha. What did her fat ass want? "Oh, hey, Martha."

"Hey, baby. Why haven't you been calling me?"

"Well, I've been busy."

"Okay, I'll forgive you this time. So when you coming to see me?"

"I don't know, Martha. You know I'm busy with school and all."

"Well, if you come over, I'll hook you up with some dinner, and I know your body's probably tired, so I'll give you a nice smooth massage."

Damn, that sounded sort of good, even coming from Martha. Hell, I'm horny as hell, too. "Martha, that does sound good."

"I'll make it worth your while, Horne. Why don't you come over tomorrow night?"

Hell, why not? Get a free meal and maybe some cat. I'll just have to diss her ass after that. "Yeah, I think I will do that."

"Oh, good. That's great, Horne." Martha said sounding real excited. Man, why did she have to gain all that weight? If she was thinner and jocking me, I would probably do right by her, but she's not, and besides, all girls are stank hoes.

"I'll call you tomorrow before I come," I said, and hung up the phone. I tried to get some sleep, but I kept thinking how I might get some tomorrow. Then the phone started ringing again.

"Hello."

"May I speak to Horne?"

"This is he."

"Hi, Horne, this is Tina."

"What's up, girl?" I was popular tonight. Tina and I talked for about twenty minutes. She seemed like she was real nice. She asked me if I wanted to go out Saturday. I told her I didn't have a car. I felt sort of embarrassed, but she had a car and said she would drive. Cool. Maybe she was the kind of girl that liked to spend money on her man. If that was the case, I would take her ass for every cent. Pull one of those Corey tricks on her ass.

After I got off the phone with Tina, I thought I was finally going to get some sleep. I was happy because I had a date with a cute ass girl Saturday, and I might be getting some ass tomorrow. Forget Shirl. I didn't need the ho anyway. Damn! The phone started ringing again. This had to be for Tim.

"Hello."

"Hey, Horne," the girl said, and I thought it was Martha, but then I realized who it was. "How are you doing, Horne?"

"I'm making it," I said, trying not to sound too excited. It was Shirl. I couldn't believe it. What in the hell did she want? "What do you want?" I asked her.

"We need to finish talking."

"What?"

"Horne, why are you doing this?"

"Doing what? You're the one who wants it this way."

"No, Horne. I want to be friends again."

"I don't want to be friends. Hell, let Eric be your friend."

"Horne, I hardly ever talk to Eric."

Hold up, I thought to myself. She never talks to Eric. "You never talk to Eric?" I asked her.

"Every now and then."

"So why do you talk like you are all on his tip?"

"Horne, I don't talk like that. I just told you I'm still in love with him. You don't fall out of love overnight."

Shirl and I talked for about two hours. We argued for almost the whole time, but my weak ass finally gave in and told her I would give our friendship another chance. Actually, I just said that shit to shut her up. I'm still going to play her cold.

I wasn't even sleepy any more. Down deep in my heart, I was happy that Shirl had called. I really felt she had to have some feelings for me.

"What are you doing up so late?" Tim asked, and he came into the room.

"I'm not sleepy. Guess who just called me."

"Well, that's simple. Only one girl calls you. Fat ass Martha."

"Nah. She called earlier, but that's not who I'm talking about. Shirl called."

"What did she want?"

"Nothing really, but I can tell, man, she wants me."

Tim just gave me his usual look like he really didn't care and his usual response. "Well, maybe you'll get to bone her." Tim looked like he was really tired. He had on mismatch socks, and his hair was a mess.

"What have Mellani and you been doing?" I asked him.

"Boning, what your ass need to be doing." Tim said, and he was always messing with me about having sex because he knew it had been a while since I last had sex. "Man, you need to go ahead and bone Shirl. If not Shirl, I'm sure you can get Martha."

I tried not to let him bother me, but deep down it did. "Well, I'll bone somebody soon enough."

"Shit. I don't know how you do it. Man, I got to have some every week."

"Well, I'm not like that. I'll get some soon enough."

Tim and I talked for about thirty more minutes. He was really making me feel bad. I don't know why, but I felt like a geek or something. Everybody doesn't have sex all the time, but still the same, I didn't want my friends to think I was getting like Fred, and besides, I was very horny. Right then and there, I made up my mind that I was going to try to bone Martha tomorrow.

Chapter Seven

It was about seven when I decided to give Martha a call. I was sort of anxious, but a little reluctant. I really didn't know what to expect. Martha had been talking straight, but I really didn't think she would give up the cat that quick. She used to be fine, and usually, girls like that, that suddenly get big, think they are still fine and try to play that role. Don't get me wrong. Martha was still attractive, but just a little too big for my taste. Also, I didn't want to keep going to see her and giving her the wrong impression. Basically, I wanted to get in and then get out. I wasn't really sure if that was possible.

I called Martha and told her that I would be right over. Tim was going to be with his girlfriend all night, so he let me use his car. She told me how to get to her apartment, and I was off.

I found the place easily and went to knock on the door. I was very nervous. I knocked on the door for several minutes. Damn, I knew she had to be home. I was starting to get mad. I was going to knock one more time, and if she didn't come to the door, I was going to leave.

I stood there another minute and finally someone came to the door. It sure as hell wasn't Martha. Who in the hell was this? I thought to myself. It was some dude who looked like he was about 25. He had a long curl, and he had two gold teeth with the initials D.J. in them. Damn! He looked crazy. Man, I was hoping that this wasn't her boyfriend. He looked like he would try to kill a nigger. She never mentioned a boyfriend though.

"What's up, player? You looking for Martha?"

I didn't know what to say. I just stood there.

"Player. You looking for Martha?"

"Yeah, she told me to come visit her," I finally said.

"Horne, right?"

"Yeah."

"Come on in and take a load off," he said, pimping away.

I didn't know what to do, so I just followed him in and sat down. He walked in another room. I was sitting there, thinking where in the hell was Martha, and who in the hell was that? I sat there for about five minutes. I was really feeling uncomfortable. The soul brother that answered the door was still in the other room. This was crazy. After about two more minutes, Martha came out.

"Hi, Horne."

"Hey, what have you been doing?"

"I'm sorry. I wasn't quite ready yet. You look so cute."

"Thanks," I said, and blushed a little. I wish I could have said the same to her, but I couldn't. Martha was dressed nice. She had a pretty green dress on, but she looked like she had gained about twenty more pounds since the last time I had seen her. Damn, she was fat. I decided to go ahead and lie and tell her she looked nice. "You look real nice too."

"Thanks, Horne. You're so sweet."

"Hey, Martha, who was that dude that answered the door?"

"Oh, that's my cousin. He didn't scare you or say anything crazy, did he?"

"Nah. I just didn't know someone stayed with you."

"Yeah, we share the apartment. Sometimes you'll just have to overlook him because he does a lot of stupid things."

I just hoped he didn't do anything stupid tonight, because I didn't plan on coming back over here. "Uh, okay," I said to her.

Martha told me that she had prepared dinner for us. She said that she had made steaks, baked potatoes, green beans, and a lemon meringue pie. Damn, that shit sounded good. I was hungry as hell, too.

"Dinner will be ready in about five minutes. Do you want a drink?"

Need she ask? I was trying to cut back on my drinking, but I knew I was going to need a drink tonight. "Yeah, I'll take one."

As I sat there, I scoped out the apartment. It was real nice. I was wondering how in the hell could they afford a place like this? Martha was still in college, and her cousin didn't look like he was too successful. He must be slanging.

Martha came back with two mixed drinks. I wasn't sure what it was, but it was strong. We sat there and talked for a few minutes until the dinner was ready. By the time I sat down at the table, I had a buzz.

"Man, Martha, this sure does look good."

"Well, I hope you enjoy it. You know, I love to cook."

No shit, this was obvious. "Oh, you do. Well, you surely out did yourself tonight," I said as Martha's cousin walked into the room.

"Damn, I'm hungry. Martha let me have some of that food," he said to her.

"Go on somewhere, Wayne."

Wayne looked like he was ready to go out. He had on a matching blue jean outfit and some suede Fila's.

"Come on, Martha, I'm tired of eating bologna," he said to her.

"I said go on, Wayne. Don't make me act a nigger." Martha looked like she was starting to get upset. She was so big, she could probably whip his ass.

"Damn, Martha, why you trippin'?" he said, and started looking at me. "Hey, player, let me get some of that steak."

"Wayne, you better get the hell out of here." Martha said, and I was glad that she said something because I didn't know what to say.

"Shit, Martha, I guess I'll eat some bologna again." Wayne said, and opened the refrigerator, grabbed a beer and some bologna, and then left.

"I'm sorry about Wayne. I told you he acts stupid."

"That's okay," I said, just relieved he had gone. I was beginning to think that I should have stayed at home.

Martha apologized for Wayne a couple more times. The food was real good. Martha could straight up cook.

After we finished eating, we went into another room and had a few drinks. This evening was turning out better than I thought it would. We were looking at some movie. I was sitting on the couch, and Martha was sitting in a reclining chair. I was wondering why she was sitting over there. I wasn't starting to like her or anything, but I was ready to make a move. I was feeling real good. I was about drunk and Martha was looking thinner and sexier by the minute.

"Martha, why don't you come over here."

She didn't say anything. She just got up and walked over by me and sat down. Man, she was smelling good and everything. Hell, what did I have to lose? Nothing! So I decided to make a move. I started kissing her on the neck. She seemed to be enjoying it. After a minute or two, we started kissing. She was a very good kisser. Almost as good as Shirl. While we were kissing, I started moving my hand up her leg. I was almost at the jackpot when she stopped kissing me.

"Horne, what are you doing?" she asked, and had a little grin on her face.

"Nothing."

"It doesn't feel like you are doing nothing."

"It feels better, doesn't it."

"Horne, we need to slow down. This is our first date."

Damn! I was afraid this was going to happen. I was so horny. I decided to lie my ass off. Maybe that would work. "Come on, Martha, baby. I want you so bad. You know I've been wanting to get with you since my freshman year."

"You have? All of last spring, I tried to get with you, but you were tripping. I thought it was because of my weight."

"Nah, baby. I was involved with someone else then, but we broke up a few weeks ago. I'm ready for us now, and don't worry about your weight. Hell, you are sexier and prettier than ever." I was lying up a storm. I was determined to get some tonight.

"Are you telling me the truth, Horne?"

"Baby, look into my eyes. I need you, baby. Tonight, tomorrow, next week, and throughout the year." Damn, I was good. I wished Corey, Fred, and Tim were listening to me; they would have been impressed.

Martha moved a little closer and we started kissing again, but only this time she was moving her hand up my leg. One thing led to another, and the next thing I knew, we were in her bedroom. Martha took all her clothes off and then took mine off. Damn, I was finally going to get some. Man! I was so excited, I was about to nut already, and we hadn't even started. I reached on the floor and got my condoms out of my pants. I had come fully prepared. While I was trying to put the condom on, I was kissing her breast. Her breast had to be the size of Texas. She had the biggest breast that I had ever seen. I was getting tired just kissing all over them. It had been so long, I was having a hard time putting the condom on.

"Let me do that for you, baby." Damn, Martha must be a freak. She was letting me get some the first date and putting the condom on me. She slipped it on fairly easy. It was time to get busy. I had a hard time trying to put it in, but finally I entered into her. DAMN!!! It felt good. I started stroking and she started moaning. There was only one problem. I was about to nut and we had only been doing it for about a minute. Man, I was trying to hold it back. There was just no use. I guess I hadn't done it in so long, I was just too excited. I held it off for about fifteen seconds, and then out it came. It felt good as hell. I was satisfied, but I felt sort of embarrassed. Martha looked at me as if she was thinking, "Is that it?"

I got off her and laid there for a while. Martha wasn't saying a word. I knew she was disappointed. I was ready to go, but I needed to satisfy her first because she might be one of those girls that goes back and tells everyone how it was. That would be all I needed, too. A reputation as a two-minute brother.

I decided to go ahead and try to please her. There was only one problem though. I couldn't get hard again. I guess after I nutted, I realized who I was with and all the excitement went away. I kissed her breast and neck for about twenty-five minutes and nothing happened. It was still limp as hell.

"Come on, Horne. Give it to me!" Martha was wanting it and I still wasn't ready.

"Now, Horne. Now!"

"I'm not ready yet," I said, embarrassed.

Martha didn't say anything. She reached down and grabbed me. She started rubbing on me and nothing happened for a few minutes. The next thing I knew I started getting ready. She rubbed me for a few more minutes and then got on top of me. I was ready now.

Martha and I had sex all night. The next day, I woke up about noon. I had missed the majority of my classes, and I was still over Martha's. I was ready to go, but I was too tired to move. Last night was great, but I just couldn't be with Martha. I decided to get up and leave while she was still asleep. I put on my clothes and was almost out the door when I heard her.

"Horne! Where are you, baby? Horne! Where are you?"

I started to say something, but I didn't have anything to say. Last night was great, but I had to leave. I didn't want to hurt Martha, but she just wasn't Shirl.

Chapter Eight

A whole month had passed, and I still hadn't talked to Martha for more than thirty seconds at a time. I didn't want to talk to her at all, but a couple of times when she called, I answered the phone and made up some lie why I couldn't talk. I told her I was sleep, on the other line long distance, or something like that. I felt bad about lying, but I had to. There was no easy way to tell Martha, so I was hoping after awhile she would get the hint.

Shirl had been calling me a lot. She really didn't say much. She would talk about her days and her problems. I would listen, but I really wouldn't say much. I didn't want it to be like it was before when I used to give her advice and trip with her all the time. I didn't want her to think that we were best friends. I had a plan, and the main part of my plan was to get her to look at me in a different way. Not as her best friend, but as a guy that she liked to be with that happened to be attracted to her. You see, I hadn't given up hope yet.

I had a big test Friday, so I decided to go to the library. Shirl had called and told me she was going to meet me over there. Even though Shirl and I had talked on the phone a lot, I hadn't seen her since that party. Needless to say, I was nervous.

While I was walking over to the library, I started thinking about my life. My grades were decent, but they could be better. I didn't have a car, but actually, I really didn't need one. I didn't have a girlfriend, but I was working on it. My conclusion was that my life was pretty damn good. I knew I was always complaining, but I was really fortunate.

I went into the library feeling good, with a lot of hope. I sat down and waited for Shirl to come. While I was there, I saw Tina. She was the girl that had come up to me while I was going to class. We had talked on the phone a lot and gone out a couple of times, but nothing serious had come out of it. I could tell Tina liked me a lot, but for some reason, I wasn't into her. She was fine and all, but my heart was still beating for Shirl.

"Hey, Tina. What's up?"

Tina walked over toward me. Man, she had on some tight ass blue jeans. I would have tried to do her, but I couldn't stand the thought of doing her wrong. I'm just not that kind of person that can have sex and leave. I know that I did it to Martha, but deep down, I felt real bad. I just wasn't like that. At times, I wished I was a dog, but the reality was that I was more like a little puppy.

"Hey, Horne," Tina said, and bent down and kissed me on my cheek. She smelled real good. "I'm surprised to see you here," she said, smiling.

"And why is that?"

"I don't know. You just don't seem like the library type."

"What does that suppose to mean?"

"I don't know, Horne. Just forget it."

"Nah, people always seem surprised to see me in the library, and I want to know why."

"Well, Horne, you're always drinking and acting silly. You just don't seem like a studious person."

"I'm not the most studious, but I don't see why it would surprise you to see me in the library."

It really didn't bother me that Tina said that. I was just giving her a hard time. It was true that people always acted surprised to see me in the library, and I knew why. It was because I was a big black man, and even other black people had stereotyped me. I guess they thought that all the big black men were supposed to be in the playground playing basketball, on the corner drinking, or in jail. Well, I had a surprise for them. Some of us are in school and go to the library, too, but I guess we were invisible in the eyes of others.

Tina and I talked for about five more minutes, and then Shirl walked in. She must not have seen us because she kept walking.

"Shirl! Hey, Shirl!" I shouted, and Shirl turned around and looked. Damn, she was gorgeous. It was like she was a goddess sent down here on a special mission, and I was that mission. She had a big smile on her face.

"Hey, Horne. What's up? I didn't even see you over there."

I felt so nervous. It felt like it was only yesterday we were outside the party arguing. "What's up, Shirl? You ready to study?"

"Yeah, let's go up to the second floor."

I started walking, and then I felt something pulling my arm. I looked back and it was Tina. Damn, I had forgotten all about her, and she knew it too. She gave me a dirty ass look. "Oh, this is why you are in the library. I knew it had to be something," she said, and she looked mad. I really felt bad. I could have been a lot smoother, but when I saw Shirl, I forgot about her. I didn't know what to say.

Shirl had turned around and started looking. "Horne, who is this?" she asked. Man, I was so scared. I really didn't know why, because I wasn't going with either one. I had gone out with Tina, but we didn't have a relationship.

"Shirl, this is Tina. Tina, this is Shirl," I said, trying to keep my voice from cracking. Damn, even Shirl had a dirty look on her face. Maybe, they would start fighting over me. Nah, but Shirl did look like something was bothering her. They said hi to each other and both of them started looking at me like they were crazy. I had to say something. "Well, Tina, Shirl and I are going to do some studying. You want to join us?"

I knew she was going to say no, but I just asked because it seemed like the only way to get out of this mess. I just knew she would say no. I would tell Shirl some lie, and then it would be over. "Yeah, I think I would like to join y'all studying."

"You would?" I said in complete surprise. I couldn't believe it. What was she trying to do. I wanted to tell her no. I wanted to tell her that I was in love with Shirl and she was only messing things up, but I didn't. "Well, come on, you two. Let's go study," I said.

Man, I knew I had to sound fake. I looked at Shirl and she seemed pissed. I was starting to wonder if she was getting jealous or if she just wanted to be alone so we could talk about her problems. When we got up to the second floor and found a table to study at, Tina sat really close to me. Then she started talking to me as if Shirl wasn't even there. I really didn't pay her much attention. I kept looking at Shirl. She seemed to get hotter and hotter.

I started thinking maybe this was good. Maybe Shirl needed to be made a little jealous. Maybe then she would come to her senses and realize her deep hidden feelings. I know it was wrong, but I started flirting with Tina a little. Tina seemed to be loving it, but Shirl seemed to be hating it. I was starting to get happy because from the way Shirl was acting, she had to be feeling something for me. After about twenty minutes, Shirl got her things together and stood up.

"Well, I need to leave. I forgot that I was supposed to meet a friend at 8:00," Shirl said, obviously lying.

"Let me walk with you downstairs. I'll be right back, Tina."

"Okay. It was nice meeting you, Tina," Shirl said, and Tina just looked and smiled. I stood up and walked downstairs with Shirl. She wasn't saying a word.

"What's the matter with you, Shirl?"

"It ain't nothing wrong with me."

"Why did you lie and say you had to leave then?"

"Why does it have to be a lie?"

"Because you would have never come to the library if you had to meet someone."

"I told you I forgot. You know, forgot. Like didn't remember," she said, sarcastically.

"You didn't forget."

"Whatever, Horne. I got to go," she said, and started walking toward the door.

"I think you're jealous," I said.

Shirl stopped and turned around. This time, she had a funny-looking smirk on her face. "Jealous of what, Horne?"

"Of Tina."

"Horne, if I wanted you, I would have had you a long time ago."

I couldn't believe she said that. I was mad as hell, but I had to say something smooth back. I couldn't let her know that she had gotten to me. "Well, you know, you better hurry up before it's too late."

Shirl opened the doors and then looked back. "I know," she said and then left. Damn! I started to go after her, but I thought it was best just to be cool. I stood there for a few minutes, thinking about what had just happened, and then went back upstairs where Tina was.

When I got back upstairs, Tina was in a pissy mood. "Isn't that the girl from the party?"

"Yeah, that's her."

"I thought you said she wasn't your girlfriend."

"She isn't. We're just close friends."

"Oh, really. Horne, I just want to know the truth!"

What was this? Shirl was acting crazy. Now Tina was really losing it. "I told you she's just a friend."

"Horne, just forget it. I'm leaving." Tina said, and stood up and started walking. I started to say something, but I didn't. I really didn't care what Tina did. I didn't want to hurt her feelings, but if she was going to trip, forget her.

I decided to leave the library since Shirl and Tina had gone. I needed to study, but hell, I wouldn't be able to concentrate here anyway.

That night when I got home, I called Shirl. I guess she wasn't home because her answering machine kept coming on. I kept calling, and that damn answering machine kept coming on. After about two hours of calling, I decided to leave a message. "Hi, Shirl, this is Horne. I'm sorry about what I said. I was just tripping. I really want us to start spending more time together. Shit, I wish you were home. I really wanted to talk to you." I was about to hang up when I heard Shirl.

"Hello."

I knew she was there. "Hey, Shirl."

"Hey, Horne."

"Shirl, I'm sorry about what I said and how I've been acting lately," I said, being weak as usual.

"Well, Horne, I was hoping that we could remain friends, but I really don't know."

Man, I knew I had been acting hard, but I really didn't want to lose Shirl's friendship. Besides, I still figured if we stayed friends, eventually, I could change her mind. "Shirl, I'm sorry. I want us to be close again."

Chapter Nine

"Yeah, man, she's great," Fred said. Fred was in the room telling me about his new girlfriend. Evidently, he had met her at that party we went to about a month ago. "Man, she's fine as hell. Did you see her? I was dancing with her at the party."

"I saw you dancing with some girl. Was she about your height and light complected?"

"Yeah! She's fine, isn't she?"

"As far as I can tell, she was cute."

"Yeah, that's my baby," Fred said, and he was so happy. I don't think Fred ever had a girlfriend here at school. This may have been his first girlfriend period. He always claimed he had a girlfriend out of town, but no one had ever seen pictures of her with him. He showed us a picture of a girl, but on the back where she had written something, it had been marked out. So I always figured she probably was one of his friends, and he just lied and said she was his girlfriend.

I was happy for Fred, though, but it was hard for me to understand why this cute girl liked Fred. Fred was straight and all, but I couldn't see her really wanting to be with him. There had to be a catch.

"How long have you two been going together?" I asked him.

"Well, we've been talking on the phone ever since the party, but we didn't start going out until about a week ago."

"Oh, so y'all just started going out. And y'all go together already?"

"Actually, we don't go together yet, but we will soon."

Now this sounded more like the truth. "Have you kissed her yet?"

"Yeah, man! Of course." Fred stood and started walking around the room. It seemed like he was getting mad about something. "Why are you asking me all these questions? You don't believe me or something?"

"Yeah, I believe you, man."

"No you don't. You, Tim, and even Corey don't ever believe me. Y'all act like I can't get anybody, but I can and I have. This girl really digs me, but I guess it's too hard for you to be happy for me. You're too busy trying to make me a liar."

"I am happy for you, Fred. I'm also concerned about you. I wasn't asking you questions because I doubted you. I was asking questions because I care about you and don't want you to get hurt," I said, and I knew that Fred knew I was lying, but I had to say something because Fred was right. We always thought he was lying. Maybe he had been telling the truth about his girlfriend out of town. Nah. I doubt it, but I did feel bad about making Fred mad. I guess I should just give him the benefit of the doubt.

"Horne, do you really expect me to fall for that bullshit? Well, I don't, Horne." Fred said, and looked at me and then left. On the way out, he passed Tim coming in and then he slammed the door.

"What's the matter with his ass?" Tim asked.

"He's mad at me because I was asking him a lot of questions about this new girl he is supposedly talking to."

"Yeah, Corey told me about her. He said she had been up to the room a couple of times. Shit. He said she was fine."

"Maybe Fred is telling the truth this time, but it's still hard for me to believe that a fine ass girl would like Fred."

"Who you telling? I guess some things just can't be explained."

"Well, you're right. I guess I'll just have to apologize to Fred later. I'll give him a chance to cool off first."

"Yeah, maybe his ass will get some."

"Yeah, maybe."

Tim and I talked for about an hour. Tim was tripping. He kept saying that Fred was going to get him some from that fine ass girl, and the only person I could get some from was big ass Martha. I told him to shut up because he had more than his share of ugly hoes, but since his girlfriend now was halfway decent, he wanted to talk shit. I didn't pay him too much attention because in actuality, his girlfriend wasn't all that. Anyway, it was just a matter of time before me and Shirl hooked up permanently.

Speaking of Shirl, we were supposed to be going to the library together tonight. She stayed in some apartments next to campus and I was going to walk over there, and then we were going to walk to the library together. I had a test the next day, and so did Shirl, so we decided to study together.

After I got ready, I called Shirl and told her I was on my way. I decided to stop by Fred's room first and apologize for not believing him. When I got to Fred's door, I heard some slow music. It sounded like The Isley Brothers. I knocked on the door and waited for Corey to answer. Fred came to the door. He had changed clothes since he had left my room. He had on some slacks and a shirt and tie.

"What's up, Fred."

"Yeah, what do you want, man?"

"I just wanted to tell you I was sorry."

"Sorry for what?"

"Man, you know what."

"Well, I want to hear you say it."

"Fred, why are you making this so hard?"

"Making it hard? You're the one who's always making it hard for me."

"Well, Fred, I'm sorry for asking you all those questions and making it seem like I didn't believe you."

"Making it seem? You didn't believe me."

"OK, Fred, I'm sorry. What else do you want me to say?"

"I don't want you to say nothing. I just want you, Tim, and Corey to start treating me with respect and believing me when I tell you things. Y'all act like every time I say something about a girl, I got to be lying. Well, I don't lie."

Man! Fred was determined to make this as hard as possible. Why couldn't he just accept my apology and leave it alone. I started to say something, but that's when I heard her. "Fred, what are you doing, and who are you talking to?"

Damn! There was a girl in Fred's room. Who was there to see Fred, not Corey. I know Tim said that Corey had told him that she had been in the room a couple of times, but for some reason, I still didn't believe it until now.

"Just a minute, Rebecca. I'm talking to one of my so-called friends."

"Come on, Fred," I said, "so-called friend? I'm sorry, Fred, and I wish you would forgive me and stop acting this way."

"I got to go, man," Fred said.

"You could at least introduce me to her."

"Nah, that's all right."

I was getting ready to leave, when Rebecca appeared at the door. Damn, she was fine! "Who's your friend, Fred?"

Fred didn't say anything. He just put his arms around her and stood there looking crazy. I decided to introduce myself. "Hi, my name is Horne."

"Who?"

"Horne. Well, my real name is Raymond Horne, but everybody calls me Horne."

"Oh, Horne. My name is Rebecca."

"Nice to meet you."

"We got to go," Fred said.

"Bye, Horne," Rebecca said. "Nice meeting you too."

Fred closed the door. I was still standing there. Man, Rebecca was fine as hell. I didn't care what anybody said, there was something fishy about Rebecca and Fred being a couple.

While I was walking over to Shirl's, I couldn't stop thinking about Fred and Rebecca. I don't know. Maybe deep down, I was just jealous. When I got to Shirl's apartment, she was standing outside. She was looking good as usual.

"Hey, Shirl."

"Where have you been, Horne? I've been out here waiting for you for fifteen minutes."

"I stopped by Fred's room. He's mad at me, and I was trying to apologize to him, but he was tripping."

"Why is he mad at you?"

"He has this new girlfriend and he was telling me about her, but you know Fred lies all the time, so I didn't believe him."

"And he got mad? What? You came out and told him you didn't believe him?"

"No, I just started asking him a lot of questions, and I guess he could tell that I didn't believe him."

"Well, Horne, Fred will get over it. Who's Fred's girlfriend anyway?"

"This girl named Rebecca, and she is cute. That's why I didn't believe him."

"She's really cute?"

"Yeah, she is."

"Damn! Well, come on. Let's go to the library," Shirl said, and we headed to the library. While we were on our way, we talked about Fred and other things. The whole time, I kept looking at Shirl. She was perfect. I just knew one day that Shirl and I would be Mr. and Mrs. Well, I wished we would anyway.

We finally arrived at the library. I really needed to get some studying done, so I tried to stop focusing on Shirl as much. We decided to study on the fourth floor since it was the study floor and everybody was supposed to be extremely quiet. When we got up there, we found a table in the corner and proceeded to start studying. I was studying Electronics II, and Shirl was studying something about child education.

I stayed focused for about an hour and then I started smelling something, and it didn't smell good. I began to look around. I was trying to find out where that smell was coming from. Behind me was this dude. He probably had farted. Damn, it was stinking!

"Horne, are you not studying?"

"You didn't smell that?"

"Smell what, Horne?"

"That fart. Somebody has farted."

The next thing I knew, Shirl was just laughing. It was probably her ass stinking the library up.

"Did you fart?" I asked her, and she was still laughing.

"No," she said, laughing.

"Why you laughing then?"

"Because of the way you are looking."

"And how's that?"

"You just look crazy."

After the farting incident, Shirl and I tripped off and on during the remaining time we were in the library. We would study some, and then we would start talking and end up tripping. We were really having fun. For a while, I forgot about all my problems. The only thing that was on my mind was Shirl. Not the Shirl that dissed me, but the Shirl that I was laughing with. The Shirl that I was comfortable with.

After spending a few hours in the library, we decided to leave. As we were on our way back, I contemplated making a move on Shirl, but I decided not to. The evening had went so well, I didn't' want to do anything to spoil it.

When we got back to Shirl's, I said good night and left with a smile on my face. Nothing serious had happened, but for some reason, I felt more confident about Shirl and me. I knew in my heart that it was just a matter of time.

Chapter Ten

It was a couple of weeks before Thanksgiving, and I was talking to Shirl on the phone about how she was getting home for the holiday. She said she would probably have to ride the bus. This was good because I was riding the bus home, and my dad was going to let me drive the car back. I told Shirl, and we agreed to ride the bus together and that she would ride back to school with me. This was really great, Shirl and I riding together back home. It was about a five-hour drive, and on the bus it took about seven hours. Usually, I would have hated to have to ride the bus, but this time, I was looking forward to it.

Shirl and I had been talking for a long time. It was Friday, and I didn't have a damn thing planned. Tim was going to be with his girlfriend. I think Corey had plans too. Fred was still mad at me. Besides, I hadn't seen much of him since he started talking to Rebecca.

I still hadn't seen the inside of Shirl's apartment, so I asked if I could come over and visit. She said yeah. So I told her that I needed to stop by the cafeteria first and get something to eat before they closed. She paused a second and then surprised me by telling me that she would cook me dinner. Of course, I said okay. I told her I would be over there in about two hours.

When I got off the phone, I laid on the bed and started thinking about the evening ahead. I was excited, but I didn't know what to do. I wasn't sure if I should play it safe or make a move. It had been about three months since the infamous kissing incident. Maybe she was ready

now. Maybe she invited me to dinner trying to give me a hint. Maybe.
Just maybe.

I got up and started getting ready. I was about to walk in the bathroom when Tim walked in.

"What up, man?" I said to him.

"Shit!" he said, and he looked like he was mad about something.

"What's the matter with you?" I asked him.

"Man, that bitch has pissed me off again."

"What did she do?"

"Man, she done got off the pill, right? She said some shit about they
were making her sick. I think it's a bunch of shit, but anyway, we were
fixing to have sex, and she told me to wear a condom."

"And?"

"Man, I ain't wearing no damn condom. Especially with my own
girlfriend. Hell naw!"

"Tim, I don't see the big deal. She doesn't want to get pregnant. Is
that so awful?"

"All I know, man, is that I ain't wearing no damn condom with her.
Shit! I'm going bare or I ain't going at all. Hell, If I want to wear a condom, I'll get with some stank ho."

"Tim, what did she say when you told her you didn't want to wear one?"

"Man, the girl told me she wasn't going to have sex with me unless I
wore one. That's all right though. If she won't give it up, there's a girl out
there that will."

I didn't say nothing else to Tim. When he was upset like this, there
was no reasoning with him. I just shook my head and went to take my
shower. When I got out of the shower, Tim was on the phone. He was
talking loud, so I could hear every word. He was arguing with Mellani,
his girlfriend.

"Naw, Mellani!"

Tim was wrong, but the more I thought about it, the more I under-
stood his point. Condoms just didn't feel the same, and if I had a steady

girlfriend, I wouldn't want to wear them either, although nowadays, you have to wear them to be safe.

"Well, Mellani, if you don't give it up, somebody will." Damn, Tim wasn't having or hearing that shit. He said a few more things and then hung up. "Man! That damn girl." Tim started walking around the room and then he sat down. "Man, what are you doing tonight?"

"I'm going over Shirl's house."

"Naw, man, forget Shirl. Let's go out and get some hoes and get drunk."

"No. I told Shirl I'd be over there for dinner."

"Well, call her and tell her you can't make it."

"No, man. We'll have to kick it another night."

"Well, all right. I'm going to get drunk and find me some ass."

"All right. I need to go ahead and get ready." I said, and started getting ready, and Tim watched television. After I got ready, I threw on some cologne, looked in the mirror, and did the final touching up. Then I left. As I was leaving, I saw Fred in the lobby. He was dressed up again. This was odd, because Fred hardly ever dressed up, but the last two times I had seen him, he was dressed up. "What's up, Fred?" I said to him.

"Hey," he said to me, sounding crazy.

"Now when are you going to forget that?" I said, and Fred didn't say anything. He just stood there. "Come on, Fred, we boys. OK, maybe I didn't believe you at first, but I believe you now, man. I'm proud of you. You got a fine lady."

He was still standing there looking dumb.

"Fred, you the boy now. You the boy, Fred!"

Fred was trying not to smile, but it was coming.

"You the boy, Fred!" I said again, and he started grinning hard as hell. "We still boys?" I asked him.

"Yeah, we still boys," he said, still grinning. I was glad Fred had finally stopped tripping. We made fun of him a lot, but he was still our boy and I didn't like him being mad at me.

"Where you going all dressed up?"

"Uh, uh." Fred was just stuttering like he was scared to tell me where he was going. "Uh, I'm going to church."

"Church. It's nothing wrong with that."

Fred was about to speak when Rebecca came around the corner with her fine ass. "Fred, let's go. We're late."

"I got to go," Fred said, and took off with Rebecca.

I watched them leave and then began my little walk to Shirl's apartment. While I was walking, I started thinking about Fred. It was good he was going to church, but on a Friday?

When I got to Shirl's, I popped a Certs in my mouth. I always had a Certs or gum on me. I believed in fresh breath at all times. I only wish everybody believed that. I knocked on the door and waited for the princess to answer the door. When she opened the door, she had on some blue jeans, a denim shirt, and some Nikes. She looked real cute. It was funny, because I was wearing the exact same thing.

She invited me in and gave me a little tour of the place, and I do mean little tour because the place was very small. It was nice though. Shirl had it looking real nice and homey, and the place smelled good, too. I could smell the food, and it was making me hungry. Shirl told me she had cooked fried chicken, green beans, and her secret rice recipe. I told her that I was ready to eat. We went to the table and got ready to dig in.

"Damn, Shirl! This food looks delicious."

"Thank you, Horne. Dig in. And you better eat a lot of everything or I'm going to be mad."

I fixed my plate and sat down to eat. Man, I was hungry. I tasted the chicken first. Damn! It was good as hell. Shirl could really cook. "Damn, Shirl, this is good."

"What did you expect? Of course, it's good."

I smiled and kept on eating. Man, I was tearing the food up. I had eaten about two pieces of chicken, a whole bunch of green beans, and drank about two cups of Kool-Aid when it happened. I tasted the rice.

It was nasty as hell. It tasted like pure D shit. Man! I was just going to have to leave this shit on my plate. I couldn't even finish chewing the little I had already in my mouth. I was just sitting there with it in my mouth. I decided to spit it out in a napkin. I looked at Shirl to see if she was looking. She wasn't. She was busy tearing that nasty ass rice up. How was she eating it, and what in the hell was the secret that made the rice taste so damn bad.

I picked up a napkin and spit the rice out into it. I started drinking some Kool-Aid to get that nasty ass taste out of my mouth. That was the nastiest rice ever.

"I see you've tasted the rice. It's good, isn't it?"

I didn't know what to say. I was about to make up some lie when she started talking again.

"I knew you would like it. My mom always makes it. I don't cook it too often, but I just felt like cooking it just for you." Now why did she have to go and say all that? I felt really bad, but what was I going to do. Ain't no way in hell I was going to eat any more rice, but I didn't want to hurt her feelings.

I decided to just eat my other food and hope that she would leave the room so I could put the rest of the rice in a napkin and throw it away. I kept eating. I was almost finished and Shirl still hadn't left the room.

"Why aren't you eating the rice? You don't like it or something?" she asked, and looked at the rice on my plate.

"I like it."

"No, you don't," Shirl said, started looking like she was upset.

I didn't want her to get mad because it would mess up the rest of the evening. I must have been really in love with her, because I started eating the rice.

"You don't have to eat it if you don't like it."

"Nah, I like it a lot. I was just saving the best for last." Damn! The rice was terrible. I ate it as fast as possible. I tried to swallow it without chewing. Shirl had started smiling again. At least somebody was getting some pleasure from me eating the rice because I sure as hell wasn't.

When I got through, I excused myself to go to the bathroom. I felt really sick. I washed my mouth in the sink. I was about to go back in there with Shirl when it started coming—the vomit. I ran to the toilet and started throwing up my guts. I must have thrown up my entire dinner, and it was all because of that damn secret rice.

After I got myself together, I put a couple of Certs in my mouth and went back out where Shirl was. My stomach was hurting, but I acted like nothing was wrong.

"I thought you had got lost back there."

"Nah, I was just taking care of some business."

"Oh, I understand now," she said, laughing, obviously thinking I meant something else.

I helped Shirl clean up, and then we sat down in her little living room and started listening to some CDs. My stomach was feeling a little better, but it still felt empty and funny.

Shirl put on a little jazz. It sounded real nice. We sat there and listened for a while before we started talking. We talked about everything. I was really enjoying myself now. I still had memories of the rice from hell, but other than that, the night was going well.

After we finished listening to the jazz, she put in The Best of Luther Vandross. Why did she have to do that? She must have wanted me to make a move. Ordinarily, I would have made a move long ago, but there was only one problem. I was sober, and when I was sober, I was sort of shy when it came to girls. I wanted to, but I was scared. Shirl was looking so damn good, though. We continued talking, and then the song came on. "A House is Not a Home." This was Shirl's favorite song, and it was one of my favorites too.

"This is my song," she said, and stood up and started dancing real slow. She was looking GOOD! "Come on, Horne, let's dance."

This was great. She wanted to slow dance. I stood up and walked over to her. She put her arms around my neck, and I put my arms around her waist. We started dancing, slow and smooth. Shirl was singing, and it was sounding good. It felt nice to have my arms around her. She smelled good and felt good; I was getting turned on. Too turned on, in fact, because I was starting to get hard. I knew she had to feel it, so I tried to move back some, but she wouldn't let me. She was holding me tighter and rubbing the back of my head. It felt really good. I had finally got up the courage to make my move, and then the song went off. Shirl let go of me.

"I just love that song," she said, smiling.

"Yeah, it got it going on," I said as I thought. Why did that song go off? Damn! Why didn't Luther make it longer. I was upset with myself for taking so long before deciding to make a move. Maybe I could get her to play it again. "Man! I love that song. That's my jam. Play that again, Shirl."

"You really want to hear it again?"

"Yeah! That shit was jamming." I said, and Shirl put it back on. "Come on, let's dance again.

"Nah, I'm getting tired. Let's just sit here and listen."

"Ah, come on. You can lean on me."

"Nah, I'll pass this time."

Damn! I thought to myself. We listened to music the rest of the night, but no more dancing took place. It was still nice, though, and I could tell that Shirl was enjoying herself. Before I knew it, it was 2:00 in the morning, and Shirl had started yawning, so I decided to leave.

"Well, I'm getting ready to go."

"OK, thanks for coming."

"Thank you for inviting me," I said, and we got up and walked to the door. When we got there, she opened it up and we just stood there. I wanted to kiss her, but I was a wimp. We started talking again. We stood up there and talked for about fifteen minutes. It was like neither of us wanted to say goodbye. I finally decided it was really time to go. "Well, I'm out of here. I'll give you a call tomorrow."

"OK," she said.

I turned around and started walking until I heard her call my name. I turned around and looked at her.

"I don't get a hug?" she said.

Damn! She had never asked for a hug before, so I walked back to the door. "Sure! You can have all the hugs you want." I put my arms around her and gave her a big hug. We hugged for a long ass time. We were just standing there holding each other. She felt so good. I decided to make that move. I moved back a little and kissed her on the cheek. She looked up. We were gazing into each other's eyes. It seemed like her lips were getting closer and closer. They must have been because the next thing I knew, we were kissing. There was no tongue action this time, but it was nice. I looked at Shirl, and she was looking me dead in the eye.

"I think it's time for me to go in. It's real late," she said, and I agreed. "Call me tomorrow," she said, still looking me in the eyes. We were still holding each other. I moved closer, and we kissed again. Her lips were so soft. They were perfect.

After we kissed this time, we let each other go, and she went back in the house. What a great night. If she hadn't served that damn rice, it would have been perfect. As I was walking back to the dorm, I kept humming the song we had danced to.

Chapter Eleven

The next few days were awesome. Shirl and I had been spending a lot of time together. Ever since that night we kissed, things were different. Things had been better than they had ever been before. For some reason, we never discussed that night, and we hadn't kissed again, but when we got together, the mood was different. It was like we knew we were going to get together, but there was no rush. It was like we knew we should be together, but we were going to let it happen naturally, at its own pace. Believe it or not, that was okay by me.

It was a couple of days before Thanksgiving break, and I was looking forward to the long bus ride with Shirl. I needed to call Shirl and ask her what time she wanted to leave, and if she could give me her money this evening because Tim was going to take me to get the tickets. It was about 4:00 and I was tired because I had been in class all day. I decided to call Shirl and then take a little nap. I called and no one answered, so I laid down to get a nap in. I would just have to call later.

I woke up at about 6:00. I must have been dead sleep because I didn't even hear Tim come in. He was over there on the phone. He probably was talking to Mellani. They were still having problems. She refused to have sex with him unless he wore a condom, and he still refused to wear one. They had been arguing every day for the past two weeks, and each conversation ended the same way.

"Okay, Mellani, fine! I keep trying to give you a chance, but I told you I ain't wearing no damn condom. And if you ain't going to give up the ass, I will get it somewhere else!" Tim said, and slammed the phone down. He had been saying that same shit for two weeks. I was surprised Tim hadn't gone out and cheated yet, but so far he had just been talking about it. "That damn girl," he said, and walked over to his closet and pulled out a bottle of whiskey. I drank a lot, but lately Tim was really overdoing it.

"You gonna drink that tonight?" I asked him.

"Yep."

"You still going to take me to the bus station?"

Tim threw his keys toward me and said, "You can drive my car." Tim was really losing it. He was going to sit in the room and drink whiskey by himself. I started to say something to him, but I could tell he wasn't going to be receptive to anything I had to say. So I decided to let him be and called Shirl. She still wasn't at home. I didn't feel like sitting in the room, and since I had Tim's keys, I decided to go for a ride.

Before I left, I called Corey to see if he wanted to roll. He did, so we broke camp. We drove around the city and talked. Since I didn't have my car, it had been a long time since I had been downtown, and it was sort of fun.

Corey and I talked about everything, but mainly, we talked about girls. Corey was telling me his secret tips on how to get girls sprung. "Man, girls are all the same. There are three types. The ones who want money, the ones who just want a good-looking man on their arm, and the legit ones."

"Yeah," I said to him.

"You see," he continued, "the ones I go after are the ones who want a good-looking man and the legit ones, because I can't do nothing with a money-hungry girl."

"I know that's right. I've gone out with a few of them, and once they found out I didn't have any funds, they were out the door."

"Don't worry about that shit. That shit has happened to me too. That's why I take these girls' money, man. Shit, they will do it to you."

"You know I'm trying to holler at Shirl, don't you?" I said, changing the subject.

"You get anywhere yet?"

"I'm making progress."

"Just be patient. She seems to be straight."

"Yeah, she is."

We talked about me and Shirl for a few minutes, and then Corey finished telling me about how he gets so many women.

"You see, first they are attracted to me because of my looks. I know I look good, and I let them know I know. When I get these girls intimidated, they will do anything to please me because they are scared to make me mad. They know I can get somebody else, and they know they probably won't get anybody as fine as me."

Damn, Corey was conceited as hell, but I liked to talk to him because so many girls had dogged me out. I liked to hear how he dogged them out. "You see, I go out with them and play that role. I act like I really like them. Don't get me wrong, I do like some of them, but I'm not ready to settle down. I act like I am, though. After a while, they start believing that shit, and that's when they let me have sex with them. They can forget it then because their asses get sprung."

"They get sprung, Corey?" I said, straight up tripping.

"Man! I dick those hoes down, and if they still don't want to give up the funds and they seem clean, I go down."

"You what?" I said, still tripping off his crazy ass.

"I go down. It ain't no shame in my game. I do what it takes, and that shit works, man." Man, Corey didn't seem like the type to go down. I really didn't know what type he was, but he didn't seem like that type. "Man, those hoes go crazy. It's like they're feenin' or something," Corey said, and I was just listening to him. I really didn't know what to say. "Man, don't tell me you ain't never went down?" he asked me.

"No, I haven't."

"You a damn lie."

"No, really, I haven't. I've never thought about it really. It seems nasty, though."

"It's not nasty."

"Well, what does it taste like?"

"Salt."

Salt. Corey was really tripping tonight, and I didn't even think he had been drinking.

"Salt?" I said. "That's all? S-A-L-T?"

"Yep," he replied. "That's all, and after you do it, they're yours. And if you're dicking them down right, they straight up get sprung," Corey said, and he was really talking a bunch of bullshit. Maybe that shit was true. Who knows? "Man, that's what you need to do to Shirl. Dick her down right and then later, go down on her ass. She'll be in love with your ass."

I didn't say anything. I just kept driving, and Corey kept talking. He talked about the previous subject for about ten more minutes, and then he started talking about Fred. "Man, I don't know about Fred. His new girlfriend is fine and all, but the girl has a problem."

"What do you mean, she has a problem?" I asked him.

"Don't get me wrong, Horne," he said. "I consider myself a Christian, and I love the Lord, but she seems to be a little too religious."

I thought to myself, this is getting interesting. "A little too religious?"

"Yeah. She goes to church every single day, and now she's got Fred going to church every day."

"Damn, that's why Fred is dressed up every time I see him with her."

"Yeah, and she goes to this little church on Northside. Fred said there's only about twenty members."

"Does he like going to church every day?"

"Nah. You know Fred never went to church before. That nigger is sprung, and I mean straight up sprung."

"I knew something was up with that girl. It's not too many girls as fine as her that would just want to go out with Fred. But really, it's nothing wrong with him going to church every day with her. I need to start going to church more myself."

"You ain't heard shit yet, Horne. The name of the church is The North 11th Holy Spirit Church of the Living Missionary of the Lord."

"And?" I said, not seeing anything unusual about that. I know I had been suspicious to begin with, but I was trying to be as positive as possible. To be perfectly honest with myself, I still didn't see anything wrong with Fred and Rebecca going to church every day. In fact, I thought it was good.

"It's like it's her personal goal to make Fred super religious, and man, I think he's giving all his money to the church."

"Why do you think that?"

"He doesn't ever have any money man. I mean never."

"Well, maybe we are overreacting," I said. "She can't be too religious. He met her at a party."

"That's what I don't understand."

Corey and I talked about Fred for a few more minutes. It was almost 10:00. We had been riding around for a very long time. We were fixing to head back to the dorm, but I decided to stop at a pay phone first and call Shirl while we were out. I still wanted to get those tickets tonight if she was going to be able to give me her money. I called, and she still wasn't at home. She had been gone a long ass time.

When I got back to the room, Tim was in there with some girl, and it wasn't Mellani. She looked pretty good, though. They were sitting on the bed watching TV.

"Roomie. Come over here," Tim said, sounding like he was drunk. I walked over to his side of the room and gave him his keys. "I want you to meet Shannon," he said.

I said hi to her and she said hi back. I turned around to walk back to my side when Tim started talking to me again.

"Yeah, this is my new friend. I met her downstairs. We talked a few minutes, and I asked her to be my friend. I've just been sitting in here telling her about Mellani," Tim said, and he was stuttering and slurring. He was really drunk, and the girl seemed to be embarrassed. She must have been real lonely to come up here with Tim.

"So you're Tim's new friend?"

"Yeah, I met him downstairs and he was tripping me out. Tim's crazy."

"Yeah, that's me," Tim said, "the crazzzy man."

"I'm going to leave you two crazzzy people alone," I said, and walked back to my side of the room and called Shirl, who still wasn't at home.

After a few minutes passed, Tim walked Shannon back to her room. While he was gone, I called Shirl a couple more times, and she still wasn't home. I was starting to get worried when Tim came back in the room. He was in one of his "I'm drunk so I got to spill my guts" moods.

"My roomie. My room dog. My boy!" he said, spitting everywhere.

"What's up, Tim?"

"Man, I love Mellani, man. I love her. I didn't even try to get on Shannon. I couldn't. All I could think about was Mellani."

"Call her and tell her you're sorry, man."

"I can't, man."

"Why not? If you love her that much, then wearing a condom shouldn't matter. You need to wear one all of the time anyway."

"It's the principle of it, man. It is principalaties and shit. If she gets her way now, then she will always think she's going to get her way."

"Get her way? When it comes down to this, there is no her way or your way."

"Whose side you on, man? Now would you want your girlfriend to all of a sudden make you wear a condom when you've been bare-dicking it all the other times?"

"No, but I would realize it is the right thing to do."

"Forget that shit. I know what I need to do. I need to get some from another girl. That's what I need to do, and that's what I'm going to do," Tim said, and walked to his side of the room and went to bed.

I was getting sleepy too. I called Shirl one more time. She still wasn't home, and her answering machine was on as usual. All night I had been hanging up when I heard the answering machine, and this time would be no different. I hung up and went to bed.

The next day was a regular old day. I went to class and came back to the dorm. This was the last day of classes before the holiday, and Shirl and I were supposed to be leaving the next morning. I still hadn't talked to her. All day I called, and all day that damn answering machine came on. I was getting mad. I started to go ahead and buy my ticket, but I was really wanting to be on the bus with Shirl, and if I went ahead and bought the ticket, there would be a slight chance that the bus I was on would fill up and she wouldn't be able to ride on the same one. I called a few more times, and she still wasn't in.

I sat there and watched television. Before I knew it, it was 12:00. Damn! It was too late to go get a ticket now. I called Shirl one last time, and the famous answering machine came on. Where in the hell was she? Her ass had been gone for two days. I decided to leave a message, then I tried to get some sleep. At first, it was hard to fall asleep because I kept wondering where in the hell Shirl was, but after a while, I fell off to sleep.

I woke up in the middle of the night because I had to use the bathroom. It had to be about four o'clock. On my way back to the bed from the restroom, the phone rang. Who in the hell was calling us at 4:00 in the morning, I thought to myself. I tried to hurry and answer it, but Tim beat me to it.

"Horne, telephone," he said, as I thought damn, who was this.

It was Shirl. "Horne, I got your message. I'm sorry, I've been busy," she said, sounding like something was bothering her.

"Well, I've been trying to call you because I wanted to go ahead and get our tickets because it would have been cheaper if we got them in advance."

"I'm sorry."

"Where have you been anyway?

"Studying."

"You've been studying tonight?"

"Yeah."

Shirl was feeding me a bunch of shit. We didn't even have class tomorrow, and I know she wasn't doing any extra studying the night before a holiday. I started to say something, but to be honest, I was scared to find out where she had really been. What if she was with Eric or some other guy. I wouldn't be able to handle it.

"Well, we need to get to the bus station early tomorrow. Hopefully Tim will take us. If not, we can catch a cab," I said, and Shirl didn't reply.

"Shirl, are you there?" I asked.

"Yeah."

"Are you still riding the bus?"

"Yeah," she said, and sounded like she was about to cry.

"What's the matter?" I asked her. She didn't say anything. She just started crying. I kept asking her what was the matter, and she just kept crying. After about five minutes, she finally stopped and told me she would be ready in the morning. I asked her again what was the matter, and she kept telling me she would be ready in the morning. I could tell that she wasn't going to tell me anything, so I told her I would call her in the morning.

Chapter Twelve

When I woke up, it was about nine o'clock. Tim was still sleep, so I woke him up and asked him if he could take Shirl and me to the bus station. He said yeah, so I called Shirl and told her to be ready. We went to pick up Shirl, and then we headed for the bus station.

The whole way over, Shirl didn't say a word. You could tell she had been crying because her eyes were swollen. I wanted to say something, but I didn't know what to say. I sure as hell didn't want her to start crying again, so I didn't say anything.

When we got to the bus station, Tim helped us take our bags in and then he left. Shirl sat down, and I went to get our tickets. While I was in line, I kept thinking about Shirl. Something had really made her upset, and for some reason, Eric kept popping in my head.

"Fuck you! Fuck all of you!!" I heard somebody say. What in the hell was that? I turned around and looked to see who was screaming. "Everybody can go to hell! Fuck all of you!" the person said again. It was some white man cursing out everybody in the bus station. He looked real dirty and was carrying a grocery bag. He just kept walking around, cursing people. He was getting closer and closer to Shirl. I started to walk over there, but I didn't want to lose my place in line because it was close to departure time. I looked around to see if there were any security guards in the area. I didn't see any. I started wondering where in the hell they were.

"Fuck you, lady!" I heard him say. Not only was he cursing, but now he was pushing people and knocking things down. He had almost reached Shirl, so I got out of line and started walking over there. He was still cursing. I was almost there when he reached her. "Fuck you too, bitch!" he said to her.

I looked around, and finally, I saw security. They were running toward him. He kept cursing at Shirl, and then he pushed her. When he did that, I lost it. I ran over and grabbed him and threw him down. Shirl was just screaming. I was about to kick him in the head when a security guard grabbed me. The dirty man got up and started running. He didn't get too far before the security guards got him. The one who had grabbed me let me go. He didn't say anything; he just let me go and ran over toward the man and the other security guards. That was some crazy shit. Shirl had stopped screaming, but now she was crying. I told her it was all right now, but the tears kept falling.

I took Shirl's hand, and we walked back to the line. It was about five minutes until departure time, so we had to hurry up. That was a wild experience, and I was hoping that Shirl would calm down. She was still crying, and everybody around us was staring.

When we got our tickets, we went straight to the bus and got our seats. I could tell already that this was going to be a long ride.

Shirl cried for the first thirty minutes of the bus ride, and then she finally stopped. I was relieved because she was really getting on my nerves. I had been looking forward to riding the bus with her. I was thinking that maybe the long ride would bring us closer together, but as long as she was in one of these depressed moods, nothing would possibly be accomplished.

I kept trying to talk to Shirl, but she wasn't very receptive. She would just nod her head. After a few minutes of this, I decided to just try and take a nap. When I woke up, we were almost in Nashville. I was happy about that because that meant we were halfway home. The trip hadn't been going as planned, but I was happy to be almost home. I looked at

Shirl and she was looking out the window. She seemed to be close to normal. I decided to try and talk to her again.

"Hey," I said, and she turned and looked at me. "How are you doing?"

"I'm better. That damn man at the bus station scared the hell out of me."

"I know. That man had a mental problem or something."

"Yeah," she said. "His ass needs to be in jail or in a mental hospital. And what makes it so bad, I was already in a bad mood."

"Now that you brought it up, what was the matter with you last night anyway?"

"Nothing," she said, and I was just happy that she was finally talking, but she was pissing me off with this "nothing" bullshit.

"Listen, don't tell me nothing was wrong. I'm supposed to be your close friend, and you keep feeding me that 'nothing' shit. What's up?"

"Horne, you wouldn't understand. You'll just get mad."

"Why would I get mad? I don't care what it's about, Shirl, I will understand." I was lying my ass off. I knew that if it had something to do with Eric or another guy, I would indeed get mad. In fact, I was already starting to get a little upset because I knew it had to be about a guy since she didn't want to tell me. I didn't say anything. I just sat there looking at Shirl.

"OK, Horne, I'm going to tell you," she said, and I was starting to get real nervous. "Eric came over to my apartment. He was finally returning some of my things that I had left over his house."

My heart started beating faster because I was getting mad as hell. I already knew it had something to do with Eric, but when she said his name, it was like an uncontrollable pain shot through my heart.

"He gave me my things, but instead of just leaving, he started talking crazy, and we ended up getting into an argument."

"And then what?"

"He just said a lot of mean things and made a lot of threats."

"Threats? Like what?"

"Nothing, really. He wants us to get back together, but I told him I'm not getting back with him. He was saying I'll never find anyone as good as him and that one day I'll realize it and want him back. I told him I won't, but he kept saying I will, and he said when I do, he will have moved on, and I'll forever regret that I let him go."

"Do you want him back?"

"I just told you I don't"

"Well, you are always saying that you love him."

"I did, but I don't think I do anymore. When I think about how he used to dog me out, I get so mad. I'll never go through that shit again, and I know he hasn't changed," she said.

I didn't say anything. I just sat there staring at the seat in front of me. She didn't say anything either. We just sat there. I was mad, hurt, and confused. We sat there for about five minutes before Shirl spoke.

"Horne, I'm sorry. I knew you were going to be mad. That's why I didn't want to tell you what happened. You shouldn't even be mad. Matter of fact, it seems like you would be glad. I dissed Eric."

Maybe I should have been glad, but I couldn't help thinking she was lying. It was hard for me to believe that she wouldn't get back with Eric if he wanted her back. I still didn't say anything. I was just thinking, maybe I should just give up. Hell, every time I started believing that maybe something would happen between us, I would get slapped in the face with harsh reality.

"Horne, I wish you would say something," she said.

I started to say something, but I didn't. I looked Shirl dead in the eyes. She looked back and smiled. I could have slapped that damn smile off her face. She was really making me mad. She must have really believed that I was going to fall for that bullshit she was saying. I decided to say something. I wasn't sure what to say, though. I didn't want to curse her out, but I wanted her to know that I wasn't falling for that shit.

"Shirl, I just don't know," I said.

"You just don't know what? There's nothing to know. I told you what happened and why I was crying."

"Well, all I got to say is if you're still messing with Eric, you're going to get hurt because he's a dog, and besides I thought, just maybe, you and I were finally developing our friendship into something more."

"I'm not messing with Eric, and I don't want to. How many times do I have to say that?"

I was waiting for her to respond to the my comment about our relationship, but she never did. She just sat there staring at me. I really didn't feel like repeating myself because I was sure she heard me. I decided to stop talking and start acting. I leaned over and kissed her on the cheek. She still didn't speak. She just started looking at me in a weird way. I wasn't sure what the look meant, but since she didn't say stop, I leaned over and kissed her again, this time on the lips, and she kissed me back. I kissed her again and again, and she kept kissing me back. Before long, we were tonguing, and it felt so good.

We kissed for a long time. I was happy, but I was also concerned. We had kissed twice before, and neither occasion led to anything, so when we finished kissing this time, I went straight to the point.

"That was nice," I said, and Shirl didn't say anything. She just smiled.

"What did that mean?" I asked.

"What did what mean?"

"That kiss?"

"It was nice," she said, but I wasn't going to let her get off that easy this time.

"This is the third time we've kissed. I want to know if it meant anything this time, because obviously, the other two times didn't mean anything to you."

"They did mean something to me."

"No, they didn't."

"Horne, I'm not fixing to start arguing."

"So what now? Are we still just friends?" I asked her, and for some reason I knew she was going to make up something about not being ready for a relationship, but to my surprise she didn't. She leaned over and kissed me again. It was so soft and wet. It was perfect, and after the kiss, I sat there more confused than ever before.

"I really like you, Horne, and I think I'm ready to give us a try."

I couldn't believe what she was saying. I had to make sure I heard her right. "What did you say?" I asked her.

She looked me dead in my eyes and said it again. "I think I'm ready to give us a try."

I did hear her right. I couldn't believe it. This was what I had been wanting for so long. I didn't know what to say, so I didn't say anything. I just grabbed her hand and smiled. I guess she didn't have anything else to say either, because she just sat there and smiled too.

While I was sitting there, I kept thinking about what we had been talking about earlier. How she said Eric had made her mad. Maybe she had been telling the truth, or maybe I was just so happy, I was wanting to believe her. I was about to say something when the bus stopped. I looked out the window. Damn! We were in Chattanooga at the bus station. We had been so preoccupied, we hadn't even noticed that we were home.

"We're home," Shirl said, and looked out the window.

"We sure are," I said, and looked at her. She was the perfect girl, and I wasn't going to do anything to mess this up. I started running my fingers through her hair. Her hair was long, soft, and pretty. This had to be one of the happiest days of my life.

"Welcome home, Shirl," I said with a big ass grin on my face. "Welcome home."

After we got off the bus, we said our good-byes and left with our respective families. I wasn't going to be able to see her over the vacation until it was time to leave because she was going out of town to see her grandmother. But believe me, I was going to call her.

Chapter Thirteen

It was good to be home. Everybody in my house was doing fine and seemed to be in good moods. My older sister wasn't home yet, but she was supposed to be home in the morning. I talked to my parents and my sister for a few hours. My dad was talking straight. He wasn't fussing, and I was real excited about taking the car back to school.

After I got settled and talked to everyone, I called my boy Stevall. I had to tell him about what had happened on the bus. His mother answered the phone and said he wasn't at home. I ended up talking to her for several minutes. She was telling me that Stevall was out on a date with some girl named Shelly. She said he had been going out with her for about two weeks, but she hadn't met her. This was odd because Stevall usually brought the girls he dated home to meet his mom at least by the second date. She must have been real ugly or something.

After I got off the phone, I sat there and thought about Shirl and wished that she was at home. She said she was leaving sometime tonight, but I decided to call anyway. The phone rang about five times with no answer, so I hung up. She was all I could think about. She was the one girl that I had really loved. The one girl that I had really lusted after and really wanted. I finally had her, and I wasn't going to do anything to mess it up.

The next day, I woke up to the smell of turkey. It was Thanksgiving, and by the noise downstairs, I could tell that my sister had arrived. I went downstairs and gave her a hug and a kiss. The day went by fast. We ate at around three o'clock, and the rest of the day we talked and watched TV. It was a normal Thanksgiving at our house, and this year, I had more to be thankful for because I had Shirl.

That evening, I went over to Stevall's house. I had called him earlier and he told me to drop by. Stevall lived in a very nice neighborhood, but they had the messiest yard I had ever seen. The grass was up to my hips. They had an old decayed statue and a couple of old tires in the yard. Their neighbors had to have complained, but every time I came over, it looked worse. I was always scared that something was going to run out of the front yard and bite me.

As I walked to the door, I made sure I stayed on the walkway. I knocked on the door a couple of times, and then Stevall came to the door.

"What's up?" I said.

"What's up, man?" he said, and we gave each other one of those quick-touch manly hugs.

Stevall looked the same except for one thing. His hair. It was straight and it looked a damn mess. I just kept staring at it. "You like my new style?" he asked.

I wasn't sure what to say. I was usually very forward with him, but since I hadn't seen him in a while, I didn't want to hurt his feelings, so I lied. "Yeah, it looks pretty good."

We went up to his room and started talking. I was very anxious to tell him about Shirl and me, but as I was about to bring up the bus incident, he started doing little things that caught my attention. He seemed different. I couldn't quite put my finger on it, but something was definitely different about Stevall besides his messed up hair style. Maybe I was just overreacting as usual, so I began telling him about everything that had happened between me and Shirl. I told him everything and he didn't even seem enthused. Usually he would have been straight tripping. Something was wrong.

"What's up with you, man?" I asked. "What's wrong?"

"Nothing, man. I'm straight."

"I know your hair is, but what's wrong with you?"

"Why you tripping?" he asked, and I had started laughing. I couldn't resist that one.

"Man, I'm just playing. Tell me about Shelly."

"Who?" he asked, seeming confused.

"Shelly!"

"Shelly?"

"Yeah, your mom said you had been dating some girl named Shelly for about two weeks."

"Oh, Shelly!" he said, the name finally ringing a bell.

"Yeah," I said. Stevall was acting strange. It was obvious that he had lied about Shelly. If Stevall had really been dating someone for two weeks, he would have been too anxious to tell me about it. "What's up? Why you lie and tell your mom you've been dating a girl named Shelly?" I asked him.

He didn't say anything. He just started looking around the room. I didn't say anything else either. I just stared at him. This lasted for a couple of minutes, and then Stevall started talking and laughing. "I just told my mom that to get her off my back."

"What? Has she been hounding you to find a girlfriend or something?"

"Well, sort of," he said, looking down.

"Sort of?" I asked.

"Yeah." Stevall just seemed like a different person. I knew something was wrong with him, but I couldn't understand why he didn't tell me what was up because he used to tell me everything.

Stevall and I talked for about another hour. The conversation was awkward, so I decided to leave. I thought about Stevall the rest of the night. Our reunion had really disturbed me. All I could think about was what Stevall was trying to hide from me. He was supposed to be my boy. He was supposed to be able to tell me everything, but he wasn't telling me anything.

My holiday visit flew by. Before I knew it, it was almost time to go. My visit home had been good with one exception. I couldn't stop wondering why Stevall was acting so funny.

Later that night, I got a phone call from Shirl. She said that she had just got in. It was good to hear her voice. I know it had only been two days since I had seen her, but it seemed a lot longer than that. We talked about our home visits, and we also tripped a little bit. We talked for about an hour. I told her that I would be over there in the morning to pick her up. I wanted to keep talking. I could have talked all night, but Shirl said she was sleepy. Right before we hung up, I told her I missed her. She got quiet for a second and told me she missed me too. She sounded so sweet.

The next morning, I left at about nine o'clock. I had enjoyed my visit with my family, but I was ready to go. Besides, I would be back in less than a month for the Christmas break. I went over to pick Shirl up, and then we hit the highway.

Shirl was looking especially good. Actually, she always looked good, but today she was looking goood! She must have been real sleepy because ten minutes after she got in the car, she was asleep. I was looking forward to talking to her, but she looked so cute sleeping. I was just happy to have her in the car. She slept for a long ass time. We had been on the road for a little over two hours, and we were already in Nashville. I usually stopped in Nashville, but since I didn't have to piss and the gas was still straight, I kept rolling.

Shirl was still asleep. I started thinking about Stevall again. I had thought about everything that had taken place while I was over there, and it all led to one thing. I had thought about this before, but I had always ruled it out. Stevall must be a homosexual. I couldn't believe I was saying this, but everything pointed in that direction. "No!" I said at the top of my voice. I must have been losing it. I looked over at Shirl. She moved a little, but she looked like she was still asleep.

My boy. My ace. My best friend since childhood. I just couldn't understand it. Maybe I was overreacting. He didn't tell me he was a homosexual. I was probably just overreacting. I had to be.

"I need to use the bathroom," Shirl said. She had finally woke up, and it was about time.

"Okay. I need to get some gas anyway. I'll stop at the next exit."

"Where are we anyway?" she asked. "Have we passed Nashville yet?"

"Yeah," I said. "We passed Nashville a while ago."

We chatted for a few more minutes until we came to the next exit. We got off the highway and went to a gas station. After we took care of our business, we got back on the road. All that sleeping and riding in the car had Shirl looking a little rough around the edges, but she still had that special glow about her. Shirl stayed awake for the remainder of the trip, laughing and tripping the rest of the way. I really felt good when I was around her.

When we got to Memphis, we decided to take our things back to our cribs and then go to Pizza Hut. I dropped my things off first, and then we went to Shirl's apartment. She told me to come in because she needed help carrying her bags; she also wanted to freshen up. Come to think of it, that's what I needed to do, but oh well.

While I was waiting for her to get ready, I looked around the room. She still had pictures of Eric and her up around the room. If she didn't want to be with him, why did she have his pictures still up. That shit was really pissing me off. Forget that shit, I said to myself. I started walking around, taking the pictures down. She had four separate ones up, and I took them all down. This was probably the wrong thing to do, but I was about to throw the pictures away. I looked at the pictures one last time. Shirl and I made a better couple anyway. As I was about to throw them in the garbage, she walked in.

"Horne! What are you doing?"

I had just been caught in the act. I stood there, trying to think of something to say while she walked toward me. She grabbed the pictures and looked at them.

"What are you doing with my pictures, and tell me the truth."

I was about to lie, but since we were going to try to have some sort of relationship, I thought I owed her the truth. "Well, when I saw those pictures, I got really mad."

"Why?"

"Why? You go with me now, and I don't want my girl having pictures of her and another nigger up," I said, and Shirl looked at me and smiled.

"So we go together now?" she asked.

"I thought you said you were ready to give us a try, so I assumed we were going together."

"You know what they say about assuming things."

"No, what do they say?" I asked.

Shirl walked right up to me. "They say this," she said. Then she leaned over and kissed me. This was a big relief because I was starting to get nervous. I was sure she was going to trip. We kissed for a few minutes. Her lips were soft as ever. After we finished kissing, we went to Pizza Hut. The evening was great. We had great conversation, and romance was definitely in the air. I felt like a lucky man.

The evening flew by, and before I knew it, we were on our way back to Shirl's apartment. We tripped the whole way back. The evening had been perfect; there was only one thing that could make it better. Hitting the skins! I wanted to real bad, but I wasn't going to rush things.

When we got to the apartment, I walked her to the door. I was going to leave because I figured she was tired, but to my surprise, she invited me in. We walked in, and she went straight to the bedroom. I was really getting nervous now. I didn't know what to do, so I just stood in the living room.

"Horne," she called to me, "what are you doing?"

"Uh," I said, not knowing what to say.

"Will you come in here?"

Damn! She wanted me to come into her bedroom. I started to walk. My legs felt so weak, and I was so nervous, it was like I could barely walk.

When I walked in the bedroom, it was like I had entered into a whole new dimension. Her room was all pink, and it smelled like a rose garden. All of a sudden, a big ass smile covered my face. I could feel it. This was going to be the night. I looked at Shirl. She was sitting on the bed, and she looked perfect. All I could think about was how good she would look in some lingerie.

"What are you smiling about? You never seen a woman's bedroom before or something?"

"No, I'm just happy."

"Why are you so happy? You used to see me on my bed all the time when I stayed on the dorm."

"Yeah, I know," I said, "but you weren't my lady then."

"Your lady? I'm your lady now?"

"Okay, Shirl, I'm tired of all this tripping. Are you my lady or not? You said you wanted to give us a try, but every time I say something about you being my lady or something, you start tripping. You trying to give me a hint or something because if you've changed your mind and don't want to be with me? I wish you would tell me now before I really start believing we're a couple."

I couldn't believe I had said that. The way that I felt about Shirl, I was surprised that I was hard enough to spit that shit out, but it needed to be said because I wasn't able to handle it if she was to lead me on for a little while and keep building my hopes up only to drop me.

"Calm down, Horne," she said. "Now exactly what is the question?"

"Are you my lady?" I asked.

She didn't say anything for a couple of minutes. She stood there, staring at me. At first, I was being hard and staring straight back at her, but after a few seconds, I started looking away. I was so in love with her, it was like the fear of not having her made me sick, and this scared me. Maybe I didn't need to be with her. Maybe I just needed to be by myself.

I started thinking when Shirl interrupted my thoughts with the words I had been waiting to hear for what seemed like an eternity. "Yes, Horne, I'm your lady."

I was happy as hell. I was about to smile, but I was trying my hardest not to, because since Shirl was my lady now, I was going to have to be a little hard at times so she wouldn't try to play me or take me for granted. I knew that she already thought she was going to be able to play me, but I was going to have to change all that. I managed to hold my smile back.

"I'm serious, Shirl. Don't say you're my lady and then change your mind tomorrow, because if you're my lady tonight, you're still going to have to be my lady tomorrow and the day after that and the day after that. I'm dead serious, Shirl. Please don't play with my emotions. Please don't."

"Horne, come here." I walked over to the bed and sat down next to her. I looked her dead in the eyes. "I'm sorry for tripping. I do want to be with you, but it just seems awkward, and I guess I trip to ease the tension."

"Well, Shirl, when you trip, it may ease the tension for you, but it makes things worse for me."

"I'm sorry. Come here." I moved a little closer. Damn, she was looking sexy! She looked into my eyes and smiled. "I'm your lady, Horne, and you're my man. Don't you forget it." Then she leaned over and kissed me. We began kissing passionately, and all I could think about was that tonight would be the night. The night I finally hit it. We kept kissing, and as we were kissing, I laid her back on the bed and started caressing her breasts through her shirt. Then I started unbuttoning her blouse. I was so damn excited.. She didn't say no, so I finished unbuttoning the blouse and proceeded to kiss her breasts. They were so soft and smelled so damn good. I could tell she was enjoying herself by the way she was rubbing the back of my neck. As I was kissing her breasts, I started trying to unbutton her pants. I was so excited, but I couldn't get the button loose. Not only was I excited, but I was also nervous as hell. I started trying to concentrate, but my hand was trembling so bad. I started getting frustrated, so I yanked the button real hard. The pants unbuttoned, but the button had broken off, flew across the room, and hit the wall. I was still kissing her breasts. Then she started moving away.

"Horne, baby, what are you doing?"

"Nothing," I said.

"No, you're doing something. Raise up for a second." She reached down and felt her pants where the button used to be. Why did I have to pull that button so hard. I knew she was going to get mad, but to my surprise, she didn't. She started smiling. "Horne, how did you tear my button off, baby?"

"Well...," I said, not quite sure how to phrase what I was trying to say.

"Don't get mad, Horne, but maybe we are moving too fast. This is probably a sign trying to tell us to slow down."

Slow down! We had been moving too slow as it was. Why did I have to be so goofy? Why couldn't I have been smooth like Billy Dee Williams, Wesley Snipes, or Denzel Washington. "I'm sorry about tearing your button off. I just want you so bad, baby."

"There will be other nights. We have forever."

"Forever?"

"I don't mean it's going to take forever. What I mean is that I'm sure we're going to be together for a long time, and there's plenty of time for that." I felt a little better, but I still wanted to hit it tonight.

We talked for a few more minutes. I kissed her and then left. Overall, it had been a wonderful night. On my way home, I kept thinking about the things that had taken place. I was fairly satisfied about how things had turned out, but there was still one problem. I had blue balls and they were killing me. Damn!! They were tearing my guts up.

Chapter Fourteen

I had almost reached my room at the dorm. I hadn't seen Tim since I got back, so I was real excited. I had so much to tell him. I knew he was going to straight up trip when I told him that Shirl was my lady. When I opened the door, all the lights were out. I turned the light on and walked over to Tim's side of the room. He wasn't there, but he had been there. There was vomit all over the bed, and a few malt liquor bottles laying beside the bed. It straight up stank. I turned around and started walking back to my side, and that's when I noticed it.

"OH HELL NAW!! HELL NAW!!!"

Tim was asleep in my bed, and he wasn't alone. Some ugly trick with a curl was laying beside him, and it wasn't Mellani. I was mad as hell. I couldn't believe he had done this. Not only were sex juices probably in the bed, but curl juices were probably everywhere too. I walked up to the bed and yanked my sheets and covers up.

"Get the hell out of my bed!" I yelled.

Tim looked up like he didn't know what was going on.

"Get the hell out of my bed!" I yelled again, and this time Tim and the girl jumped up. That's when I recognized her. It was Holly, the campus freak. I was really mad now. No telling what kind of germs were floating around on my bed. "Man, what the hell were you thinking? Fucking this bitch on my bed?"

Tim didn't say anything, he was so drunk. He looked like he was about to fall out, but the freak gave me a funny look and started talking crazy. She was sitting on the bed, butt naked, looking nasty as hell.

"BITCH!" she said. "I ain't nobody's bitch. You the trick ass bitch!" I couldn't believe she had the nerve to be talking crazy. I looked at Tim. He was sitting there with a pillow in between his legs, fucked up.

"You need to get this bitch out of here now!" I said.

"There you go with that bitch shit again. I'm going to show you who's the bitch." She started reaching for her purse, so I went in the closet and grabbed my bat. Girl or not, I wasn't going to let her hurt me. I was just hoping that she didn't have a gun. She started pulling something out of her purse. It looked like a knife. That's when Tim grabbed her.

"Put your clothes on, Holly, and let's go," his drunk ass said. She had the knife in her hand, but Tim was holding her arm down.

"Hell naw!" she yelled. "He ain't going to call me bitch and get away with it. I'll slice that trick ass nigger up into fifty pieces."

I started swinging my bat at the air. I was mad as hell, but I didn't really want to have any violent confrontation because this greasy ass bitch wasn't worth going to jail for. I was just trying to scare her so she would hurry up and get the hell out of my room. "Man, get this bitch out of here 'fore I knock her ass silly!"

"Hell naw! Let me go, Tim!" she said, and she was really trying to get to me, but Tim was holding her down. They were still naked, and she was flinging curl and pussy juice everywhere.

"Okay, Horne!" Tim said. "I'll get her out of here, but leave so I can calm her ass down."

"All right. You got five minutes, but if that ugly ass, jheri curl creature ain't out of here when I get back, I'm putting this bat upside her head, and I may put it upside yours for having that greasy hoe on my bed."

"All right, man. All right!"

I left and went downstairs to the lobby. I was so furious. I was going to curse Tim's ass out. He had really went too far this time. I couldn't believe he had done that shit. I waited in the lobby for fifteen minutes. I really didn't want to see Holly the freak again. I couldn't believe that she had pulled a knife out on my ass. It had truly been a crazy night.

When I got back to the room, Tim was still gone. The room straight up stank. It smelled like vomit, feet, ass, and curl activator. Believe me, it was a deadly combination. I felt like I was about to pass out. I started to take my sheets off, but then I stopped. I wasn't going to touch these nasty ass sheets. I was about to sit down in the chair at my desk when Tim came in.

"What the hell is your problem?" I asked him.

He didn't say anything. He just kept walking toward his side of the room, so I grabbed his arm. He stopped and looked at me.

"Don't start, Horne. I'm not feeling well."

Oh, hell naw! No he didn't. Tim was my boy and all, but I was going to have to wax his ass if he kept talking crazy. "You need to shut the fuck up and listen. Don't you ever bring a girl up in here on my bed. Better yet, don't you ever be on my bed."

"OK. Whatever, man," he said, sounding like he didn't even care and wasn't even sorry.

"Damn, Tim! You could at least say you're sorry."

"Man, you need to let my arm go and stop acting like a bitch."

Hell naw! He had just messed up. I was trying to stay calm, but when he said that, I lost it. I bent over, grabbed him by the legs, and dumped him. Then I wrapped my arms around his neck and started jerking it. "Punk, I'll kick your ass all over this motherfucking floor! You better start respecting me, motherfucker!"

He was trying to get up, but he was too skinny and weak. After a couple more seconds, I raised up off him, jerked his ass up, and threw him against a wall. He was still trying to retaliate, but with no success. I looked at him one good time, and then threw his ass to the floor. He just sat there looking mad. I didn't want to have to resort to force, but he was treating me like a bitch and I was not having that shit.

"Clean up this damn room, and get that vomit up with something," I said to him. He didn't say anything. He just kept laying on the floor. I felt like kicking his ass, but I didn't. I started taking the sheets off my bed and straightening up. By the time I finished, Tim had got up and walked over to his side and laid on the floor. I didn't say anything else. I wanted him to hurry up and get that vomit up, because it was smelling, but if he wanted to lay over there by it, I wasn't going to bother his drunk ass. I put some fresh sheets on my bed and tried to get some sleep. It was hard at first, because I had a lot on my mind. It had truly been a day full of excitement. Good and bad.

The next day, I woke up to the buzz of my alarm clock. It was eight o'clock, and I had a nine o'clock class, so I started getting ready. I looked over at Tim, and he was still asleep on the floor. The vomit was still on the bed, and it smelled like pure D shit in the room. I didn't even say anything. I was to the point, if he didn't give a damn, I wasn't going to give a damn, as long as he stayed on his side of the room.

After getting dressed, I left for class. The day went as usual. I went to all my classes and tried to pay attention to the teachers, but half the time, my mind was elsewhere. I kept thinking about Shirl and what had happened yesterday. I was supposed to go over there later on and study with her. I was planning on studying more than my books and notes. I had plans of studying Shirl.

After my classes, I went back to my dorm. When I walked in, I noticed the smell. The stint of vomit was gone. I walked over to Tim's side, and he had cleaned up. He wasn't in the room, and I was glad because it was going to be awkward to face him. I didn't know where he was, but I was going to try to leave before he came back. I got my things together, and then I called Shirl. I told her I would be over there after I went to the cafeteria. I made it out of the dorm without seeing Tim

The more I thought about it, the worse I felt about the incident, but I really had no other choice. Tim kept acting crazy, so I had to straighten his ass out. I was just hoping that he wouldn't hold a grudge.

I was mad, but I was willing to forgive him and just forget the whole thing had ever happened.

I went to the cafeteria and ate; then I broke out to Shirl's. When I got there, I knocked on the door. She answered the door, looking good. She had on some nicely fitted blue jeans and a sweatshirt. She wasn't fixed up or anything, but she was naturally beautiful. I gave her a kiss and walked in and sat down. We tripped for a few minutes and then began studying. It was really hard to study because Shirl was turning me on. She wasn't doing anything but studying, but I kept thinking about last night and what I wanted to do tonight.

We studied a little while longer before I interrupted her to tell her about Tim. She acted real surprised at first, but then she said the more she thought about it, the more it sounded like something Tim would do. We talked about that a while and then started back studying. I had stopped gazing at Shirl and started really focusing on my work.

After we got through studying, we went into her bedroom. I had got over the initial shock of being in her bedroom yesterday, but I was still getting excited. Shirl laid down on the bed, and I sat on the bed. She had my full attention. It was like she kept moving her body every few minutes in a slow, gyrating, sexy sort of way. I didn't know why she was doing that, but all I knew was that she was making me hard.

"Horne, baby," she said, "I'm so sleepy."

"You are?"

"Yeah. You not tired?"

"Yeah, a little bit," I said.

"Well, you can spend the night if you want to."

"What?"

"You can spend the night if you want to," she repeated.

I had a big ass smile on my face. She had just told me I could spend the night. Naturally, I said I would and started getting ready for bed. I didn't have a change of clothes, so I just went to the bathroom and washed up. I was going to have to get up early and go back to the dorm so I could take a shower and change clothes.

After I got out of the bathroom, Shirl went in it. I had washed up all the main areas, and I was ready! I laid down on the bed. I had to have the biggest grin on my face ever. Tonight was going to be the night. I started thinking about the activities that were destined to take place later on that night, and I couldn't wait.

Shirl was taking forever in the bathroom. She must have had to take a dump. Well, anyway, I kept laying on the bed, thinking about us doing the nasty, and a funny thing happened. The more I thought about it, the more I started getting scared. All types of crazy shit started running through my mind. What if I didn't perform well? What if I came too quick and she started thinking I was a forty-five second brother? These thoughts kept racing through my mind, and for every negative thought, I got limper and limper. Before I knew it, I had gotten all the way limp, and that's when Shirl came out of the bathroom. As soon as the door opened, I could smell the freshness. She looked like a priceless picture when she was coming through the bathroom doorway. That's exactly what she was to me. Priceless.

She had on a short gown, and I mean real short. It just came down to her upper thighs. I could see all of her legs, and they looked damn good. I had forgotten about all my doubts and fears. I was ready to get it on. Shirl walked over to the bed, sat down, and looked at me. I was still laying down. I was giving her the "let's not waste time, let's get it on" look.

"What are you doing?" she asked.

"I'm relaxing. I was just waiting on you so we could go to bed."

She looked at me real hard and then busted out laughing. I didn't know what she was laughing about, but I started laughing with her. We kept laughing for a few more seconds, then she stopped, but I continued.

"I don't think you understand," she said, smiling. "When I told you that you could spend the night, I didn't mean in my bed with me."

I looked at her like she was crazy. She couldn't be serious. She had to be playing. "What?" I said.

"When I asked you to spend the night, I meant out in the living room on the couch."

"You're not serious, are you? I know you're just playing."

"I'm sorry, Horne, but I am serious. I'm not ready to have sex with you yet."

I couldn't believe this shit. I was all excited, thinking that I was going to finally get the cat, and she throws this shit at me. I didn't know what to say. In actuality, there was nothing to say, so I grabbed a pillow and headed for the damn couch. I was mad as hell, and she knew it.

"I don't think it's right for you to get mad. I don't want to rush things, and if you don't understand, then damn you!" she said, and slammed the door behind me after I left the room.

If I had to go to bed mad with blue balls, I was glad the queen of tease had to go to bed mad also. I put the pillow on the couch and laid down. The pillow smelled just like Shirl. Damn! I had blue balls bad as hell, and all I could think about was what should have been going on. I envisioned myself going to work on Shirl, and started getting madder. I guess I just needed to be patient. If she wasn't ready, then she just wasn't ready.

I started thinking about how she had just got mad at me, and I was hoping that she wouldn't get the wrong impression of me and think that's all I wanted, because it wasn't at all. I wanted a long, lasting relationship that would last for eternity, but the way I had acted, I was sure she didn't get that impression. I had started feeling really bad about how I had acted.

I started to go and tell her, but I figured if I told her tonight, she would just think I was saying that to try and change her mind, so I decided to wait until morning and tell her. As I laid there, thoughts of Shirl raced through my mind until I finally fell asleep.

The next morning, I woke up at about six o'clock. My class wasn't until nine o'clock, so I had plenty of time. I decided to do something nice for

Shirl. I decided to cook breakfast and serve it to her in bed to show her that I wasn't mad. I walked to the kitchen to see what she had to eat. I guess it would have been nice if I had bought and cooked my own groceries, but the sad fact was that I was flat broke. She had some eggs, sausage, and bacon, so I decided to cook that. I also made some toast.

After I finished cooking, I put the food neatly on a plate and put the plate on a dinner tray. It looked too plain, so I went outside and looked for some type of flowers growing. I had barely walked out of Shirl's small yard, when I spotted some pretty wildflowers across the street. I picked the flowers and went back inside. I placed them on the tray. The tray looked much better now, so I went into Shirl's room. She must have been knocked out, because she didn't even hear me come in. I laid the tray by her bed and woke her up. She looked peaceful, but sexy as hell.

"Shirl. I made you some breakfast," I said.

She didn't say anything. She just kept laying there. I think she was still half-asleep.

"Wake up," I said.

She finally looked up. "What, Horne?"

"I made you breakfast."

"You did what?"

"I made you breakfast," I said, and pointed at the tray.

She started smiling. I was both happy and relieved. I was worried for a second that she was going to be mad at me for waking her up, but the smile on her face let me know that she wasn't.

"Good morning, Shirl."

"Good morning, Horne. Thanks."

"You're welcome," I said, and got up and went back to the kitchen to get my own breakfast. When I returned, we sat on the bed and ate. I told her I was sorry for getting mad and that I respected her for wanting to wait. She seemed to appreciate my saying that.

After we finished eating, I decided it was time for me to leave because I needed to go get ready for school. I told Shirl that I would talk to her later and made my way to the door. Before I got there, she called me back to the bed and gave me a kiss. It was nice and seemed to be filled with passion, but I didn't want to carry it too far, so I left it at that, not trying to make a move. I raised up to leave, but she kept pulling me back, and kissing me. I was really getting turned on. One kiss led to another, and before I knew it, I was on top of her on the bed, rubbing her breasts. It felt right, but I wasn't sure if I was making the right move. I had just told her I respected her choice to wait, and here I was rubbing her breasts. I wanted to keep rubbing, but I decided to stop. I raised up.

"I'm sorry, Shirl," I said.

"Sorry for what?" she asked.

"I don't want to rush you. It's just that I love you so much." I couldn't believe I had just said what I had said. I had just told Shirl that I loved her. I knew I loved her, but I wasn't planning on telling her this soon. She was looking at me with a shocked expression on her face. I wasn't sure what to say next. Damn! I was stupid as hell. Why did I have to go and say something like that. I stood up and started to turn toward the door when she grabbed my legs. I turned around, and she was staring me in the eyes with a look that I had never seen before. I sat down next to her. We didn't say anything for five whole minutes. We just sat there, looking into each other's eyes.

"Shirl, are you all right?"

"Yeah," she said, and paused a minute, then continued. "Did you mean it when you said you loved me?"

I wasn't sure what to say. I didn't want her to get the impression that I was sprung, but I was in love with her. Instead of playing hard, I decided to tell her the truth. "Yeah, I meant it."

Shirl put a small smile on her face, then leaned over and kissed me. I felt so awkward. I couldn't believe I had told her that. Why couldn't I have kept my big mouth closed.

Shirl and I kissed for a few more minutes. I was wanting to rub her body down, but I was trying to be Mr. Nice Guy. The funny thing about it was while I was trying to be Mr. Nice Guy, she was rubbing my whole backside down, and it was making me horny as hell. I didn't want to disrespect her, so I tried to raise up, only this time she wouldn't let me. She was holding me down, and had started kissing my neck. It felt so good. Damn, she was acting like she wanted to make love, but every other time, I thought she was ready, I got slapped in the face with blue balls. I decided to tell her that I thought it would be best if I just left.

"I think I'd better go," I said, and I was still laying on top of her. She stopped kissing my neck and asked me why I was ready to leave.

"I just think it's best because I'm getting highly aroused, and I want to make love to you so bad, but I know you don't want this. So I think it would be best if I just left."

"How do you know that?" she asked.

"Well, last night, you said…"

She interrupted me. "That was last night, Horne."

"What?" I asked.

"That was last night."

I was shocked. I didn't know what to do. It was like my whole body and mind just froze. This was what I had been wanting for two years. What I had been dreaming about. What had made my underwear unexpectedly wet in the middle of the night. It was finally going to happen. I started to get it going, but then a thought popped into my mind. What if she was teasing me again? Then again, what if she wasn't?

We started kissing, and I started going up under her gown. After a few moments of kissing and fondling, I started undressing her. I would pause every few minutes, thinking I heard her say stop, but she never said it. I was just imagining things. Before I knew it, she was butt naked. She looked awesome. I just stopped and stared at her. I was scoping her out from head to toe. She had started smiling. I could see her well too, because her blinds were open and the sun was shining on her body. She was pure perfection.

"What are you doing?" she asked, and I just ignored her and kept staring. It was like I was a kid in a candy store. I didn't know where to start.

"OK, you are sure having a good time checking me out, but now it is my turn," she said, and pulled my shirt over my head. I was so busy admiring my catch, I had forgotten that I had all my clothes on. My shirt was almost over my head when I stopped her and put my shirt back on. "What are you doing?" she asked.

I raised up and got off the bed, walked over to the window, and closed the blinds.

"What did you do that for?"

"I wanted to set the mood," I said, lying. The real reason was that I was self-conscious about my body. I was tall, and at 234, about five pounds over my ideal weight. I had a little belly. It didn't stick out or anything, but in the nude, it was fairly noticeable.

I walked back over to the bed and took all my clothes off. It wasn't that dark, so I could still see Shirl pretty well. I was ready. I got on top of her and proceeded to do my business. It was great!!! We really didn't do any foreplay though. We got right down to the main event, and I was proud of myself because I straight up showed out. I had been worrying about how my sexual performance was going to be, but evidently, I had been worrying for nothing because I was straight up boning.

We made love for a couple of hours, and then we laid in the bed, talking. This had to be one of the happiest moments of my life. I had skipped class and everything, but I didn't even care. In fact, I was going to skip my classes for the rest of the day. Shirl and I talked about everything. There's something about making love that opens a person up. I told her about how I used to dream about making love to her, and it seemed like I was dreaming now. She smiled and told me to hold her.

Chapter Fifteen

On the way back to the dorm, I stopped at the liquor store and bought two bottles of Cold Duck, my favorite champagne. It has a nice, robust flavor, plus it only costs $1.99 a bottle. It was a school night and only seven o'clock in the afternoon, but I was still going to celebrate. I had been at Shirl's apartment all day, and oh, what a day it had been.

I got back to the dorm and went to my room. Tim wasn't there. Usually, I would have wished he was in, so I could have told him what had happened, but we were still on bad terms. I put one bottle of Cold Duck in the refrigerator, and then I sat down on the bed. I was alone, but I didn't feel like it. I felt like I was in a room full of lovesick guys. Guys who were all in love with the girl of their dreams, and I was the guest of honor. The one who had succeeded in his hunt for love. I sat there feeling very happy and very proud of myself.

After a few minutes of reflecting, I opened the bottle. It didn't have a cork, but that was okay. I preferred the screw tops anyway. The liquor went down smooth as usual, and before I knew it, I was swallowing the last drops. I had straight up killed that bottle, and I was feeling good.

I decided to go to Corey and Fred's room. Hopefully, Corey would be there. I knew if Fred was there, either his girlfriend was there or he was talking to her on the phone. I went upstairs and knocked on the door. When Corey answered the door, I went in and sat down. I had barely sat down when I blurted it out.

"I boned Shirl this morning," I said.

Corey looked at me crazy. "You what?" he asked.

"I boned Shirl this morning."

"You did?" he said, smiling. Then he walked over and gave me some dap. "It's about time. Well, tell me about it, man. Was it worth the wait?"

"Man, it was great. I was straight up boning her, man. Shiiit, she's probably sprung now." I was talking much shit, but I felt I deserved to talk a little trash. After all, I had been after that ass for over two years.

"So you say you got her sprung?" he asked.

"Yeah, she probably is. Hell, she was holding me tight as hell."

"I know you was loving that shit."

"Shiiit, you know my ass was."

Corey and I talked for about another hour, and then Fred and Rebecca came in. Fred was looking goofy as usual, and Rebecca was looking upset. I spoke to them, then continued my conversation with Corey. We had changed the subject by then. We were now talking about Tim. I told Corey about what had happened. He was tripping, but he said I did the right thing.

We kept talking until Fred and Rebecca interrupted us. She had started talking loud, and Fred was trying to calm her down. I was going to ignore them and keep talking, but Corey whispered to me to be quiet so he could hear what was going on.

"Fred, I'm tired of this. You don't ever have any money. What are you doing, spending it on sinful things?" she asked him, loud as hell.

"No," he answered. "You know where my money goes!"

"Where, Fred?"

"To the church and to you. Besides, I don't have a job. I only have the money that my folks send me."

"You know what we talked about before."

"Will you hold it down?" Fred said. "And can we talk about this later?"

"Fredrick, you don't tell me to hold it down, and no we can't talk about it later!" She was sounding like his mother. I was on the other side of the room, straight up tripping. I looked over at Corey, and he was just shaking his head in a disappointed sort of way. I shook my head also, and kept listening.

"Fred, I told you that I have needs, and if you can't fulfill my needs, then I will find somebody else that can."

"Please, Rebecca. Let's talk about this later when we're alone."

"And that's another thing. You need to stop worrying about what your friends think and worry about what I think. If you can't satisfy my wants now, then I advise you to get a job real fast, because if you don't, you won't be with me anymore, and I'm not playing, Fred."

"Well,..." Fred tried to say something, but she cut him off.

"Well, nothing. If you want to stay with me, you'd better do it because I'm the best you have ever had or will ever have. I'm ready to go!" she said, and walked across the room and stormed out the door. Fred followed her. He looked ashamed. His head was facing the ground, and it looked like his eyes were watery.

Damn! Fred was a true sucker. I couldn't believe he had let her talk to him that way. Actually, I could believe it, but I didn't understand it. Fred was fat and goofy, but he didn't have to take the shit she was dishing out.

"Damn!" I said. "Does she always talk to Fred like that?"

"At first she didn't," Corey told me, "but I know yesterday, she was talking crazy too. Shiiit, at first she seemed nice, but you know, she be straight up going off on him." He paused for a second as I stood up and walked across the room. Then he continued. "You heard what she said about money?"

"Yeah, I heard her," I said.

"She's straight up taking that fool's money."

"I thought she was real religious."

"She is, but in her own way. She still makes him go to church and pay the church their share of money, but you heard her. She needs to have her needs fulfilled too."

"It sounds to me like she's straight up playing Fred for a fool."

"She is, and I really don't think Fred's getting any ass either," he said.

"Damn, I was sure Fred was hitting that shit."

"Nah. I honestly don't think he is."

"You ever ask him?"

"I've asked him a few times, and each time he tried to play it off like he was getting some, but I knew he was lying."

"I was sure he had to be taking that shit because he was pussy whipped, but he ain't seen no parts of the pussy and being played?"

"Yeah, and you can't talk to him. If you try to tell him to be careful or something, he gets defensive and sensitive."

"Well," I said, "I guess all we can do is keep trying to talk to him and hope he starts listening. He will probably have to learn for himself though."

"Yeah, I hope he learns before he gets too deep."

Corey and I talked for about an hour before Fred came back. When he got in, he didn't say anything to us. He just walked over to his side of the room and laid on the bed. I started to say something to him, but I could tell he was in a pissy mood, so I didn't say anything. I talked to Corey for a few more minutes, and then I left.

I went back to the room and Tim was still gone. He was probably somewhere drunk. Speaking of drunk, I had one more bottle of Cold Duck. I opened the refrigerator, picked up the bottle, and proceeded to empty it. I had sat there drinking for about an hour by the time I took the last swallow. It was good, and I was feeling good.

I picked up the phone and called Shirl, but her phone was busy. She was probably talking to one of her girlfriends. I called a few more times, and the line was still busy, so I decided to go down to the lobby and see who was hanging out. There was always some people down there playing cards.

When I got down to the lobby, to no surprise, the regulars were playing cards, and there were a few people hanging out. I saw a couple of my friends, so I hollered at them for a little while. After I got through chit-chatting, I decided to walk over to the girls' side before going back to the room to call Shirl. As I was walking through the girls' side, I saw a few fine honeys, but none compared to my baby.

I was about to head back to the room when I heard some girl call my name. When I turned around, I saw this cute girl standing in front of me. I recognized the face, but I couldn't remember where I knew her from.

"Hi, Horne, how you doing?" she said.

"I'm straight, how are you doing?" I said, looking at her crazy because I still couldn't remember where I knew her from. Usually, I had a good memory, but I was buzzing, so my thoughts weren't straight in my head.

"You don't remember me do you?" she asked.

"Yeah, I remember you," I said, sort of lying. I remembered her face, but I still couldn't remember where I met her. It was probably at a party, and I had probably tried to talk to her or something.

"No you don't, but if you do, tell me where you met me."

"At a party. I can't remember which one, but I remember meeting you at a party." She started smiling, so I thought I had guessed right. "See, I told you I remembered you. So how do you feel now?"

"Wrong!" she said. "You didn't meet me at a party. You met me in your room about a week ago. Tim introduced me to you."

Now I remembered. I must have been really buzzed because that was just a week ago, and I couldn't remember. She was cute, too. That's what made it so bad. Tim didn't bring too many cute girls to the room. It seems like I would remember the cute ones he did bring. "Oh yeah! Now I remember you. Your name is Susan."

"Wrong, again! My name is Shannon, and I can tell you're just like Tim."

"Nah, I ain't nothing like Tim, but what makes you say that?"

"You smell like you've been rolling around in some booze, and that's how Tim always smells."

"Well, I've been drinking tonight because I'm celebrating."

"Celebrating? Well, you know what they say. Drunks hang with drunks, and Tim's your roommate."

"Hold it a second," I stopped her. "If that's true, you must be a drunk because you came to the room with Tim."

"No, I'm not a drunk. I was bored, and Tim seemed like a nice, innocent guy, so I came to the room to just talk to him."

"So every time you're bored, you find somebody that you think is nice and innocent and go to their room?" I asked.

"No."

"Well, then, it must have been something special about that drunk that made you go to the room with him."

"Well, actually, I felt sorry for him," she said. "He kept talking about his problems with his girlfriend, and I thought he needed somebody to talk to."

"Yeah, tell me anything."

"It's none of your business anyway, but if you must know, I don't like Tim. He's just a friend."

I talked to Shannon for about an hour. She was cool and easy to talk to. She told me she was just a freshman and that she was from Little Rock, Arkansas. She didn't look like a freshman, though. I thought she had to be at least twenty, but to my surprise, she was only eighteen. We talked about everything. We could have talked for another hour, but I told her I had to go and that I would see her around. I was sure Shirl was probably off the phone, so I rushed to the room to call her. I had enjoyed my conversation with Shannon, but Shirl was constantly on my mind the whole time we were talking.

Tim was still gone when I got back to the room. He must have made up with Mellani unless he was over that freak's house. I hoped not, because I knew already that if that freak ever came back to the room, we were going to have to go at it.

I picked up the phone and called Shirl. Her damn phone was still busy. It had been that way for over an hour and a half. The funny thing about it, though, was that I didn't even get mad. After what had happened that morning, I had a great feeling about us and nothing was going to change that. I was sure she was probably just talking to one of her girlfriends.

I turned on the television and laid down on my bed. I needed to be studying, but today was like a holiday for me. It wasn't my first time having sex or anything like that, but it was an experience that I would never forget. I must have watched television for about fifteen minutes before falling asleep. I awoke to the sound of the door opening. Tim had just come back. I raised up and looked at the clock. I had been asleep for two hours. I looked at Tim. Something seemed different about him. He wasn't drunk. I was still mad at him, but I spoke anyway.

"What's up, man?" I said.

"What's up?"

"What you been doing?"

"I've been over Mellani's."

"Oh."

"Yeah," he said. "I really love her, man."

"You sure don't act like it."

"I know. I really messed up the other night." He walked over and stuck his hand out as if he wanted me to shake it. Then he continued. "I'm sorry, man. I was real drunk, and you know how I get."

"That's no excuse, Tim. Is that the same shit you're going to say the next time you get drunk and mess up?"

"No, man. I ain't going to mess up. I knew it was wrong, but I just did that shit anyway. I didn't think you would get that mad."

"You didn't? What if I was on your bed with some freak? You wouldn't get mad?"

"Yeah, you're right. I promise I ain't going to do no more messed up shit, man."

"I hope not," I said.

"Okay, you gonna leave me hangin'?" he said.

I gave Tim some dap. I was still a little upset, but I decided to give him the benefit of the doubt. Although if he ever did some crazy shit like that again, it was going to be on. We talked for a few minutes more, and then he went over to his side of the room. I laid back on the bed and was about to fall asleep again when the phone rang. I answered it, and it was Shirl.

"Hey, Shirl."

"Hey, Horne"

"What you been doing?" I asked her.

"Oh, nothing really. I've just been watching TV. I also did some homework. What have you been doing?"

"Chillin. I tried to call you for over two hours, and your phone was busy."

"Oh yeah," she said. "I talked to a couple of my friends."

We ended up talking on the phone for about two hours. We talked about several things, but the main topic was what had taken place earlier that day. She told me that she was impressed. She didn't think I could whip it like that. That shit tripped me out. I told her that it was only the beginning—that I was just warming up. She laughed a little, but I was dead serious.

After we got off the phone, I got up and started getting ready for bed. All I could think about was Shirl laying in that bed, all alone with nothing on but a gown. I was trying to brush my teeth, but I was steadily getting turned on. Fuck it, I decided to go over to Shirl's and make a surprise visit.

I finished brushing my teeth and was about to leave when I remembered that I hadn't taken a shower since yesterday morning. I was dirty as hell, too. I know I had to smell. I had been sweating, fucking, and drinking. Shit. If I had gone over Shirl's like this, she probably wouldn't even have let me in. I know she wouldn't have let me lay in the bed with her.

I took a shower and changed clothes. I was about to walk out the door when Tim started talking to me. "Where you going, man?"

"I'm going over Shirl's crib."

"Shirl's?" he said. "What y'all going to do?"

"Man, you're going to trip."

"What?"

"I go with Shirl now," I said. Tim looked at me like I was crazy. "I'm serious, man. We go together."

"Y'all go together?" he asked, still in disbelief.

"Yeah, we started going together on the bus."

"On the bus? That's not exactly the most romantic place."

"Yeah, but that's when it all materialized and came together. THE BUS!" I said, and Tim smiled.

"Well, I guess you finally got her, man. I know your ass is happy."

"You know it."

"So you're fixing to go over there now?"

"You know it."

"You going to try and hit that shit tonight?"

"Try?" I asked. "Nigger, you got me in the mix. Try?"

"Oh, so you know you're going to hit that shit tonight?"

"I've already conquered that mountain, and oh, what a climb it was," I said.

"You already hit that shit?" he asked, and I nodded my head. "Man, you're bullshitting. You ain't hit that shit."

"Whatever," I said. I got up and walked to the door. Tim was looking at me as if he was waiting for me to say something so I did. "Time to go," I said, and walked out the door, slamming it behind me. I heard him call my name, but I kept walking.

It only took me a couple of minutes to get over Shirl's. I had to knock on the door several times before she answered. She finally came to the door, wearing a robe and a frown. She didn't look the least bit excited or happy to see me.

"Hey Shirl, I thought you might need a little company tonight."

"What made you think that?" she asked.

"I could just sense it."

"Why didn't you call?"

"I wanted to surprise you."

"Well, next time, please call first."

"What? You don't like surprises?" I asked.

"Just call next time," she said.

Damn. I was sure she was going to be happy to see me, but once again, I was wrong. I stood there for a minute, staring at her. She just stood there, looking at the ground, not saying a word. I took it that she didn't want me to stay. I told her that I was sorry and that I was only trying to make her happy. I turned and started walking off, but she stopped me and told me to come in.

Shirl explained to me that it wasn't that she didn't want me to come in. She just didn't want me to start popping up all the time unexpected because she was a very private person and sometimes she just liked to be alone. I felt that I should be able to pop up whenever I wanted to, but since our relationship was in its beginning stages, I said okay to avoid an argument.

I walked in the apartment and followed her to the bedroom. I was still somewhat excited, but a lot of my enthusiasm had gone away. We sat on the bed and started talking. She was sweating me about drinking. She must have smelled it on me, but anyway, she was telling me that she wanted me to cut down on my drinking. I told her that I had, and that tonight was an exception because I was celebrating. She asked what I was celebrating.

"I'm celebrating making love to you this morning," I said, and I just knew that was going to put a smile on her face. Wrong again.

"So every time we make love, you're going to go out and get drunk?"

"No! And I'm not drunk." I said. Well, I was drunk, but she couldn't tell, or at least I didn't think she could. She didn't say anything else. She just laid back on the bed. She was in a pissy ass mood. She sounded straight on the phone. Something must have happened between then and now. The only thing I could think of was that Eric must have called.

"What's the matter with you?" I asked, and she didn't say anything. She just kept laying there, so I said it again, only a little louder. "What's the matter with you?"

"Nothing, Horne."

"Something's wrong."

"Yes, and I've told you what it is."

"Nah, you had to be upset about something before I came."

"Why?" she asked.

"Because of the way you are acting."

"I was getting that way because I didn't like the fact that you didn't call first. I told you that."

"Nah, that's not it. Did you talk to Eric tonight?"

"What?"

"You heard me," I said. "Did you talk to Eric tonight?"

She didn't say anything. She just raised up off the bed and started walking toward the bathroom. She was really pissing me off.

"Shirl! Did you talk to Eric tonight?" I asked again.

She was almost at the bathroom when she turned around and walked back to the bed. "No, Horne, and will you stop sweating me?"

"Oh, hell naw. Sweating you? You've been sweating me since I got here."

"Well, maybe you should leave," she said.

I didn't say a word. I just stood up and left. She had really pissed me off by the way she was acting.

Chapter Sixteen

The next day, I managed to get up and go to class. I was really trying to focus on what the teacher was saying because exams were coming up in about a week. I was doing pretty good in all of my classes except this one. I had a low C in Physics. I would have been satisfied with a C; I just didn't want it to slip down any lower.

The teacher was talking about vectors, and I was really trying to pay attention, but I couldn't. I was still upset about Shirl, and I was getting more upset because I couldn't concentrate on the lesson. She was the only thing that my mind would focus on. I kept trying to forget about her, but it was impossible. She had always been my ideal woman. Why did we have to fight, and if we had to fight, why did it have to be so soon?

Before I knew it, I was making up excuses for what had caused last night's argument. I had started blaming myself, but in actuality, I knew I hadn't done anything wrong. I was trying to rationalize things so I wouldn't think I was acting like a sucker when I went to apologize because that's exactly what I had decided to do. Maybe I was wrong. I guess I could have called first, and I should not have asked about Eric.

After my classes were over, I went back to my dorm room. Tim wasn't there, so I sat down on the bed and started watching television. I was still thinking about Shirl and what I was going to say to her. After a few minutes of deep thought, an idea popped into my head. Well, actually, a commercial popped on the TV. The commercial was about saying things with roses, and the store had a sale on roses. You could get a dozen for twenty dollars.

This was perfect. I would tell her I was sorry with a dozen roses. I had given her roses last summer, and that had led to me getting a little play. I could just imagine what a dozen roses would lead to this time. Yeah, it was going to be on, but there was only one problem. I didn't have twenty dollars. I only had ten. I was just going to have to borrow it. Since Tim wasn't in, I went up to Corey and Fred's room. Fred was gone, and Corey said he didn't have any money at the time, and all his girls were gone, so he couldn't get any.

I had to get that ten some way. I thought about waiting on Tim, but there was no telling what time he was coming back. His ass was probably broke anyway. There was only one other way I could get the money, and that was to sell one of my books back to the bookstore. I knew I didn't need to do that, but I was getting desperate.

I started thinking about which one of my books I could sell. We used all of them in class except for one—my Physics book. The only thing about that was that Physics was the class I was doing bad in. Fuck it, I said to myself. We didn't use that book anyway. I would just have to take good notes.

I grabbed the book and jetted out the door. Five minutes later, I was handing my Physics book to the man behind the counter. I just knew I was going to get at least thirty dollars for the book because when I bought it, it had cost fifty dollars. I stood there as the man typed the name of the book into the computer.

"I can give you fifteen dollars for it," he said, making me look at the computer screen.

"What?" I asked in disbelief.

"Fifteen dollars. I can give you fifteen dollars for this book," he repeated.

I couldn't believe he could only give me fifteen dollars. Usually, they gave you at least half-price for the book. They were really trying to cheat me, and I was mad. "Is that what the computer says?" I asked him.

"Yes," he replied.

"May I see it please?" He looked at me as if I was crazy, so I asked him again. "May I see where it says fifteen dollars, please?"

"Sir, I don't think that's necessary. I can give you fifteen dollars for the book. Do you want it, or are you going to keep the book?"

"I think it is necessary. If you are not going to let me see where it says fifteen dollars on the computer, I would like to see the manager."

"Sir, I don't think…"

"I don't care what you don't think! The manager, please!" I was really showing my ass, but I honestly felt I was being cheated. The man turned around and walked to the back of the store. I stood there, waiting. There was hardly anybody in the store. I was glad because at least nobody I knew would see me acting a fool. I stood there for about five minutes before this short, fat man walked to the counter.

"May I help you, sir?"

"Yes, I would like to see the computer."

"The computer?" he asked.

"Yes. This dude keeps telling me I can only get fifteen dollars for this book, and I find that very hard to believe. I just want to see where the computer says that."

"Well, sir, it does say fifteen dollars, but if you wait until the end of the semester, the prices usually go up."

"Well," I said, "may I see where it says fifteen dollars?"

"I really…"

"May I see it on the damn computer!" I said, and the man turned the computer to the side and pointed at it. There it was—fifteen dollars. I really felt stupid. The man who was waiting on me at first was standing behind the short, fat man, smiling. I really felt like slapping his ass.

"Well, do you want to sell the book, sir?" he asked. "As you can see, the computer says fifteen dollars."

There was another bookstore a block away, but it was already closed for the day. I really didn't want to sell the book, but I had to buy Shirl those roses. "Yeah, I'll sell it. Give me my fifteen dollars," I said, feeling real stupid. I took the money and left the store.

I barely made it to the shop in time. It was a few minutes before closing time when I walked in. The store was pretty large. I went back to the counter to purchase the roses. There were two men behind the counter. They seemed a little different at first glance, but I didn't pay it much attention.

"May I help you, dear?" one of the men asked me.

Dear? This man was calling me dear. These men were different, all right. They were feminine as hell. I just took a good look at them. They looked a damn mess. One of them was wearing red tights and heels, and the other had a little eye shadow on and a big ass bow on his head.

"What can I help you find?" the one with the bow asked.

I didn't know what to say. All I could do was laugh, because these men looked straight up like a couple of fools. I tried to stop laughing, but I couldn't. Every time I thought I had it under control, I would glance up and see that big ass bow and start laughing again. After about five minutes of this, tears were running down my face.

The two men were starting to get frustrated. They kept asking me why I was laughing and if I wanted to buy something because they were about to close the cash register. I tried to say the word roses, but I looked at the man's red tights and shoes and started laughing all over again. So I just pointed at the sign that advertised the sale.

"Is that what you want, dear?"

I finally stopped laughing and shook my head yes. I was too tired to talk from all the laughing.

"What is wrong with you? You think something's funny?" one of the crazy looking dudes asked me.

I didn't say anything. I just handed him my money and got the roses. As I was walking out, I heard the two men talking. "I don't know why he was laughing," one said to the other. "If he hadn't bought anything, I would have cursed his ass out."

"Hell, I know he wasn't laughing at us with his tall, goofy ass," the other jumped in. "Shit, he…" I just ignored them and kept walking. They had really tripped me out.

I went back to my dorm room before going to Shirl's apartment. I needed to freshen up some. After I took care of that, I was off. I got to Shirl's place and knocked on the door. When she answered, she had a strange look on her face. I just stood there with the roses behind my back.

"What do you want?" she asked.

"I'm sorry," I said.

"Sorry? You're not sorry, Horne, because you have done it again."

"Done what again?"

"You came over here without calling first."

"I came to apologize."

"And? You came to apologize, doing the same shit that started the problem in the first place?"

I didn't know what to say, so I just showed her the roses. She didn't do anything at first. She just looked at them, then at me.

"These are for you," I said.

"Horne, I…" she started, but I cut her off.

"Just listen to me for a second. I am sorry for making you mad, but I didn't intend on you getting mad. I really care about you, and I just wanted to see you. I didn't know that not calling first would cause all of these problems, because if I did, I would never have come over without calling. I'm telling you that I'm sorry, and I'm hoping that you will accept my apology. What we have is new, and it's going to take some time and effort. I'm willing to give it that, and I hope you are too."

I gently laid the roses on the ground in front of her. I turned and started walking off. I had just laid some straight up rap on her ass. I was hoping that she would stop me before I reached the car, but if she didn't, I was sure she would call me later that night. I slowed up, waiting on her to say something, but she didn't. As I was driving off, I saw her pick up the roses and smile. I knew that she would be giving me a call later.

When I got back to the room, Tim was in there with Mellani. They were supposedly back to normal. Mellani must have given in and gave him some ass, or he must have caved in and put on a condom. I wasn't sure who did what, but by the way they were acting, I could tell that somebody gave in. I talked to them for a few minutes. I was beginning to feel like a third wheel, so I decided to leave. I started to leave a message with Tim to tell Shirl in case she called, but I could tell by the way they were acting that no phone calls would be answered tonight anyway, so I left without saying anything.

I went up to Corey and Fred's room, but no one was there, so I headed to the lobby. When I got down there, the first person I saw was Shannon. I walked over to where she was standing.

"Do you live down here?" I asked her.

"No," she said, smiling. "Do you?"

"Nah, but I think you do. Every time I come down here, I see you."

"You've seen me two times."

"I know, but I've only been down here two times."

"You've been down here more than two times. You need to stop that damn lying."

"Well, anyway," I said, "how are you doing?"

"I was fine until you came over here talking crazy."

"Come on, Shannon. I was just playing."

"I know. I know. I just don't want people to start telling people that I'm a regular."

"You are a regular."

"Horne!" she said.

"Nah, I'm playing. So what's up?"

"Nothing. I'm just taking a study break."

"Me too," I said, lying. I hadn't been studying, but I was perpetrating as usual.

Shannon and I talked and talked. We talked a little about everything. Well, actually she talked, and I lied a little about everything. I don't know why. She seemed like a real nice girl. In fact, as I talked to her more, I started liking her a little. She was real easy to talk to, but for some reason, I was in one of those lying moods. I told her so much bullshit.

When I got up to my room, I put my head to the door to see if I could hear what Tim and Mellani were doing. I wanted to know if they were still busy or not. I listened for about two minutes, and I didn't hear anything. I started to go ahead and open the door, but I decided to knock first to make sure they were gone. Usually, you could hear the bed squeaking or something, but they could have been asleep, so I knocked. Tim didn't say anything, so I opened the door. I turned on the light and looked over to Tim's side to make sure they were gone. They were and that was quick. They didn't waste any time. They did what they had to do and then left.

I sat on my bed and started thinking about Shirl. I was sure she had been trying to call me. I picked up the phone and gave her a call. She answered it after the first ring.

"Hello," she said.

"Hey."

"Hey."

"What are you doing?" I asked.

"Nothing," she said. There was about a minute of silence, and then she spoke. "Where have you been?"

"You been trying to call me?" I asked.

"Yeah. Where were you?"

"I was downstairs in the lobby."

"Doing what?"

"Just talking to a few of the fellas," I said, wondering why she was asking so many questions.

"Who?"

"The fellas. What's wrong with you?"

"Nothing. I just know that I've been calling you for an hour, and I wanted to know where you were all that time." She was acting jealous as hell. It was weird, but I liked it.

"Well, Shirl, I was just down in the lobby talking to Corey and a couple of the guys I shoot hoop with," I said, and I was lying my ass off again, even though nothing was going on between me and Shannon. I wasn't about to be dumb and tell Shirl that I was in the lobby talking to another woman. I couldn't take any risks.

Naturally, Shirl bought the lie. We talked for about three hours. She told me that the reason she had been acting mean the other night is that she was having a hard time accepting what was going on between us. We had been close friends for so long. It was weird for her to think of me as a lover instead of her best friend. At first, this alarmed me because it sounded like she was trying to say that we should just be friends, and that was the last thing I wanted to hear. She didn't say that, though. She told me that she still wanted us to be together, but maybe we were moving too fast. She thought we had made love too early, and that maybe we should get to know each other in this new way before we had sex again.

I didn't agree with her suggestion at all, but basically, she didn't give me much of a choice. We had been very close friends for two years. We already knew each other well. Just because we moved things into the bedroom doesn't mean that all of a sudden, we are strangers. I tried to change her mind, but it was no use. Her mind was made up, and in so many words, she told me that if I wanted to stay with her, I would have to go along with what she said.

I was a little upset. All I could think about was her nude body next to mine, but I would just have to be patient. I had waited for two years; I guess I could be patient a little longer. Just as long as she didn't break up with me. I didn't think that I would be able to handle that. I could tell already, though, that I would have to put up with a lot of stupid shit that I didn't understand, but I was willing to, because I really loved Shirl. I really did.

Chapter Seventeen

Finals week was finally here, and I was stressed all the way out. Not only was I stressed out, but I was hornier than a dog in heat, and I wasn't getting any ass. Shirl wasn't playing when she said she wanted to slow things down. Not only had things slowed down, they had damn near stopped completely. I rarely even got a kiss, and when I did, no tongue was involved. It was really frustrating. It made it very hard to focus on my schoolwork, but I tried my hardest.

Shirl and I had been going to the library every day, and that was the major problem right there. I probably should have gone by myself. I knew I would have gotten more accomplished that way because all I did when we went together was stare at her and imagine that we were naked, doing the wild thing down one of the library aisles.

Well, besides the sexual part of our relationship, things seemed to be improving. We were getting along great, and it did seem as if we were getting closer. Maybe she was right after all. I just hoped that this not having sex thing would stop soon. Hell, I bet when she was with Eric, she screwed her ass off.

My exams came and went. I did well in all my classes except for Physics. The teacher ended up letting us use our books on the test, and ain't that a bitch. I had sold my book back to the bookstore to buy Shirl those roses. I was starting to think that maybe selling my book was a dumb move.

Exams were over. That meant the semester was over, and it was time to go home. The semester had flown by as usual, but all in all, it had been a good one for me. I may have made an F in Physics, but I had gotten my girl.

I was leaving for home the next morning, so I was busy packing my things. I expected Shirl to be riding with me, but she said that she had so much stuff to carry home that her dad was going to come get her. I told her I had enough room, but for some reason, she insisted on having her dad take her home, so I just left it alone.

Tim had left four days ago. He said he was exempt from his exams. I found this hard to believe. I was pretty sure Tim was lying, and I was also concerned about him coming back next semester. I knew I didn't do just great in school, but semester after semester, it seemed like he never went to class and never studied. The only time I ever saw him studying was when Mellani would come over and make him study. Mellani was good for Tim, but he was so damn foolish. Sometimes, I really worried about him. Maybe he did better in school than I thought he did. Hell, this wasn't the first time I didn't think he would be back, and he had always returned.

After I finished packing, I called Shirl. She wasn't at home. Her dad wasn't supposed to get there until tomorrow, so I was really wondering where she was. I called her constantly for an hour, and she still wasn't at home. I was starting to get frustrated, so I decided to go and see if Corey and Fred were still here. I had been so busy over the past week, I hadn't gotten a chance to go and holler at them.

I didn't even know what was the latest on Fred's romance. I only hoped that he would come to his senses. It was so obvious that Rebecca was trying to play him. She was fine and all, but damn! I sure as hell wouldn't take that shit she was trying to pull. Telling Fred that he'd better start taking care of her or she would leave him. Fred needed to tell her to go to hell. Damn, I just don't understand people sometimes. I knew I was sprung, but I sincerely hoped that I would never get like he was. Maybe he was so in love that he didn't realize what kind of fool he had become. I guess people have to learn for themselves, because if I had gone to Fred and tried to talk to him, I knew he would get mad at me and accuse me of trying to mess up his relationship or something, so I wasn't going to say anything. Corey had been trying to talk to him, and I know if he wouldn't listen to Corey, he sure as hell wouldn't listen to me.

Maybe one day, Fred would realize that he didn't have to take that shit, and that he deserved better. She looked good as hell, but looks weren't everything. I knew that was hard to realize at times. I sometimes forgot it myself, but when it got down to it, looks weren't going to make me happy. Don't get me wrong. I would have loved to have a fine woman, and I did, but if she had a nasty attitude, she would have to get kicked to the curb.

Speaking of kicking girls to the curb, it was time for my girl to be at the crib. I called Shirl again and she answered on the first ring.

"Hello."

"Hey."

"Hey, Horne. What are you doing?"

"Never mind that," I said. "Where have you been?"

"What?"

"Where have you been?"

"I was just out with one of my girlfriends."

"Who?" I asked.

"Horne, don't start that jealousy shit," she said.

She was always telling me not to act jealous, but every time she called me and I wasn't there, she would give me the third degree, and I wasn't about to be played like that. If she was going to ask me twenty questions, then I sure as hell was going to have twenty of my own for her. It wasn't that I was trying to be hard or anything. I was just making sure that I kept her ass in check. Besides, she wasn't giving me any ass, so I had to make sure she wasn't giving somebody else some.

"Never mind that jealous shit," I said. "Just tell me which girlfriend you were out with." You see, I wasn't about to let anyone play me like Fred was getting played. I had never been close to a mack or anything, but I had always made sure I wasn't played like a fool.

"I was with Angie. Damn! You are going to have to stop that shit for real, Horne. I don't like having to answer to you every time I do something."

"Well, hell, I have to answer to you every time I do something."

"No, not really."

"No, yes really. Every time you call me and I'm not in, I get twenty questions when I get back."

"You're not me, and you can't be trying to do everything that I do," she said.

I couldn't believe she had said that shit. I was already fired up about Rebecca and Fred, and she had to go and say something messed up like that. I was about to curse her out, but I stopped myself. I figured cursing her out wouldn't help anything. I already wasn't getting any ass, and if I cursed her out, I sure as hell wouldn't get any. I figured it would be best just to let her know I didn't appreciate her attitude and that I wasn't going to put up with it.

"I don't appreciate that comment, Shirl," I said, "and if you are going to think that way, then maybe we shouldn't be together."

"Oh, so now you're going to break up with me because I hurt your pride?"

"No, that's not it at all. I'm not breaking up with you, and my pride isn't hurt. I'm just tired of the way you talk to me and treat me." She tried to say something, but I cut her off. "Just listen for a change, please. Ever since we've been together, you have been treating this relationship like it's a dictatorship. Maybe it's because you know I've been in love with you for over two years and that I would do about anything to be with you. You constantly disrespect me. You make all the decisions and all the rules, and that's not right. A relationship is supposed to be a fifty-fifty thing, not a ninety-ten thing. Maybe it's my fault, Shirl. Yes, I thought I would do anything, but now I realize that I deserve better and that I shouldn't put up with all the things you do."

After I finished, silence dominated the room for a few seconds. Shirl wasn't saying anything, and I was waiting on her reply. She sighed a couple of times and then finally spoke in a low tone.

"What things do I do, Horne?'

"For starters, you jump on my case it seems like every time I act concerned about how you spend your time. I'm not trying to keep up with your every move, but sometimes I'm going to wonder where you are, and I don't see nothing wrong with me asking, if that's what I want to do."

"Horne, it's the way you ask," she said.

"Okay, maybe I said things the wrong way today, but hell, I got it from you. If you want me to show you some respect, then you need to show me some. And if you want to be in a relationship with me, then you are going to have to answer some questions at times about where you are and what you are doing. I don't think that's too much to ask, and if you're not going to be able to do those things, then you need to really think about if you want to be with me."

She just sighed again. When I first started talking, I didn't intend to say all of these things, but they just seemed to flow from my mouth. I sort of regretted some of the things I had said, but deep down, I knew that they needed to be said.

"And another thing," I continued. "That night I came over to your apartment without calling. You acted like I had committed a crime or something, and all I was trying to do was surprise you, not spy on you. And what if I just pop up. I'm your boyfriend, and I'm supposed to be able to do that."

"Not necessarily," she responded.

"I bet you didn't say anything when Eric used to pop up."

"What?"

"You heard me," I said.

"Yeah, and I'm tired of listening to you," she said, and hung up the phone.

Damn. I was tired of arguing, and I knew a lot of our arguments could have been avoided, but I was not going to just take orders from her. She basically wanted to do what she wanted to do when she wanted to do it, and she wanted me to do what she wanted me to do when she wanted me to do it. Man, things were so much easier when we were just friends.

I got up and started walking around the room. I picked up the phone a few times to call Shirl back. I would dial six digits and then hang up before pressing the last button. I just didn't feel right calling her back. I was really feeling confused. I knew I loved her probably more than I had loved any girl, but I didn't feel like I was getting any love back. If I would have been straight up honest with myself, I would have had to say that she didn't want to be with me. It was like she felt obligated to me. Like she was repaying me for all the times I had helped her out by being my girlfriend, as if she was going with me out of pity. That was honestly how I was feeling, and it didn't feel good at all.

After pacing the room about twenty times, I decided to leave. I wasn't sure where I was going. All I knew is that I was going to keep driving from place to place until I came up with some answers. My first stop was the store up the street to pick up a forty. After that, I drove around town, drinking my forty and doing some serious thinking. The more I thought about the situation, the more depressed I got. I came to the point that I wasn't sure what the hell to do, so I did the only thing I could think of. I turned my car around and headed to Shirl's apartment.

When I got to the door, I just stood there. I wanted to knock, but I was scared to. I was afraid of what was going to happen when she came to the door. No, I wasn't worried about her complaining that I didn't call, because at that moment, I could have cared less about that bullshit. I was afraid of what might have happened after that. I was scared that Shirl might have realized what I had already realized and say to me those famous words that had broken guys' hearts worldwide. We would be better off just being friends. The fact is that this was probably true, but I just couldn't deal with it. I had wanted Shirl for so long, and to think that I had finally had her, and for it to end so soon would truly be messed up.

I stood outside Shirl's apartment for nearly an hour. By this time, I had stopped thinking about everything. I couldn't move. It was as if I was paralyzed. I wanted to leave, but my legs wouldn't move. I was just standing there, freezing my ass off. I just stood there like a fool, staring at the door, and then I heard a noise. It sounded like a car door being closed, so I ran behind the nearest bush.

I could hear the person's footsteps getting closer and closer. My heart started beating faster and faster in anticipation of who it might be. For some reason, though, I already knew who it was. It had to be Eric. This was probably the reason why I wasn't able to leave. It was fate for me to catch her in the act and come face to face with the reality that she wasn't the girl for me.

The mystery person was almost in sight. As the figure took another step into my view, I saw Shirl's friend Angie, not Eric. I was so relieved. I jumped up by mistake. Angie turned and looked straight at me. At first, she seemed startled, as if she was about to scream, but then she recognized me.

"Damn, Horne!" she said. "What in the hell are you doing?"

Man, I felt so dumb. I had to think of a good ass lie fast. "Well, I dropped my keys on the way to the door, and I was trying to find them."

"All the way over there?"

"Well, when I dropped them, I accidentally kicked them over here."

"Uh-huh," she said. She was looking at me like I was crazy or something. "Well, while you look, let me see if Shirl's home." She knocked on the door. I was still behind the bush, acting like I was looking for my keys. When Shirl came to the door, I raised up and acted like I had found them.

"Here they are," I said. Angie, just turned around and gave me a funny look.

"What's up, Angie?" Shirl said.

"Hey, girl."

"Who's that out there?"

"Girl, it's Horne. He was behind the bushes as I was walking up, girl. Scared me half to death."

"Behind the bushes!"

"Yeah, girl. He said he lost his keys or something."

"Horne, what are you doing?" Shirl asked me.

I walked up to the door. "I came over here to talk to you."

"How can you talk to me behind the bushes?"

"Didn't you hear Angie? I lost my keys."

"Yeah, sure. You were probably trying to spy on me."

"Spy?" I said. "Girl, have you lost your mind?"

"Well, why were you behind the bushes?"

"I told you I lost my keys!" Damn! Shirl was really pissing me off.

"Shirl, I think I'll just come back later, okay?" Angie said.

"Nah, you don't have to leave," Shirl said. "Let the spy go!"

"Spy?" I said, loudly.

"No, I'll leave," Angie said, and started walking to her car.

I just stood there looking at Shirl, shaking my head. She just looked back at me, shaking her head. By this time, I was way beyond cold, so I asked her if I could come in. She hesitated for a few seconds and then said yeah. I walked in and sat down.

She was looking beautiful as usual. She even had rollers in her hair, but it didn't phase her. She was glowing as brightly as ever, and it was starting to make me sick. Why did she have to be so damn perfect, and why did things have to be so hard between us? Shit, why did things always have to be so hard every time I was trying to have a relationship with a real pretty girl. It was like there was a law against me having a pretty girl on my arm because every time I came close to having one, I would end up getting dissed. I was damn tired of it, too.

"Well, Horne," Shirl said, "what do you want to talk about?"

I wasn't sure what to say. A million things were running through my mind. I would start to say one thing, and then I would stop myself. I would start to say another thing, and then I would stop myself again. I was just so tired of all of it. I just wanted to know…Shit, I didn't even know what I wanted to know. I was truly frustrated.

"Horne, I guess I was right," she said. "You obviously don't have anything to talk to me about. So you must have been spying on me."

Damn, there she went again with that spying shit.

"Shirl, do you like me?" I asked.

"What?"

"Do you like me? And think about it before you answer. I want to know the honest truth. Just forget about everything that has taken place. Forget about everything that has been said. Forget about everything, and just answer my question honestly. Do you like me?"

She looked at me real hard, and then she looked around the room as if she was hoping to find the answer to my question written on the wall. I just sat there looking at her, waiting. She looked like she was about to speak when the phone rang. She gazed at me and then walked over and answered the phone.

I heard her say hello, and then it was like she started whispering. I was trying very hard to make out what she was saying, but she was talking too damn low. Man, I was so pissed, I was about to just give up. Things seemed really hopeless. Shirl had been tripping. Now her ass was standing in my face, whispering on the phone. Ain't that some shit? I wanted to stand up and leave, but my brain wouldn't give my legs the order. I really felt like I should leave, but something kept telling me to wait for the answer to my question.

A few minutes passed before she finally hung up the phone. Then she started that damn looking around the room again.

"Hello," I said. "Hello! Now that you're off the phone, will you answer my question?"

"Question?" she asked.

"Yeah, my question. Do you like me?"

"Yeah, Horne, you know I like you."

"Better than Eric?"

"Will you stop asking me all these stupid ass questions?"

"Stupid! That's the damn problem. You think everything is stupid, including this relationship."

"Relationship? Oh, is that what you call this?"

"Go to hell! I try and try, Shirl, and you don't give a fuck about me. Just go to hell!" I shouted, and got up and started toward the door. I had truly made a mistake thinking that Shirl and I could be more than friends.

I had the door half-open when I felt a tug on my shirt. I turned around and looked. Before I could even blink, Shirl's open hand met my face with enormous force. That damn girl had just slapped the hell out of me.

"Fuck you, Horne! Fuck you!" she screamed. "All you ever do is worry about yourself. You never worry about me. Never!"

"What is your damn problem?" I said. "That's all I do, dammit, is worry about your sorry ass. My whole damn day consists of worrying about you and your ass better not ever slap me again."

Shirl just fell on her knees crying. I was mad as hell at her, but I still didn't like seeing her cry. She just kept crying, louder and louder. I closed the door and sat back down. Shirl was really losing it. I had never seen her like this before. I wanted to say something, but I wasn't sure what to say. My face was still hurting, and I was still mad about what she had said, but she was looking so pitiful.

A few moments passed, and Shirl had calmed down a little. She was still crying, but not as loudly and wildly. I stood up, walked over, and sat down next to her. I wanted to put my arm around her, but I was reluctant because I didn't want to get slapped again.

"Are you okay?" I asked her, and she didn't say anything. She just sniffed.

"Are you okay? Damn, I hate to see you like this." I said, and put my arm around her. She grabbed it and threw it off. "Shirl, I'm just trying to help. I do worry about you because I deeply care about you. I'm sorry that I made you cry, baby, but you make me so mad by how you treat me. Shirl, look at me."

She didn't. She kept looking at the ground. So I gently put my hand on her chin and lifted her head up so that I could see her eyes. I was relieved that she didn't resist me. "Look at me, baby."

She gradually looked up. We looked in each other's eyes for several seconds. With every passing second, I got more nervous, and a little sweaty because I was about to say something again that I just knew I would probably regret.

"Shirl, look at me," I said. She looked everywhere except at me. "Shirl, look at me. Shirl. Shirl. Shirl!!" I shouted.

She turned her head around and looked my way.

"Look me in the eyes, please!"

She slowly looked into my eyes. Tears were still slowly running down her face. At times, Shirl seemed so cold-blooded, but now she seemed so sensitive and delicate.

"Shirl, I love you. Did you hear me? I love you," I said, and I was really looking at her hard to see what kind of response I was going to get. The tears that were running down her face in a slow manner had suddenly doubled in pace, and the little crying murmurs that had gone away were back. Damn, I just didn't understand it. You tell a girl that you love her and she cries harder than ever. "Shirl, please stop crying. Let me go get you some tissue."

I walked to the bathroom and rolled some tissue off the roll. I started thinking about the night's events. The more I thought, the more I realized that Shirl wasn't crying over me. I had thought she was, but she wouldn't be going that crazy over the little argument that we had. She didn't really loose it until after she had gotten off the phone and I said something about Eric. Damn! I had just realized that she was in there crying over that motherfucker. I started walking back to the room to give her the tissue, and dammit, I was getting hot.

When I walked back in the room, Shirl had gotten off the floor and sat down on her couch. I walked over to her and handed her the tissue. She looked like she was about to stop crying. I wanted to say something, but I wasn't quite sure what to say. I was mad, but I didn't want her to start crying again. We both sat there on the couch, speechless for what seemed like an eternity. In reality, it was only about twenty minutes. The whole time, I was thinking of how I thought Shirl was crying over me, and how I had told her I loved her like an idiot. The worst part about it was that she still hadn't said shit about it.

Shirl had finally stopped crying. She got up and went into her bedroom. I stayed on the couch. I assumed that since she didn't say anything, she was coming back in a few, so I waited. And waited. And waited. After about thirty minutes, I came to the realization that she wasn't coming back, so I got up and went into her bedroom.

Shirl was sitting on the floor, resting her back on the bed, talking on the phone. By this time, my anger had turned into frustration. I looked at her for a few seconds, then walked over and sat down on her bed. As soon as she realized I was in the room, she murmured a couple of words and hung up the phone. She sat there for a few seconds and then turned and looked at me. The tears were completely gone, and her eyes were now swollen. I looked dead into her eyes. They were so red, and she looked extremely tired. Tonight had truly been a depressing night. It had been a major set-back.

"Well?" she said, finally saying something. Not much, but it was something.

"Well, I'm glad you're through crying," I said.

She smiled a little. I tried to smile back. It was hard to, but I managed to fake a little one.

"Shirl," I said. I was about to say something else, but I stopped myself. I was depressed enough, and I didn't see any reason to make things worse. Shit, there was really nothing else to be said. Everything seemed quite self-explanatory.

"What?" she said.

"What?" I repeated.

"Yeah, you said my name. What were you going to say?"

"Nothing."

"Dammit, Horne. This is one of the things that pisses me off. You used to tell me everything, and now you act like you can't open up around me."

"No, it's nothing like that."

"Well, what were you going to say?"

I looked around the room, preparing myself for the conversation that would be inevitable once I said what I was about to say. I knew it wasn't going to be to my liking, but she insisted, so I went ahead and said it. "What's going on with you?" I said.

"What do you mean?" she asked. "Between us?"

"Nah, I sort of know what is happening between us," I said.

"What?"

"You know what."

"No, what?"

"Just forget that right now," I said. "I want to know what is going on with you. I know you weren't crying because of the argument we had. So what's up, Shirl?"

She didn't say anything. She just started that damn looking around the room again.

"Shirl, what's going on?" I asked, and grabbed her hand, and she gradually looked at me. "Don't forget, Shirl. I'm your friend. One of your best friends. You can tell me anything."

She abruptly stood up and began pacing the room. I just looked at her like she was crazy.

"Shirl," I said. "Shirl, come on. Tell me what's going on."

She stopped pacing and turned toward me. "I can talk to you?" she asked, sarcastically.

"Yeah, you can talk to me."

She looked at me as if she was trying to see right through me. "Like hell, I can."

"What?" I knew I had heard her right, but I couldn't believe what she had said. It had really caught me by surprise.

"Horne, I can't talk to you. Shit, I can't talk to no damn body. OK? That's what's going on, dammit."

"You can talk to me."

"Horne, everything has changed right now. I really do need a friend. It's too much shit that's trapped up inside of me, and I really need to talk to somebody about it. You used to be the person I could come to, but not anymore."

"Not anymore? It doesn't have to be like that."

"Horne, wake up! It's like that. Yeah, you were my best friend. I used to be able to tell your ass everything, but not anymore."

"You still can!" I insisted. "Just because we started a relationship doesn't mean we have to end a friendship. I'll always be here for you, baby."

"Hell, can't you see it, Horne? I can't talk to you because you're part of the problem. I'm so damn confused. Half of me is mad at you for ever wanting to get romantically involved with me, and the other half of me hates myself for doing it. Damn!" She sat on the floor. The tears were back. This scene was becoming far too familiar. I sat there with my head down, trying to think of something, anything, to say.

"Shirl, I said this earlier, and you didn't say anything, so I'm going to say it again. I love you, Shirl. I really do. I want us to be more than friends, but if that is not possible, then I still want us to be very close friends."

"Stop!" she shouted. "Just stop! You been yelling you love me all night. You don't even know what love is."

"Like hell, I don't. For two years, I listened to your problems and did anything and everything you asked of me. Each day getting to know you. Wanting to be with you. Wanting you to let me love you. Dammit, don't tell me I don't know what love is!" I was really hot. I loved this girl more than I had ever loved anybody, and she had the nerve to tell me I didn't know what love was.

"You don't. You don't love me, Horne. You just want to love me."

"How in the hell can you say that shit?"

"Because if you loved me so much, you would have never messed up our friendship."

"What? What the hell are you talking about. Messed up our friendship? Hell, I wanted more. I still want more. I don't just want to be friends, but I will settle for that if that's what I have to do."

"Well, that's what I want you to do. Hell, I'm not even sure if I want that."

"So you don't even want to be friends?"

"Horne, we fucked," she said. "Things will never be the same."

I started thinking about what she had just said. The more I thought about it, the more I realized that she was right. Things couldn't ever be the same, and I didn't want them to be the same. I know I had told her that I would settle for just being close friends, but in actuality, I had more planned. I figured that as long as I stayed close to her, she would realize that I was truly the right man for her.

Shirl and I talked for a couple more hours. She kept insisting that we should end our romantic relationship and that we shouldn't try to hang on to our friendship. I agreed just for the sake of agreeing. I was frustrated and very pissed, but I wasn't about to give up. Not yet, anyway. I suggested that for that night and that night only, we should act like we did when we were close. I told her that I knew something was bothering her, and that she needed to open up. I was hoping that if we started talking about her problems, maybe I would be able to help her; then she would remember how important I used to be to her, because I was always giving her advice and making her feel better when we were close friends.

She was resistant to my suggestions, but as the evening dragged out, she began to open up. She told me that for the past week, she had been seeing Eric. She also said that she had been talking to him almost every day since we had sex. She said that when we made love, that really upset her. Shit, I couldn't tell. She said that it just didn't seem right, and that it really made her realize that she wasn't over Eric. I asked her why she didn't just tell me that and get back with him. It would have hurt, but in the long run, it would have made things easier. She told me things were more complicated than they seemed. It turned out that the reason they broke up was because Eric had cheated on her. I asked her how she found out, and she said that he had just come out and told her. I didn't believe that shit because Eric didn't seem like the type to admit anything. He seemed like a sneaky snake in the grass. Don't get me wrong, I think it's messed up what he did, but even though I couldn't stand the punk, I respected him for being honest with Shirl.

She told me that she still loved him and that she wanted to get back with him. She just couldn't put what had happened behind her. She didn't think she could ever trust him again. So I asked her if the only reason she was with me was because she was scared to go back to him and to make him a little jealous. She denied it. She said that she had felt alone. She went on to say that she really cared about me and that for a little while, she really thought that she and I could have made things work. But now she knows that things would have been best if we had just remained friends. I asked her if she was going to get back with Eric. She said that right now, she just needed time to herself to sort things out.

We talked way into the night. Shirl just couldn't shut up. She was telling me every detail about Eric, things that I could have done without knowing. I guess she needed to get it off her chest. Things were really messed up. Not only had I gotten dissed. I had told her I loved her, and her response was to try and make me look like an idiot. Now

I was up here listening to her damn problems and giving her advice while I'm feeling lower than shit. And she had the nerve to tell me I don't know what love is. If that wasn't true love, then I didn't know what was.

Chapter Eighteen

I had just woke up, and I was still at Shirl's apartment. I looked over at her; she was asleep. I must have fallen asleep listening to her, and she probably got so tired of talking that she fell asleep. I wasn't sure what time it was, but I knew it had to be late as hell. I stood up and got ready to leave. I decided not to wake her up. I really didn't have anything to say. Shirl was right when she said that we could never be close friends again. I had realized that last night as I was listening to her problems. I had been listening to her and giving advice, but I wasn't really into it. I was faking, and I knew it would always be like that.

I started walking toward the door. When I passed the window, I noticed that it was light outside. I had spent the whole night there. I was supposed to be leaving for home early this morning. I started looking for a clock. It seemed like every clock in the damn place was unplugged. After about a minute, I realized that it would be quicker to just go to my car, because I had a clock in it.

I was about to walk out the door when someone knocked on it. I looked through the peep hole; it was Shirl's father. I wasn't quite sure what to do at first, so I just stood there and looked at him through the peep hole. He was a crazy looking man. It was like the front part of his head was bald and the back part had an afro. He was also tall and very thin. Shirl didn't favor him at all. Come to think of it, she didn't favor her mom either.

I was still staring at his head through the peep hole when he started banging on the door again. I went back to Shirl's room and woke her up. She was looking rough. I told her that her dad was out there banging on the door. It took a couple of minutes before she realized what I had said. When she finally came to, she jumped up and began panicking. She looked at me like I was crazy and then asked me what in the hell I was still doing there. I told her I had fallen asleep just like she did. She gave me another crazy look and then asked me what time it was. I told her I didn't know because all of her damn clocks were unplugged. I mentioned that it had to be after six, because the sun was out.

She started panicking again, and I just stood there. Her father was not only banging on the door now. He was also yelling her name out. She told me that she had to get me the hell out of there. I was to the point that I didn't give a damn anymore. Last night had pushed me over the edge. I gave her a look of sheer frustration and told her that I was fixing to go.

"No, Horne, you can't leave!"

"The hell I can't," I said, and I started walking toward the door.

Shirl ran ahead of me and stood dead in my way. "Horne, you're going to have to go out one of the windows." I was about to speak when she started begging. "Please, Horne. Please! Don't do this to me! If you go out the front door, my dad will go crazy!"

"Just tell him that nothing happened," I said. "Hell, just tell him the truth. Nothing happened!"

"Horne, you know how my dad is. Even if I tell him nothing happened, he won't really believe me. He may act like it, but deep down, he'll have some doubts. Come on, Horne. You can go out the window in the back."

I stood there thinking about what I should do. Damn! Shirl had really made me feel like I was nothing. It was like I was her servant or something. I did whatever she wanted. She kept trying to pull me toward the back, but I wouldn't budge. I kept standing there, thinking.

The more I thought, the more I started rationalizing. I really didn't want to get Shirl in trouble. After all, I really did love her.

I was about to go to the window when she said something that made me mad as a motherfucker. She told me to hurry up. She then said that I would do it if I really loved her. Man, I almost lost it. I couldn't believe that she had the nerve to say some shit like that. I stared her down with a look more fierce than any wild animal could have. She faked a smile and began to back up. For a minute, I thought about slapping her, but I erased that from my head because it wasn't my style. I looked at her one last time and then headed for the front door. She realized that I was about to go out the front door, and she started begging me not to. I didn't say a word. I opened the door and walked out.

I didn't see her dad at first, but then I glanced over to the side and there he was. He had gone from banging on the door to the side window. I just looked at him for a brief second. I didn't even look long enough to notice his facial expression. We knew each other because I had been over their house several times. He didn't say anything. I sure as hell didn't say anything to him. I was almost to my car when I heard Shirl's dad ask her what in the hell was she doing.

Chapter Nineteen

When I got in my car, I saw what time it was and realized that I was running late. I wanted to be on the road by 9:00, and it was already 8:30. I went back to the dorm and got my things together. I threw them in the car, and I was off. I didn't get a chance to shower or anything, but I was right on schedule.

The ride was long, but it gave me a chance to get my thoughts together. I had told myself before that I was through with Shirl, but I was serious this time. She had showed me how little my feelings meant to her and how she was willing to manipulate me to get what she wanted. I was really through with her. The damn bitch. I tell her how much I love her, and she doesn't even have one positive thing to say about it. To hell with her.

I got home at around 3:00 in the afternoon. The drive had taken six hours, but it had seemed a lot shorter, probably because I was preoccupied with that Shirl shit. When I got to the house, my mom met me at the door, fussing.

"Hello, and where have you been?"

"I've been on the road," I said. "Where do you think I've been?"

"Don't get smart with me, boy. I mean, all night and all morning."

"All night and all morning?"

"Yeah," she said. "I called you all night and all morning, and nobody was there."

"Well, Tim left last night, and I was on the road all this morning."

"Boy, don't treat me like I'm dumb or something. Tell me where you were all night."

My moms was sweating me. She must have been calling me all night, and I had been over Shirl's the whole night. Something must have happened for her to be sweating me like this. I immediately started panicking and asked in a nervous voice if dad was hurt or something. I don't know why I asked that. I guess her questions had gotten me scared, but she reassured me that everyone in the family was okay.

I was relieved and starting to feel comfortable again when she said that dreaded word. But. When I heard that word, I knew something bad was soon to follow, and I was right. She told me that something had happened to one of my friends. I got very nervous and anxious. I asked her who it was, and what had happened. She looked at me for a few seconds and then told me that Stevall was in the hospital. I asked her why. She said that he had tried to kill himself. I heard her, but it was like I didn't want to hear her, so I stood there, hoping that I hadn't just heard her say what I thought I had. She walked up to me and put her arm around me.

"Yeah, Stevall tried to take his life yesterday morning."

When she said it this time, it was like I heard the words in slow motion. Stevall had tried to kill himself. I felt terrible. I walked over to a seat and sat down.

"I just don't understand it," my mom said. "He always seemed so happy."

I just listened. She didn't understand it. I sure as hell didn't understand it either. I knew sometimes he got a little upset about having girl problems, but trying to kill himself? What in the hell could have caused that? I asked my mom why he had tried to kill himself. She said she really didn't know.

My mom and Stevall's mom were close friends. My mom said that his mom had called her last night wanting to know if I was home. My mom had told her that I wasn't at home, but I would be here today for the

Christmas break. Stevall's mom went ahead and told my mom that Stevall had tried to commit suicide. I asked my mom if that was all that Stevall's mom had told her, and if he was all right. She said that his mom said he was doing better, and that she didn't go into any details. She told me that Stevall's mom wanted me to come by and see him. She thinks maybe it will cheer him up. I told my mom that I was exhausted and that I would go see him tomorrow. She asked me why I couldn't go see him today.

"Mom, I told you, I'm exhausted."

"Just because you are a little tired, you can't go see your best friend in the hospital?"

"I'm going to go, but tomorrow."

"Well, I don't think a little tiredness should keep you from going to see your best friend."

"Mom, it's not just the tiredness. I just don't feel like I'm ready to see Stevall."

"Why?" she asked.

"You hit me with this news as soon as I get home. I mean I have hardly had a chance for it to sink in. I'm still trying to comprehend Stevall trying to commit suicide. If I see him, I won't know what to say or do."

"You say and do what comes natural."

"Well, what if asking him 'What in the hell was you thinking?' is what comes natural?" I asked.

My mom gave me one of those 'Boy, you better chill' looks. "Boy, you best remember you're talking to your mom and not one of your friends."

"Mom, I was trying to get you to understand why I don't want to go see him today. My feelings are all tangled up, and the more I think about it, I start getting upset."

"Well, since you seem to be so determined not to go today, you just make sure to be there early tomorrow, okay? Okay?"

I tried to say okay back to her, but I was starting to get choked up. The news had really started sinking in. I started thinking, what if Stevall had died? He was my best friend. Actually, it felt like he was the brother I had never had. The more I thought about what might have happened, the lump in my throat grew bigger and bigger. My eyes started filling up with tears. I didn't want my mom to see me, so I managed to mutter an okay and got up and walked to my room. My mom said something else, but I was so busy trying to get to my room that I didn't hear her.

By the time I reached my bed, tears were coming down my face. I must have cried for an eternity. I ended up crying myself to sleep. I was awakened by my little sister. She was screaming my name out. I turned over and looked at her. She said hi and told me that dinner was ready. I said hi back, and told her to tell mom I would be down for dinner in a few minutes.

I laid there in bed for a few minutes, and then I sat up. My eyes were tired, probably from crying, but I felt a lot better. It was like all the stresses, pressures, and disappointments had been washed away by the tears. Not only had the stresses from hearing what had happened to Stevall been washed away, but the stresses from my problems with Shirl had also been washed away. I really felt relieved.

I got up and walked to the kitchen table. My whole family was present. It really felt good to sit down and eat with them. Stevall was in the back of my mind, but it really was good to be home.

Chapter Twenty

The next morning, I got up at around 10:00. I felt really good. It was a little cold outside, but all in all, it was a pretty day. There was only one thing that I had to do that day, and that was to go see Stevall. I decided that I would do that around 2:00. In the meantime, I washed my clothes and tripped some with my little sister.

Time flew by and before I knew it, it was almost 2:00. I had told my mom earlier that I was going to leave at 2:00, so she had been bugging me all morning about it. So at 2:00, I was ready and out the door.

It only took me about twenty minutes to get to the hospital. As I pulled into the parking lot, I started getting very nervous. What in the hell was I going to say? How was I going to react if he started talking crazy and shit. I didn't know what to do or what to expect. I just went in hoping that everything would go smoothly.

On my way to Stevall's room, I ran into his mother. She was standing in the hall, talking to a nurse. I spoke to her, and she spoke back. She seemed really happy to see me. She said a couple more words to the nurse and then focused her attention on me.

"Hey, Horne. It is good to see you."

"It's good to see you too," I said.

We hugged and then looked at each other for a couple of seconds. It was like we both were trying to find the right words to say. She must have found hers first, because she started talking.

"Horne, I'm so glad you're here. I just don't know what's the matter with Stevall." She went on to tell me that Stevall had tried to kill himself over a girl. She said that he had met this girl named Susan about two weeks ago. They had been seeing each other almost every day, and he thought they were serious, but the girl met somebody else and broke it off with Stevall, and he just lost it. She said it was as if he was having a nervous breakdown. She said that she knew he felt terrible, but she never imagined that he would try to kill himself.

I asked her how did he try to do it. Her reply was that he had taken a lot of pills and drunk a lot of liquor. She said that Stevall was lucky to be alive. When she said that, I got a lump in my throat, and the tears started gathering in my eyes again.

Stevall's mom told me that she had gone to his room to put his tennis shoes in there when she saw him lying on the floor. She said that she saw an empty liquor bottle on the floor and got mad because she thought that he was just drunk. As she was yelling and walking toward him, she said she saw an open pill bottle on the floor. She looked closely and saw that it was empty. Then she pushed him, yelling at him for about a minute, but he never replied. She said that she really didn't think much of the empty pill bottle at first, but after about a minute, she started to panic. After a couple more minutes, she said she had regained control and called the ambulance. She said that they barely made it there in time to save his life.

Stevall's mom was still talking, but it was like I couldn't hear a word she was saying. Her lips were moving, but the only thing I could hear was my mom's voice telling me that Stevall had tried to kill himself. It was like I was losing my mind or something. I turned away from Stevall's mom and headed toward the restroom. When I got there, I went to the sink and started splashing water on my face. After a minute or so, I stopped and looked in the mirror. My eyes were red and I just looked real crazy.

I started thinking to myself, what in the hell was going on? Why were all these messed up things happening? I had really fooled myself. After I cried last night, I thought I was okay. I thought my problems had been washed away, but they were still here. They had only temporarily vanished. I had really thought I was going to be able to come down here and see Stevall and not get emotional. That was a big ass mistake.

Stevall's mom was now at the restroom door, calling my name. I moved away from the mirror and went to the door. I stood there for a minute and thought about my life. I was going through some rough times, but I thought about other people's lives. There were people whose problems were probably ten times worse than mine. I decided that I needed to suck things up and carry on. I took a deep breath and then opened the door.

"Are you okay, Horne?" Stevall's mom asked.

"Yes, ma'am," I said.

"Are you sure, baby? Do you want to sit down and talk?"

"No, I'll be all right. I just got a little upset, but I'm okay now."

"Are you really?"

"Yes. Now let's go see Stevall."

I started walking down the hall to Stevall's room. When I got to the room, I turned and looked at his mother. She asked me if I was sure that I was okay. I told her yes and went inside the room.

Stevall looked pitiful. It wasn't that he was looking sick as much as it was that he was looking sad. I put a big fake ass smile on my face and pimped up to his bed. I looked at him, and he looked back at me. I had this fake ass smile on my face, and he had a real ass frown on his. I felt like frowning with him, but I needed to be strong. I broke the silence by saying what's up.

He looked at me like I was crazy or something and then murmured something under his breath. That's the way it was for about twenty minutes. I would say something, trying to start up a conversation, and he would mumble something. After a while, the conversation started flowing more naturally. We started tripping and talking like we used to. The conversation was good, but it was odd. It was odd because here Stevall was, lying in a hospital bed, and we were talking about everything except what had happened to him to bring him to this point.

After a while, I got tired of being fake, so I just asked him what was up. Why did he try to kill himself? I didn't beat around the bush or nothing. I just asked him why. He tried to bullshit around the answer, but I was onto his shit, and I wasn't going to let him. I knew that he probably felt bad, but I wasn't going to let him off the hook. I felt that he owed me some answers. After he realized that I was serious and that I wasn't going for his bullshit, he told me he didn't know why he did it.

"What do you mean, you don't know?" I asked him.

"I, I…" he started, but I cut him off.

"Naw, naw, Stevall. I'm your boy. It's time for you to come clean. All this shit you've put me through. I've been worrying my ass off and I want to know what caused this," I said, and Stevall just stared at the ground. He didn't say a word. I told him that I didn't have a damn thing to do, and if it was going to take all day, I would just sit there until he told me something. It didn't take long before he started talking.

"Well, Horne," he said, "I was real depressed. It seemed like everything messed up was happening to me. I just got tired of it all. It didn't make sense to me anymore why I always had to be depressed."

"You don't always have to be depressed," I said. "Shit, you get depressed over little shit."

"Yeah, sure it's little to you. But the shit is major to me."

"What was it? What was so damn major that you would take your life over it?"

He just laid there with his head down.

"Tell me, Stevall," I continued. "What was so damn major that you wanted to kill yourself?"

He didn't respond, so I decided to let him off a little.

"Okay, Stevall, maybe at that time, you really thought it was major, but it couldn't have been that major. You're my boy, Stevall. My best friend, man. I don't want to lose you, and I'm not going to lose you," I said, and Stevall still didn't respond. He was still lying there with his head down. I stopped talking and just sat there. We sat there, not saying a word for about an hour, and then his mom came in with the nurse. She told me that it was time for Stevall to get some rest. I told her okay, and got up to leave. Before I left, I looked at Stevall and told him not to forget what we had talked about, and that I would be back tomorrow.

That night, I thought about my day and realized how special it was. I had spent a lot of time with my family. A lot of quality time, and I had really enjoyed myself. I had also spent some time with my best friend. I really felt blessed because he could have easily been dead. I know that may sound a little harsh, but it was true. Stevall could have been dead.

That night, I thanked God for all my wonderful blessings. I started thinking that maybe this had happened for a reason. Maybe this event would make Stevall a better and stronger person. I knew it was going to make me a better and stronger person. I already felt like I was seeing things differently.

The next day, I went to visit Stevall at around noon. When I went into his room, he was talking to his mom. He stopped talking when he saw me. I traded hellos with his mom and then she left.

"What up, Stevall?" I said.

He didn't say anything. He was still giving me the cold shoulder, so I spoke again. He still didn't say anything.

"Well, I guess we'll just have to sit here in silence like we did yesterday," I said, and that's exactly what we did. We sat there, speechless for an hour. I guess he was mad at me for being rough on him, but I felt it was necessary. I wanted him to know that I cared, but I also wanted him to know that there was no excuse for what he had tried to do. I wanted to know exactly why he had tried to do it, but it was quickly becoming apparent to me that I was not going to find out today. We sat there for a few more minutes and then the nurse came in and said that it was time for him to get some rest. She told me that I could come back later on that evening if I wanted to. So I got up and told Stevall that I would see him later on. I knew that if I persisted, it wouldn't be long before he opened up.

I returned to the hospital at about six o'clock. Stevall's mom was not there this time when I went to his hospital room. He was in there by himself, looking at TV. I walked in and sat in my usual seat.

"What up, Stevall?" I said. As usual, he didn't say anything, so I continued. "You are going to talk this time. I've been over here two times to see you and you keep acting like a bitch. I'm your boy. Tell me what's up or I'm just going to say forget it and not come back. Hell, I'm only doing this because I care about you."

Stevall didn't say a word. He kept looking at TV, so I got up and walked out of the room. I wasn't really mad, but I acted like I was because I knew this would probably make him talk. I thought he was going to stop me before I left the room, but he fooled me. I stood outside the door for a couple of minutes. I was beginning to feel stupid, so I went back in the room.

"Okay, Stevall, this is your last chance. When I leave this time, I'm not coming back."

He kept looking at TV. I walked up to the TV and turned it off. He looked at me as if I was crazy.

"Okay!" I said. Now that I have your attention, I'm going to say it one more time. When I leave this time, I'm not coming back, so this is your last chance." I looked at him and he looked away, so I started walking to the door real slow and grabbed the doorknob.

"Come back over here and sit down," Stevall said in a soft tone and I obeyed. "Horne, the reason I haven't been talking to you is because you pissed me off."

"I figured that," I replied.

"Damn, Horne, you think everything is so easy. Well it isn't!"

"All right. Tell me what happened that was so major that you had to try and kill yourself?"

"What happened?" he said. "What happened? A lot of things have happened. Hell, everything has happened. I just turned twenty-one not too long ago, and I have never had sex."

"So you're telling me that you tried to kill yourself because you are a virgin?"

"Nah, that's not all of it."

"Well, tell me all of it."

"Man, it's just how people treat me when they find out I'm a virgin. They either think I'm gay or a real geek."

I sat there waiting for him to say that he wasn't these things, but he didn't. He just stopped talking. I didn't care if he was a geek. In fact, I knew he was a little geeky, but I sure as hell hoped he wasn't gay. I was really worrying because ever since Thanksgiving, something in the back of my mind kept telling me that he was gay. It was the way he was acting over the Thanksgiving holiday. I decided to ask him straight up.

"Are you gay?" I asked him.

He gave me a crazy look. "Nah, man, I'm not gay."

I still wasn't convinced. "I'm your boy, Stevall. You can be straight with me. I'm still going to be your boy."

"Horne, I told you I'm not gay. Hell, I am being straight with you. I like women! I ain't with that gay shit"

"Okay, I believe you," I said.

"No, it's not okay. You're my best friend, and you don't even believe me."

"I just told you that I believe you."

"Whatever," he said. I could tell he was upset.

"Okay, Stevall," I said. "Let's just say I didn't believe you, and nobody believed you. Hell, that's no reason to commit suicide. As long as you know the truth, and just because you're a virgin now doesn't mean you're always going to be one. Hell, no one has to know you're a virgin."

Stevall looked at me and then turned away. As he turned, I saw a tear roll down the side of his face. He was really upset. Maybe to him, being a virgin was something awful. Hell, I didn't really see anything wrong with it. At least he knew he didn't have AIDS or anything. That was one of my greatest fears. I feared that one day, I might get a call from one of my ex-girlfriends telling me that she had AIDS, and that I needed to go get checked. If I was a virgin, I wouldn't have that fear, and when I did have sex, I could always wear condoms.

"Stevall, man, there is truly nothing wrong with being a virgin. One day, you will meet a fine ass girl that you really want, and she will want you too. Eventually, y'all will do it, and it will be very special because you waited, man. Shit, sometimes I wish I had waited."

I watched him wipe the tears from his face and look at me. "You a damn lie," he said.

"Nah, I'm straight up."

"Yeah, right!"

"You don't have to believe me, but you do have to realize that it's not the end of the world because you're twenty-one and haven't had sex."

"Whatever," he said. He was beginning to piss me off with his negative attitude.

"Listen to me, Stevall. You're just twenty-one. You're still young! During your lifetime, you will probably have so many women, man!"

"That's hard to believe."

"Man a lot of ladies like you. You're a nice looking dude."

"Yeah, they like me all right," he said. "Usually for about a week and then they diss me. Why is that?"

"You're being too hard on yourself."

"No, it's the truth, and since you know so damn much, tell me why. Why do girls always dump me after about a week?"

"Okay, I'll tell you why. It's because you try so damn hard. You try so hard that you forget to be yourself and end up acting like an idiot, a fool, or a jerk."

"Fuck you, man." Stevall was upset, but at least the tears had stopped.

"I'm just being real with you. If you just relax and be yourself, I'm sure you will find a girl that will be crazy about you."

Stevall and I argued back and forth for about another hour. I knew I was being hard on him, but I felt that it was what he needed. His family, and probably everybody else that came to visit him, had been babying him. In my opinion, this wasn't going to help him. I wanted him to know that what he tried to do was stupid. I was not going to feel sorry for him, and I didn't want him to feel sorry for himself either.

Although we argued the majority of the time I was there, I felt that I had accomplished what I was trying to do. He might not have agreed with me then, but I felt that I had left some important points with him. I was confident that once I left, he would be laying in his hospital bed, thinking about some of the things I had said, and sooner or later, he would understand what I was saying. Before I left, I told him to hang in there, and that I would see him tomorrow.

Chapter Twenty-One

A few days passed, and it was almost Christmas. In fact, it was Christmas Eve. I was going to have to go to the mall today, because I still had to buy a couple of presents. I had waited until the last minute as usual. My intent was to go early, but I messed around as usual and ended up running late. I was finally ready. I grabbed some bologna and headed out the door.

When I got to the mall, I had to drive around for what seemed like an eternity before I found a parking space. I guess everybody else had waited until the last minute. When I got inside the mall, it looked like a big traffic jam. There were so many people in there, everybody had to walk shoulder to shoulder and very slowly. Man, I started wishing that I had taken care of my shopping earlier. Oh, well, I would just hurry up and get these presents and break. I had to get my family something. I had intended on getting Shirl a gift, but I was beginning to change my mind. I went ahead and got the presents for my family, and debated with myself about whether I should get Shirl something. I wanted to, but I didn't want to. I wanted to because I really cared about her and we had exchanged presents last Christmas.

I wasn't sure if she was even going to get me anything this year, though. She was probably pissed at me for getting her in trouble with her dad. I really didn't care if she was mad because, hell, her ass dissed me anyway. Hell, yeah! She did diss me, and as I thought about it, it became easier and easier for me to make my decision. I decided to say to hell with Shirl and buy myself a present. I bought myself some black tennis shoes. I had them wrapped and everything. Damn Shirl.

I was finished with my shopping, and was making my way to the parking lot. There were so many fine ass women in the mall, but it was so damn crowded, I couldn't really scope them out like I wanted to. I could see their faces and breasts, but it was almost impossible to see the asses.

I was almost out the door when I heard someone calling my name. I turned around to see who it was. Whoever it was called again, but I didn't see who said it, and nobody looked familiar. I heard it again, and this time I saw who it was. It was a big black girl. She was just smiling and waving, and she didn't look familiar at all. She began walking toward me. The crowd didn't seem to bother her at all. She was just bumping people, knocking them out of her way.

The whole time she was coming, I was wondering who in the hell she was. When she reached me, I finally recognized her. Before I could say anything to her, she grabbed me and gave me a big hug. It felt like she was crushing my ribs and taking my breath away. When she let go, I gasped for air and tried to put a little smile on my face.

"Hey, Belinda," I said. "What are you doing in town?"

"My family is here, spending Christmas with Shirl and her folks."

It was Big Belinda, Shirl's cousin that went out with Stevall. If Belinda was here in the mall, then Shirl was probably somewhere close by. I started looking around to see if I saw her. Belinda kept talking. I didn't pay her any attention. I kept looking around to see if I saw Shirl until Belinda said something that caught my attention.

"Shirl and I was just talking about you. Yeah, she was trying to find you a nice present."

A present? Shirl was going to get me a present after all.

"She got you something good too," Big Belinda said.

"She bought me a present?" I said.

"Yeah, and you better buy her one if you haven't already, because she got you something good."

Damn, Shirl had got me something real good according to Big Ass Belinda, and I had spent the money I was going to use on her to buy myself something. I started wondering if I should take my shoes back and buy her something.

"Where is Shirl?" I asked Belinda.

"She's around the corner in one of those stores."

I knew I was supposed to be through with her, but I had to admit that I wanted to see her. I asked Belinda to walk around there with me so I could see Shirl. While we were walking, I asked Belinda how long she had been up here and if she had talked to Stevall. She said that she had just got in last night, and that she had not talked to him, but she planned to call him tonight. Maybe she could cheer him up. Hell, maybe she would give him some ass. That would really cheer him up. Belinda was big, but she looked like she could throw down a little.

When we got around the corner, we went into a women's clothing store looking for Shirl. She wasn't in there, so we went in a couple of other stores looking for her. She wasn't in any of the places we looked. Big Belinda said that she couldn't be far, so she suggested that we just wait a couple of minutes for Shirl to walk around this way.

While we were waiting, we talked and tripped a little. By the way she was talking, it sounded like she thought Shirl and I went together or something. They must not have had a chance to really talk yet. I thought about straightening her up, but I didn't even feel like being bothered. I knew that if I told her, then I would have had to go into a long, drawn out explanation. I would leave that job for Shirl.

Belinda and I stood there and talked for about five minutes before she spotted Shirl. She hollered to Shirl so loudly that half of the people in the mall could hear her. I turned to look, and there was Shirl coming out of Frederick's of Hollywood. She was looking sexy as a mother-fucker. She started coming toward us, and when she got a little closer, Big Ass Belinda started showing out.

"Hey, girl, what you doing coming out of Frederick's?" Belinda said, and Shirl didn't say anything. She just kept walking as if she didn't hear

Belinda. Belinda turned to me and smiled, and then said it again, loud as hell. "Girl, what you doing coming out of Frederick's?"

Shirl gave her a look like 'Belinda why don't you shut your fat ass up', but the look had no effect on Belinda. She just kept on talking.

"Girl, let me see what you got in the bag," Belinda said. "I know Horne wants to know what's in there. Don't you, Horne?"

I looked at Belinda with the same look on my face that Shirl had. The look that said, 'Shut your big ass up'. But oh, no. Belinda continued to show out. She asked Shirl one more time, and then she grabbed the bag. Shirl told her to stop and tried to hold on to the bag, but Belinda was too damn big. She got the bag from Shirl. Shirl looked real pissed, and for a second, I thought she was going to sprang on Belinda. She didn't, though. She just stood there and watched Belinda go into her bag and pull out her stuff. Belinda immediately started tripping.

"Ooh, girl, look at this," Belinda said. "Ooh, girl, what is this?"

I felt a little awkward, and I could tell that Shirl was embarrassed. That didn't keep me from looking, though. What I was seeing was really turning me on. It was a bra & panty set. The bra was basically a regular bra with a design or two added on. The panties, on the other hand, were something else. They were G-string type panties with a snap on the flap in the front for easy access. They were the bomb.

I looked at Shirl, and she looked humiliated. I looked at Belinda, and she was laughing. The laughter was disturbing enough, but then she started talking again.

"Damn, Shirl, you and Horne are kinky, aren't you?" Belinda said, and I couldn't believe she had said that. I didn't know what to say, so I stood there looking dumb.

"Man, you going to wear that shit out, ain't you?" Belinda said, looking at me. She had a fat, crooked grin on her face.

By this time, Shirl was ultimately pissed. She grabbed the panties and the bra from Belinda and then gave her a word or two. "Belinda, you need to just chill. Damn! Why does your big ass always have to embarrass me?"

"Embarrass you?" Belinda said, with a confused look and a shaky voice. "I was just playing with you."

"Well, you embarrassed me," Shirl said, and looked at me. Her eyes were intense, and she had a frown on her face as wide as Belinda's ass. "I'm sorry, Horne. Just ignore Belinda," she said, and turned and looked at Belinda. "I don't know what she is thinking about sometimes."

Belinda tried to reply, but Shirl cut her off.

"Anyway, I got something for you, Horne," Shirl said, and put her bra and panties back in the bag and started going through her other bags.

As she was rambling through her bags, my thoughts focused on those panties. I started thinking about the flap on them and who she was going to wear them for. Damn! She talked all that talk about needing time to her self. People that need time to themselves don't wear G-string panties with a flap in the front for easy access. I knew who they were for. That damn Eric.

My thoughts were interrupted when Shirl handed me a box. It was sort of small, so I assumed that it was probably some cologne. "It's not much, Horne, but I just wanted to get you something to let you know I was thinking about you."

I faked a smile and told her thanks. The gift was nice and all, but I was still thinking about those easy access panties. She was just standing there smiling at me. I think she was waiting for me to give her a present, but I didn't have anything for her. After a few seconds of awkwardness, Shirl started talking.

"Well, Horne, what have you been doing?"

"Nothing really." I didn't feel like telling her about Stevall. Actually, I didn't feel like talking at all. Those panties had really pissed me off. After about five minutes, she started picking up on the fact that I didn't have much to say. Actually, she didn't have much to say either. It was like she was trying to make conversation, but it all seemed fake. I don't know if it was because of what happened at school or those damn panties or the fact that I didn't give her a present or even mention anything about a present. We eventually said goodbye and went our separate ways. As I was walking away, I heard Belinda whispering to Shirl.

"Girl, you pissed at me?" Belinda said. "You need to be pissed at that nigger. He didn't give you nothing, nor did he mention anything…"

I just ignored her and kept walking toward the parking lot. I probably would have taken the shoes back and bought Shirl a nice present, but not now. Shit, she owed me this damn present anyway, and it was probably just some cheap ass cologne anyway. Some Jovan Musk or Brut or some bullshit like that. Hell, it probably attracted flies.

Christmas day came, and it was great as usual. I got my usual Fruit of the Loom underwear and calf-high tube socks, plus some other nice things. I was very pleased. As I had anticipated, Shirl gave me some cologne, and it wasn't the cheap kind either. It was Obsession. It had to run her about fifty dollars. She had also got me a little Christmas card. I especially liked the card, probably better than the cologne. The card was average, but the note made it really special to me. It read:

> Horne,
> I have been really thinking about you a lot lately. I admit I
> was really pissed at you. You know you almost got me in
> trouble, but I managed to explain my way out of it. Anyway,
> I couldn't stay mad at you long because you are so special to
> me. I know things aren't the way you would want them to be,
> but I know we will remain friends. Why? Because we have a
> special bond. A friendship that will last forever. You're proba-
> bly still mad at me, but just remember all the good times we
> have had. I care about you so much, Horne. I really do.
>
> > Love,
> > Shirl
>
> P.S. Have a great Christmas and tell your family I said HI.

I really liked that note. It had me smiling all day. I still wasn't going to buy her a present though.

Chapter Twenty-Two

Christmas flew by and so did New Year's Eve and the rest of my Christmas break. I had enjoyed my stay at home, but now I was ready to go back to school. I had spent most of my break chillin with my family and my boys. I especially spent a lot of time with Stevall. He seemed to be doing a lot better. He was supposed to be coming up to see me in school in about a month. I wasn't sure if that was a good idea or not. I didn't want him to come all the way to Memphis and then flip out. I knew I was wrong for thinking that, but I couldn't help myself. Anyway, I didn't say anything to him, so he was still going to come to Memphis to see me at school. Maybe I'll find somebody to hook him up with. Yeah, I think that is what I'm going to do. When I get to school, I'm going to start looking for someone to hook Stevall up with.

I hadn't talked to Shirl since the day she had given me my Christmas present. I had called a couple of times on Christmas day and the day after, but nobody had answered the phone. I would have kept calling, but Stevall had talked to Big Belinda, and she told him that Eric had come down for Christmas and was going to stay for a few days. Stevall said that he thought Belinda said he was staying at a hotel and not at Shirl's house. He also said that Belinda had felt so embarrassed and stupid about the incident at the mall. She had thought that Shirl and I were still messing around. She didn't know that Eric was back in the picture. Hell, she didn't know! I didn't know either until I saw those kinky ass panties.

Anyway, the day had come for me to head back to school. I said goodbye to my family, packed up the car, and headed out. It took me about six hours to get to Memphis. The drive was long, but it gave me an opportunity to think about a few things. I thought about Shirl as usual. I also thought about Fred and Tim. I wondered if Fred was still with that religious girl. He probably was, but I hoped he wasn't. That girl had Fred looking like a fool. I guess it was good that she was religious and all, but she treated him like he was a servant or something. It was true that Fred was not a Denzel Washington or anything, but he deserved to be treated with the same respect. He had got hold of that ass and lost his damn mind. Shit, to be honest, he probably hadn't even hit it yet.

When I finally got to school, I unpacked my things and tried to get a little rest. It was Sunday and classes didn't start until Thursday, so I had the majority of the week to chill and kick it. I rested for about three hours, sleeping for about two hours, and watching TV for another hour. I started wondering what time Tim was coming back and if he was even coming back on that day. Knowing him, he probably wouldn't come back until Wednesday.

As the sun went down, I became restless. I had rested about all day, and now I was ready to find something to do. I wanted to hook up with a girl, but I had been chasing Shirl's ass for so long, I hardly had any girls' numbers. I think I had two—Shirl's and Martha's. I sure as hell wasn't going to call either of them. I used to have more numbers, but I lost all of them. I wished I had Shannon's number. I wondered if Tim had it. I got up and walked over to his side of the room and started looking through his shit. I was sure he wouldn't mind if I called her. They were only friends. Nothing more. I was sure that would be all Shannon and I would end up being, but I still would like to give her a call even if all we did was trip.

Tim had a lot of junk in his drawers. Most of it looked like trash. I started going through it thinking maybe he had her number written down on one of the pieces of paper. I sure hoped he wouldn't come in while I was doing this. He would be mad as hell.

While I was looking through his shit, I came across something interesting. It was his transcript, and it had his GPA on it. His grade point average was low as hell. He had a 1.87. I knew that I wasn't a brain, but my GPA was a lot higher than that. Tim was no dummy. He just concentrated on other things more than his schoolwork. Things like Mellani. He should have been worrying about his schoolwork instead of spending all his time worrying about his problems with her. I knew I worried about girls too, but I did manage to pass and do well in the majority of my classes.

Tim also drank too much. So did I, but I didn't drink as much as he did. The more I looked at his transcript, the more I started realizing that Tim probably was only going to be coming back to get the rest of his stuff because it didn't seem like he had been doing anything last semester. Maybe he had done better than I thought. I kept looking through those junky drawers. After a couple of minutes, I figured that I wasn't going to find the number, so I shoved his junk back into the drawers and went back to my side of the room.

I sat on the bed and started looking around the room. I started thinking of how I could rearrange the room after Tim came back and got his stuff. Maybe I was wrong, but I was almost sure he had flunked out. I really didn't feel any sympathy for him because I had told him several times that he needed to straighten his shit up. Don't get me wrong. I would miss my boy, but I couldn't do anything about it. Besides, I would be happy to get a room of my own. I would hook this place up.

I started thinking about how I could hook the room up. Everything I thought about doing required money to do. I really needed a job. Not only to hook my room up. I just needed a job because I was always broke. The money my folks would send me, I would spend quick as hell. I thought about trying to get a job at the desk in one of the dorms. That seemed fairly easy, and it would probably be a good way to meet girls, especially if I could work in a girls' dorm. I would try to do that sometime in the next week. I needed to meet some new girls to get Shirl off my mind anyway. Hell, getting some from one of the girls would be a better way to get her off my mind.

Man, it seemed like it had been ages since I had last had sex. In reality, it had only been a couple of months, but it sure as hell seemed longer than that. Man, Shirl had felt so damn good that night. Her little ass was working it out. I really needed to get some girls' numbers. I was horny as hell. I sat on my bed with a smile on my face, thinking about the night that I had knocked Shirl's boots for a couple more minutes.

After a while, I decided to go see if Corey and Fred were back. When I got to their room, I heard loud music and a lot of laughter. It sounded like they were having a party or something. I knocked on the door. A couple of seconds later, Corey came to the door with a cup in his hand.

"What up, Horne!" he said. "Come on in."

I said what's up and walked in the room. When I got in there, I saw three young guys that I had never seen before. Each of them had a forty-ounce in his hand. There was a fifth of Crown sitting up on Corey's desk.

"Hey, man," Corey said with a drunken slur, "I want you to meet my cousin Terrell and my two boys from back home, Derrick and E.J."

I greeted my new acquaintances and just laid back. Corey went into the refrigerator and got a forty for me. This was cool, because I needed a drink. I hadn't drunk that much when I was at the crib, and my body was calling for a cold one.

Corey's friends and cousin seemed pretty cool. They were talking about some girls they were messing with. By listening to them, I could tell that they thought they were macks. I just sat back, drank my forty, and listened to them talk. However, I did get a chance to ask Corey where Fred was. He said that Fred had called him earlier and told him that he had gotten it cleared so that he wouldn't have to check into the dorm until Wednesday. Then Corey asked me where Tim was. I just told him that Tim hadn't made it back yet. I didn't go into all the details about how I thought that he had flunked out.

After everyone had finished their drinks, Corey suggested that we go over one of his freaks' crib because she was supposed to be having a birthday party. He said that there was going to be plenty of babes and booze there. That shit sounded straight to me as well as everyone else. Corey grabbed the fifth of Crown off his desk and we rolled out.

Corey's cousin Terrell had a minivan, so we all rode with him. While we were rolling, we passed the fifth around and hit it straight. After a couple of hits, I started to get a pretty good buzz. By the time we got to old girl's crib, I was drunk as hell.

When I got out of the minivan, all I heard was loud music and all I saw was young brothers and honeys. They were all in the driveway, the yard, and the house. We all looked at each other and smiled. This was definitely on. As we walked up to the house, I was just looking around, and all I saw was fine ass girls everywhere. It was cold outside and these people were still hanging outside. I couldn't see the girls' bodies like I wanted to because of their coats, but I could tell that most of them were pretty stout.

As soon as we got in the yard, some girl started walking toward us, yelling Corey's name. She was very pretty. I assumed that it was the girl throwing the party.

"Corey," she yelled. "Hey, Corey!"

Corey turned toward me and mumbled that he wished the girl would stop yelling his name. I thought to myself, Damn, I wish she was calling my name out, especially if she was laying her back flat on the bed, screaming Horne while I was working it out. Well, anyway, Corey was getting pissed because this girl kept yelling his name. When she finally reached us, she grabbed hold of Corey and gave him a big hug and kiss. Corey just smiled and looked around, trying to look cool.

Corey was talking to this freak. Terrell, Derrick, and E.J. were chilling nearby. I decided to walk around and scope out the scene. I saw a couple of people that I knew from school, but the majority of the faces were new. As I was walking, my nose instinctively led me to the keg. It was inside the house in a room that I assumed was the basement. This seemed like the place to chill because the honeys in here had their coats off and were not ashamed to flex. It was definitely on.

I chilled there, drinking on brew, watching the girls dance. While I was watching, my eyes zoomed in on one honey. She was fine as hell. There were a lot of girls there, but this girl stood out. She was about 5'10 and had a smooth, chocolate complexion. Her legs were long and thick. Her stomach was flat and her breasts were just right. To top it off, she had long, pretty hair, back for days, and the cutest face. She was damn near perfect. I sipped on my beer and lusted after her in my mind. She was dancing with some guy. I wondered if it was her boyfriend. I sure as hell hoped not because I was going to have to say something to this girl. Even if I only said hi to her, I was going to have to say something or I wouldn't be able to live with myself.

I continued to scope this woman's every move, and with her every move, my desire to talk and touch her grew greater and greater. I began to think of ways that I could approach her when I saw Corey, Terrell, Derrick, and E.J. coming down the stairs. They spotted me and walked over.

"What up, Horne?" Corey said. "We been looking for your ass."

"Well, I've been down here chillin', man, sipping on some brew," I said, and Corey looked at my cup. "Where did you get that from?" he asked.

"It's over there." I pointed at the keg and then refocused on the fine ass girl that I was lusting over. Corey and his boys grabbed some cups and started drinking some brew. It didn't take long for one of them to notice the girl. Terrell was the first to notice. He was sipping from his cup, and all of a sudden...

"Damn!" he said. "Who in the hell is that? She is fine as hell."

Corey looked at Terrell and asked, "Who are you talking about?"

Terrell pointed at the girl and Corey went crazy. He immediately went over there to talk to her. She had just stopped dancing and was standing up talking to another girl. I couldn't believe that Corey was going over there. My ass had blown it. I had waited too damn long.

Corey was almost over there when some girl started calling his name. I knew he heard her, but he tried to ignore her. That only made her yell louder. He turned around slowly, trying to look cool. He had a 'Damn, what now?' look on his face. He strolled over to the girl, and they began talking. This was a different girl than earlier. Whoever she was, she really saved me. I decided that I would make my move now before anything else happened.

I was almost a nervous wreck, so I tried to calm down. I looked around and thought about how I was going to make my move. I started walking across the room, trying not to look drunk, when I heard Corey calling my name. I didn't want to look because I was afraid he was going to stop me and then walk over there himself, but I looked anyway. He was still standing by the same girl, motioning for me to come over there.

When I got over there, Corey introduced me to the girl. Her name was Candy, and she was the one throwing the party. This explained why Corey didn't want the other girl screaming his name. Candy was fine, and she was all over him. He didn't seem too interested though. He kept looking at the girl that I was lusting after, and this was making me more anxious to hurry up and take care of my business.

I talked to Candy and Corey for about a minute, then I walked over to the keg of beer. I got another cup of beer, guzzled it down, crushed the cup, and walked over to the sexy ass girl. I stopped a couple of feet away from her and admired her body. It was definitely all that. I stepped next to her. She was standing by some other girl, bobbing her head to the music, so I started bobbing mine and looking at her. She turned toward me and smiled. I smiled back and proceeded to make my move.

"Hi," I said with a smile on my face.

"Hi," she said, and I asked her what her name was.

"Kim," she said in a smooth, sexy tone.

"My name is Horne."

"What?"

"Horne," I repeated in my best macking voice.

"Oh, Horne," she said.

After that, I wasn't sure what to say. She had turned away and started saying something to her friend. While she was talking to her friend, it gave me a chance to throw a couple of Tic Tacs in my mouth. I sucked on them a little bit. Once I was feeling comfortable about my breath, I tapped her on the shoulder and asked her to dance. She seemed to have to think about it, but she said yes. This was my chance to dazzle her with my moves. I wasn't the world's best dancer, but I could jook a little bit.

We walked to the dance floor and began to dance. The area that everybody was dancing in wasn't too big, plus a lot of people were dancing, so it forced us to dance sort of close. This was just fine with me. We danced for a long time and I enjoyed every second of it. This girl could move. She was doing all the dances like the Bankhead Bounce and the Tootsie Roll. I couldn't do all of that stuff, but I was hanging in there by doing some old school dances, like the Network and the Reebok. I hadn't really macked up on her yet because I was waiting on a slow song. I was keeping her laughing, though, by acting silly from time to time. Fast song after fast song kept coming on, and I was starting to get tired, but she didn't seem to be phased even a little.

Finally after about ten songs, the D.J. played a slow one. When it first came on, she just stood there like she didn't know what to do. So I grabbed her hand, and looked into her eyes. "I know you are going to dance with me, baby," I said.

She said yes, and it was on. I wrapped my arms around her waist and she slid her arms around my neck. Damn, she felt good! She smelled good as hell too. This girl had it going on, and she was most definitely turning me on. I began my macking by telling her that she smelled good.

"Thank you," she replied.

"Not only do you smell good, you feel good too," I said, and she moved back a little, looked me in the eyes and gave a little chuckle. "I'm serious, baby," I said. "You feel good."

She chuckled again. "Well, thank you," she said, and she must have thought I was joking, but I was dead serious. This girl felt so damn good, and the way she moved! Hell, all I could think about was how good she probably was in bed. In fact, this girl could probably make me forget about Shirl. I moved my arms around her and held her closer. She seemed to like it because she began to caress the back of my neck, and it felt so damn good. We danced like this for the rest of the song and for two more songs. I wanted to put my hand on her ass, but I wasn't that bold. After the last slow song was over, her friend came over and tapped her on the shoulder.

"You ready to go, girl?" she said, with a tired look on her face.

"Well, are you ready?" Kim asked back.

"Yeah, girl. I'm a little tired, and plus I have to get up early tomorrow and go to work."

"Well, Okay. Here I come."

Damn! She was getting ready to go, just like that. Man, this girl was like a girl straight out of my dreams. I couldn't just let her leave. I wanted to ask her to let me take her home, but my dumb ass didn't even drive. She turned around and looked at me, smiling.

"Well, I guess I have to go."

"Do you really?" I asked.

"Yeah, I didn't drive, and my friend is ready to go."

I grabbed her hand and held it gently, while looking at her with a sad expression on my face. "You could talk her out of it," I said.

"Nah, she's really tired, so I'm not even going to try to," she said, and put her hand on mine and shook it. "Well, it was nice meeting you."

"Hold up," I said. "You're saying that like we're never going to see each other again."

"Well, we probably will," she said, as she started walking away.

"Wait!" I said, and she turned around and looked.

"I really have to go."

"At least let me get your phone number."

"I don't know? I don't even know you."

"I promise you that I'm a nice guy. And besides, you will never get to know me unless you give me your number. Who's to say we will ever see each other again?"

"I don't know," she said, looking confused.

"Please. Please. I want to get to know you," I said desperately.

Her friend waved to her to come on. "Okay," she said. "It's 327-1134. I got to go."

"Wait a second and let me find a piece of paper."

"No, I have to go."

"Okay, tell me one more time."

She repeated the number and then she was gone. As she was walking away, my eyes focused on her ass. Damn! It was all that and a bag of Fritos. After she left, I went to find Corey and the boys because they were no longer in the basement. I walked upstairs and looked around until I found Derrick and E.J. They said that Corey had went in the back in some room with Candy, and Terrell had met some girl and walked outside with her. It seemed like we were going to be here for a while, so I went back down to the basement.

I walked back over to the keg and began to drink a little more. At first, I was sort of pissed at myself for not driving, but I thought about it and realized the drunken condition I was in and started feeling glad that I didn't drive. Besides, she probably wouldn't have let me drive her home anyway.

People were still dancing. There were a lot of good looking girls, but none could come close to Kim's fine ass. I danced a few more times with a couple of girls I didn't know. The entire time, I kept repeating Kim's phone number in my head. I just knew I was going to forget it because I was drunk as hell. When I got through dancing, I went back upstairs to see if the boys were ready to go. Corey was no longer in the back with Candy. He was outside talking to Derrick and E.J.

The first thing I did was ask Corey for a pen and a piece of paper. I knew he had both of them. I wrote Kim's number down and then asked them if they were ready to go. Corey said that he was, but we had to wait on Terrell. He had drove somewhere with some girl. While we were waiting, we talked and tripped. Corey told us that he had to break down and give Candy some because she kept begging for it. We all laughed and kept tripping.

Then the conversation focused on me. They wanted to know what was up with Kim. I told them that she seemed straight and that I got the digits. This seemed to please everyone except Corey. He kept saying that he was the one who was supposed to get up on that. He had just got through knocking the boots with fine ass Candy, and here he was tripping about Kim. Some guys just want all the ass.

We talked for about thirty more minutes before Terrell came back. He got out of the car and walked the girl back to the party. Meanwhile, the rest of us hopped in the minivan. I must have fallen asleep because the next thing I knew, we were at the dorm. I managed to get up and drag myself to my room. I was so drunk and tired, I didn't even take my clothes and shoes off. I just fell out on the bed.

Chapter Twenty-Three

The rest of the days before school started back up, I didn't do too much. Basically, I just chilled. Tim never came back or called, so I assumed I was right about him flunking out. I wanted to rearrange my room, but he still had a bunch of his junk in there. He was going to have to hurry up and come get his stuff. I decided that I would give him a call one day to see what was up.

Fred came back the day before classes. I had been up there a couple of times, but I hadn't gotten a chance to really talk to him. The word from Corey was that Fred's girl had dumped him. I hadn't verified it with Fred, but both of the times I had been up in their room, he seemed really sad. He was probably depressed and lonely. I sure as hell knew how that felt. I was a little depressed and lonely myself. All I did was sit up in the room and watch TV. I had seen enough of Fred Sanford and Shaft in the last two days to last me a lifetime. I had called that girl that I met at the party a few times, but she was never at home. I was starting to get frustrated because I really wanted to talk to her. I was just going to have to keep trying. She was too damn fine to give up on.

The first day of class finally came. I put on my good school clothes and combed my hair just for the occasion. As I was walking to my first class, I took my time and looked around. There were babes everywhere. I started thinking that there was no reason why I couldn't find another girl and fall in love because there were so many nice girls in the world.

Forget Shirl. Shit, she wasn't all that anyway. I would just mack up on some of these other girls.

I continued scoping out all the girls on my way to class. When I got to class, I sat down and tried to pay attention. There was only one small problem. I couldn't keep my eyes and ears open. I kept falling asleep. I was tired, but the class was also boring as hell. The teacher was dull and there were no fine hoes in the class to look at.

After that class was over, I managed to wake myself up and walked to my next class. This class looked like it was going to be interesting. My teacher was fine as hell. She was young and had pretty long hair. Also, she was built and had a nice, caramel complexion. I would really be paying attention to what she had to say because her lips were big, full, and luscious. When she talked, you couldn't do anything but hang onto her every word. It seemed like all the guys were sitting on the front two rows. Even the ones that usually sat in the back and slept were sitting up front. There I sat, attentive, with a big smile on my face, lusting over the teacher.

We were about ten minutes into the class when two girls walked in late. Both of them were fine. One of them was Shirl. She walked right by me and toward the back of the class since there were no seats up front. I don't think that she saw me because she didn't speak. She was looking as good as the teacher. She had on some tight ass blue jeans and a tight ass sweater. It looked good. Between lusting over the teacher and thinking about Shirl, I did manage to learn a little. Even if I didn't learn anything, at least I stayed awake.

After the class was over, I stayed in my seat and waited for Shirl to walk by me so I could thank her for the Christmas present that she had given me. She walked up to me smiling.

"I didn't even notice you was in here until halfway through the class," she said, in her usual casual way.

"Yeah, you walked right past me when you came in late."

"I did? I was just trying to hurry up and get a seat. I was outside tripping with my friend Tosha and fooled around and ended up being late."

"I just wanted to thank you for the Christmas present."

"Oh, you know you're more than welcome, Horne," she said, with a cute ass smile on her face. "I know you're not going to sit here all day."

"Nah," I said.

"Get up and walk with me," she said, and I got up and we walked out of the classroom together. "You got another class?"

"Yeah, I got a basketball class."

"What?"

"A basketball class," I repeated.

"Why are you taking a basketball class?"

"I have one more P.E. that is required, so I chose the basketball class."

"Come to think of it, I think I heard some more people talking about a basketball class," she said.

"Well, it should be straight," I said, as we continued walking.

Shirl said that she had a class over toward the P.E. building, so we walked together. Instead of me being the gentleman, she was the gentle-woman because she walked me all the way to my class. When we got to the door, we talked for a few more minutes. She asked me if I had read the little note that she had put with my Christmas gift. I told her that I did and that it was a sweet note. Don't get me wrong. I wasn't trying to be soft, but I just couldn't act hard and mean toward her. It was true that she kept dicking me around, but I cared too much for her to be mean to her.

While we were talking about the note that she had written, she suddenly lost her attention and began looking at something behind me. I turned around to see what had distracted her. It was Eric. He was walking directly toward us.

"What up, Horne?" he said to me, then he looked at Shirl. "Hey, Shirl. What you doing over here?" he asked her.

"I walked over here with Horne. We were just tripping."

"Come here for a second. I need to talk to you," he said, and Shirl looked at me and told me that she would see me later, and then she walked up to Eric. He put his arm around her and they started talking.

Eric just thought that he was the shit. I guess I could see why Shirl liked him. He was cool and he was a good dresser. Also, he was a fairly good-looking dude. The only thing wrong with him was that girls did like him—a lot of girls, and he wasn't good at turning them down. So he was always fucking off. Shirl didn't want to hear that, though. She knew that he was no good, but for some reason, she thought that she could change him. At least that's how I saw it. I glanced over at them one more time. They were both smiling and hugging and looking so happy. Damn them!

I went ahead and went to class. We weren't going to play basketball today since it was the first day. We sat on the bleachers and listened to the teachers talk. The teacher had been talking for about ten minutes when Eric walked in. Damn. Why did he have to be in this class? I could tell already that this was going to be a different kind of semester. I had the girl that I was in love with in one class, and the guy that she was in love with in the next.

After basketball class, I had one more class for the day. Fortunately, there were no surprises in that one. I really didn't pay too much attention because I kept thinking about Shirl. I knew that I was supposed to be over her, but it was very tough to stop thinking about her.

When my class was over, I went back to my dorm room and chilled. I called up to Corey and Fred's room, but nobody was there. I still wanted to talk to Fred to see what was up with him and his girl. I guess I would have to wait.

I started getting bored. I wanted to call Shannon and trip with her, but I still didn't know her number. I had been looking for her all week, but I had not seen her. I decided to call the girl I had met at the party. Maybe she would finally be at home. I picked up the phone and dialed the number. Her phone rang about four times before somebody answered it. It was a lady. It didn't sound like an old lady, but a young lady. My heart started beating fast and my hands suddenly became sweaty. I was getting nervous because I hadn't prepared what I was going to say. I had figured that she wasn't going to be home. She said hello twice and I didn't say anything. She said hello one more time and then hung up.

Man, I had straight up acted like a punk. I decided to wait a few minutes and call back, but this time I was going to be fully prepared. I started going over my game. This girl was fine as hell, so I would have to spit some clever game on her. She probably wouldn't fall for any hard shit because she probably heard that from brothers all the time. I decided that it would be best to come with the sincere, 'but I ain't no straight up punk' approach. That is, come off real nice and understanding, but not too nice, because girls don't seem to like overly nice guys.

At least, that is what I had noticed from my experience. It seems that when a brother is real nice, the girl takes advantage of him and then usually dumps him after she has drained him dry emotionally, mentally, physically, and financially. Hell, that is what had happened to Fred. It had also happened between Shirl and me. When I first met Shirl, I was so nice to her. She began to see me as a buddy, not as a lover. She would rather be with that no good Eric. I guess she feels like there is a challenge with him. Maybe as the college girls got older, they would realize that it's better to have a nice guy than a challenge that is constantly dogging them out.

Well anyway, I was going to be the challenging nice guy and see how that approach worked. Hopefully it would work great because I really wanted this girl bad. Once I got my game together, I picked up the phone and called her back. This time a man answered the phone. I asked to speak to Kim, and he told me to hold on. A couple of seconds later, she picked up the phone and said hello.

"Hello, how are you doing?" I said to her.

"Fine," she said, in her sexy ass voice.

"That's good. This is Horne."

"Uh, who?" she asked. Damn! she said who. 'I know this girl hasn't forgot who I am already,' I thought to myself.

"Horne. I met you Sunday night at Candy's house party."

"Candy's house party? Oh! Yeah, I remember you. What's your name again?"

"Horne."

"Horne, yeah. I'm so sorry. I had forgot your name."

"Well, it's Horne," I said, and I was starting to feel bad. Kim had forgotten my name and by the way she talked, it seemed like she had a lot of guys calling her. I should have expected that, though, because she was so damn fine. We talked for about fifteen minutes. It wasn't a bad conversation, either. It was just okay. I lost all of my enthusiasm and spirit when she didn't remember me at first, so she seemed to be going through a routine or something. It just wasn't personal. I wasn't going to give up, though. I asked her if I could call her again, and she said yes. I was going to keep calling her. I was sure that my charm and game would break her down.

The rest of the day I didn't do too much. I went up to Corey and Fred's room later that night. I saw Fred for a brief minute, but I didn't get a chance to talk to him because he was on his way out the door. So I ended up tripping with Corey. We talked about women as usual and he was telling me about how he had sex with three different girls the day before. He said that he had one for breakfast, lunch, and dinner, and that they all gave him the full treatment. Here he was having sex for lunch, breakfast, and dinner, getting the full treatment, and I couldn't even get a little sex on a holiday. Damn!

After I finished listening to Corey brag about all his sexual encounters, I went back to my room. I watched some television and then decided to call Tim to see what was up with him. His mom answered the phone on the first ring. I asked if I could speak to Tim. He came to the phone soon thereafter.

"Hello."

"What up, Tim?"

"What up, Horne?"

"I just called to see what was up. Your ass coming back to school or what?"

"Nah, man. I got a once-in-a-lifetime offer that I couldn't pass up," he said, and I knew that he was about to tell me a big ass lie, but I asked him anyway.

"What once-in-a-lifetime offer?"

"Man, I got this internship making fourteen dollars an hour."

"Straight up?" I said. "Where?"

"It is at this shoe manufacturing plant up here at the crib."

"How did you get that job?"

"Man, well it's a trip how I got it."

When he said 'it's sort of a trip', I knew that this was where he was going to throw out the lie and I was going to either catch it or drop it.

"You see, I met this girl one day at the mall. Man, she was fine as hell, and she was all up on my jock. You know me. I was chillin', but she was jocking me so hard, I had to lay down a little mack," he said, and I interrupted him.

"What's up with Mellani?"

"We still cool, but you know, sometimes you got to try something new." He continued with his story. "Well, anyway, I started knocking the boots with this girl. So we become all cool and shit and she invites me over to some holiday family get-together. While I was there, I met her older sister's husband and he works at the shoe plant. We talked a little bit and the next thing I know I got the hook-up. He told me to come down to the plant and that he would see what he could do for me."

"Oh, so you told him that you wanted a job?" I asked.

"Nah, he just offered. I guess I impressed him when we were talking, and when I went down there, the offer was so good, I couldn't turn it down. That's experience in my field, plus a nice ass wage. Man, I couldn't pass that up."

Normally, I wouldn't have believed him because he lied so damn much, but this sounded like it could have been true. Well, even if it wasn't true, he was getting better at lying.

"I guess it would be hard to pass up an offer like that," I said. "You didn't want to finish school first and then try to get that job?" I asked him.

"Nah, because I got about two more years of school and the job was available now. I had to take it, man."

"Well, I guess you had to take it."

"Yeah, I had to."

"When are you going to come and get your stuff?" I asked.

"I'll be up there next weekend," he said.

"Next weekend?"

"Yeah, can you keep my stuff until then?"

"Yeah," I said, and I talked to Tim for a little while longer. He was supposed to be coming up next weekend to get his stuff. He also said that he was going to kick it with me and the boys while he was here. I didn't expect him to be doing a lot of kicking it because Mellani was down here. He would probably end up being with her the majority of the time.

After I got off the phone, I chilled and thought about my day. It was indeed an interesting day. The girl I loved was in one of my classes. The guy she loved was in another class of mine. And the girl I'm lusting over, I talked to on the phone. It was most definitely an interesting day.

Chapter Twenty-Four

The days seemed to pass by fast. Day after day, I did basically the same thing. It was like I was in a rut or something. I would go to class and come back home. When I got home, I would do a little homework, watch TV, sleep, and eat. That's all I did. I called Kim a couple of times and had the same boring ass conversation every time. Although I had a class with Shirl, I really didn't talk to her much. I kept sitting in the front and since my teacher was a sex goddess, all the seats by me were taken by all the perverted guys in the class. I guess I could have sat in the back by Shirl, but I had once again realized that I had to get over her. Shit, she didn't seem to care that I didn't sit by her. Her ass was so into Eric. To her, he could do no wrong. I didn't even get a chance to walk with her after class because he was always there waiting on her.

The first full week of school flew by and the weekend was finally here. I had tried to set up a date with Kim. She said that she was busy or some shit. I started to get the feeling that she didn't want to get with me. Hell, I would just try a couple more times, and if she was still tripping, I would just forget it.

Well, there I was on a Friday night with no plans for the weekend when I got a couple of phone calls. The first call was from Stevall. He was calling to tell me that he was going to come down in two weeks. I told him that sounded cool and that he could stay with me since I had an extra bed and no roommate. He sounded good, like his old self. We basically just tripped. We didn't even get into any serious conversation, and that was just fine with me. I was tired of all the emotional, serious shit. I was ready to trip.

The next call I got was from Tim. He was in town. He said that he was going to stay in a hotel with Mellani tonight and tomorrow night, but that he would be through to holler at me and to get his things. I told him that was cool. I already knew that he was probably going to be with her all weekend. That's why I hadn't made any plans for us to kick it over the weekend. I couldn't blame him, though. I knew I wished I was somewhere knocking boots.

The rest of the night, I chilled. I went up to Corey and Fred's room. Corey wasn't there, but Fred was. I tried to go in and talk to Fred, but he was acting like he didn't want me to come in, so I started thinking that maybe he had that girl in there. I asked him if he had company and he said no. He also said that he was asleep and that my knocking had woke him up and that he was going to go back to bed. I knew he was lying because it wasn't even late and he seemed wide awake. Fred had really been acting strange since he had been back. I rarely saw him, and when I did seem him, it was as if he didn't want to be around me. I had to know what was up, so I asked him.

"Fred, man, what's wrong?"

"Nothing, man, I'm just a little sleepy," he said, and looked down toward the ground.

"Man, I'm not talking about you being sleepy. I want to know why you have been avoiding me."

"Avoiding you?" he asked. "I haven't been avoiding you."

"I think you have. We haven't really talked since we've been back to school this semester."

"Horne, we really didn't talk too much last semester, and it wasn't because I was avoiding you. We've been busy doing our own thing," he said, and glanced up to me.

"Actually, we didn't see each other because you were always busy with your girl."

"And?" he said. I couldn't believe he was trying to get smart.

"And if I heard right, the two of you are not together anymore, so I was hoping we could be friends again," I said, and he looked up quickly, looking me dead in the eyes.

"Who told you that, Corey?"

"Yeah," I replied, looking him right back in the eyes.

"Corey needs to stay in his own damn business and not mine."

He moved back and tried to slam the door, but I kept him from doing it. I put my feet and hands on the door and pushed it back open.

"What in the hell do you want?" Fred said, loud as hell.

I was about to say something when I happened to glance over to Fred's bed. He had on his bed a box of Oreo's, some popcorn, some barbecue Fritos, a large box of granola bars, and a three-liter Diet Coke. He was already big as hell. If he started eating like that, he was going to be bigger than hell.

"What are you doing with all that food on your bed?" I asked him.

"None of your damn business," he said loudly.

"You trying to eat your troubles away or something?" I said and I must have hit a nerve when I said that because he put one of the meanest and ugliest expressions on his face.

"I'm going to say this one time," he said. "Get the hell out of my damn room." His voice was louder and meaner this time.

"Okay, Fred, but I have one thing to say. I'm your friend, remember? You can talk to me about anything. I can see that you're hurt, and when you feel like talking, you know where I stay."

"Okay, whatever," he mumbled.

I walked out the door and back to my room. I thought about how Fred was tripping the whole time as I was making my little walk back. Fred really wasn't himself. He hadn't been himself since he had met Rebecca. It wasn't like she had drained him of his personality and filled the space back up with someone else's personality. I knew that I really didn't see Fred that much last year. I really missed my buddy. I missed the Fred that I used to kick it with.

When I got back to the room, I watched television a little bit. It was only ten o'clock, and I was bored to death. For a brief second, I thought about calling Shirl, but I realized that that wasn't the answer. I decided to walk around downstairs to see who was in the lobby. When I got down there, I saw a whole lot of people playing cards. I knew quite a few of them, so I stayed down there and tripped with them.

I had been there for an hour and had played a couple of games when I decided to go get a forty. This dude I knew named Lemont was thirsty too, so he wanted to ride with me to the store. We decided to leave through the girls' side to scope out some of the honeys. There weren't many of them out, but there were a couple that made the extra walk worthwhile.

As we were walking out the door, I saw Shannon walking up toward the door. I wanted to say something to her, but I didn't because she was with some guy. She was looking good! She had always been cute to me, but tonight, she looked more than cute. She looked fine! She had on some tight ass black pants with some long black boots. She also had on a long black leather coat that covered her ass. I couldn't even see her ass or her tits and she was still looking fine. The guy that she was with looked like a geek and he had his hand on her shoulder.

I smiled at her and said hi. She did the same. She looked like she wanted to stop and talk. I know I wanted to talk to her, too, because I wanted to ask her for her phone number. She didn't stop, though. She kept on walking with the geek. Lemont was straight up tripping. He was going crazy over Shannon. He kept talking about how he would love to get in those panties. I didn't really say anything. I just smiled and said that she was looking good and kept walking.

It took us about ten minutes to get to the store and back. Since it was supposed to be illegal to drink on campus, we couldn't drink downstairs where everybody was playing cards, so we went upstairs to my room. I had got a forty of Bull, and Lemont had bought some punk ass coolers. He said he didn't like the taste of beer and that hard liquor made him sick, so he drunk coolers. To each his own, I always say.

While Lemont was playing around with his coolers, I was taking my forty to the head. I was straight up guzzling. I finished it in no time and was ready to go back downstairs. Lemont was on his second cooler and wanted me to wait for him to finish before we went back downstairs. Since he wanted me to wait, I drank his other two coolers to pass the time. He didn't seem to mind at all.

Lemont was sort of a different kind of guy. He was cool and all, but he acted and talked like he was white, although he hung around black people. He couldn't have been mixed or anything like that because he was black as tar. My final assessment of him was that he must have grown up around white people. He didn't seem to want to be like them. He probably just always grew up around them and picked up their ways.

Well, by the time he finished his cooler, I had a pretty good buzz. I was really ready to go downstairs to the lobby. I was hoping there would be some girls down there because I was in the mood to mack. When we got downstairs to the lobby, we walked back over where everybody was playing cards. There were a few honeys down there. About half of them were cute and the other half were a bunch of sandwich-eaters.

I sat down and eyeballed the cuties. While I was scoping these honeys out, Lemont was straight up tripping. He kept acting crazy and everybody was laughing at him. He seemed to think everybody was laughing at what he was doing, but they were really laughing at how he talked and the way he acted. If you closed your eyes and listened to him, you would swear that he was a white guy from the deep south.

While I was sitting there watching Lemont make a fool of himself, I was startled by somebody suddenly rubbing my shoulders. It felt very good and relaxing, but I turned around sort of quick to make sure it wasn't one of those sandwich-eaters. When I turned around, I was pleasantly surprised. It was Shannon. She had sneaked up on me. She was wearing the same thing that she had on earlier, but this time she didn't have the leather coat on. She had a black body suit on with the tight pants and boots. Damn, she looked goood!

"Hey, Shannon," I said to her.

"Hey, Horne," she said, and stopped rubbing my shoulders and walked around and sat down beside me.

"Why did you stop?" I asked, and smiled and looked her over. "That shit was feeling good."

She got back up, walked back around me and started rubbing my shoulders again.

"Thanks," I said.

"You're welcome."

I didn't say anything else for a few minutes. I was pretty buzzed, and her rubbing my shoulders was putting me in a trance or something. She didn't say anything either. She was busy laughing at Lemont like everybody else. After a little while, she stopped rubbing my shoulders and came back around and sat by me.

"Well, I hope you enjoyed that because that is all you're getting because I'm tired," she said, and I told her thanks and started smiling at her.

"I've been trying to get your number," I said.

"You have?"

"Yes, I have," I said, and for some reason, things seemed different between us. Every other time we had talked, things seemed real friendly, but this time, they seemed more intense. The more I looked at her, the more I wanted her. She seemed a little more interested too.

"You look real good tonight," I told her.

"Thank you," she said.

"I mean you look really, really good tonight."

She started blushing real hard and said thank you again. I asked her who was the guy I saw her with earlier. She said that it was some guy that she was dating. I asked her if it was serious, and she said no. She said that they were more like friends than anything. We kept talking, and eventually,

we distanced ourselves from everyone else. We talked about everything—
love, romance, politics, religion, school—everything

An hour had passed. My buzz was starting to fade and my thirst buds
were starting to fiend, so I told Shannon that I was about to go to the
store and asked her if she wanted to come with me. She said yeah. I
started to ask Lemont if he wanted to go, but he was still over there tripping. Hell, if he got another drink, he would probably end up hurting
himself, so I didn't ask him.

Shannon and I walked outside to my car and headed to the store.
When we got there, I bought another forty-ounce, and she bought some
Gatorade. I asked her if she wanted a quart or a cooler or something. She
said no thank you and that Gatorade was her drink, but she did say that
she was hungry. I asked if she had eaten on her date. She said yeah and
that she was hungry again. So we stopped by Krystal and I treated her to
two cheese Krystals, a Chili Pup and an order of Kriss-Kross Fries.

When we got back to the dorm, we decided to go back to the room
since I couldn't drink my forty downstairs. As soon as we got to the
room, Shannon started snooping around, especially around Tim's old
side of the room. I had told her earlier that he wasn't coming back to
school and that he was here to get his stuff. She seemed real interested
in knowing when he would be coming to get his things, so I straight out
asked her something that we had discussed before. I knew what her
answer was going to be, but I asked her anyway.

"Do you like Tim?"

She gave me a crazy look. "Boy, nah," she said. "Don't start with that."

"Don't start with that?"

"Nah, please don't."

"You've been asking about him ever since you walked in the room."

She walked back over toward me and sat down on my bed. Man, she
was looking good. I was leaning on my desk, so I raised up and then sat
down on the bed beside her.

"Horne, the only reason I have been asking questions is because I care about Tim. Tim's a good friend of mine, and that's all. Just a friend."

I opened my mouth to say something to her, but she put her finger on my mouth.

"Wait a minute," she said. "Why do you keep asking questions about Tim and me anyway?"

"Well, uh…"

She smiled and then cut me off. "Well, uh, nothing. Tell me, Horne. Why are you so interested in Tim and me?"

It was becoming clear to me that Shannon wanted me. Why else would she be asking me this? I decided to give her a hard time. "I'm so interested because Tim is my friend, and I care about him," I said to her with a serious look on my face.

"Yeah, right," she replied.

"Yeah, right? You don't believe me or something?" I said, and she didn't say anything. She just smiled, shook her head, and finished eating her food. I didn't say anything else either. I opened my forty and started gulping. A few minutes passed, and I was already half finished with my forty. She was finished eating. I was really feeling good now, so I started staring at Shannon. She looked so damn good.

"Why are you looking at me that way?" she asked me.

"You look so damn good," I said.

"What?" she said, in a shocked sort of way.

I was just as shocked as she was. I couldn't believe I had just said that. I always seemed to surprise myself when I got drunk. "I said that you look good," I repeated.

She smiled and said thank you. When she said thank you, a sudden urge to kiss her took over my body, so I did. I leaned over and kissed her on the cheek. She turned her head slowly toward mine. I didn't back up, and our lips were nearly touching. I leaned a little closer and kissed her again, this time on the lips. She moved back away from me and looked me in the eyes with a dazed expression on her face. I thought to myself,

'I know I'm a good kisser, but if that got her dazed, wait until she gets the tongue action'.

"What was that?" she asked with a confused look on her face.

"What do you think it was?" I said, smiling.

"I know what it was," she said. "What did it mean?"

"What do you want it to mean?"

"I'm not sure. I wasn't expecting anything like that to happen."

"I wasn't either. It just seemed like the natural thing to do. It felt right, too."

She didn't say anything. She just looked at me. She wasn't smiling, but she wasn't frowning either. It was more of a confused look. I wasn't sure what the look meant. All I knew was that her lips were wet and looking good. So I leaned over and kissed her again. This kiss was longer than the first one. Plus, there was some tongue action this time. She was a very good kisser. She didn't use too much tongue or too little tongue. She used just the right amount. We kissed for a long time. As we kissed, I did a little roaming with my hands. I roamed all down her back and on her thighs and knees. I couldn't reach her butt like I wanted to because she was sitting down in a way that her whole but was flat against the bed. I was trying to get her to lean in a way that I could get my hand on that ass, but she wouldn't budge. So I gave up trying to rub her ass and went for the breasts.

I started rubbing on her breasts on the outside of her blouse. She didn't say stop, so I kept on. We were still kissing, stopping every so often to catch our breath. I was really horny now. I decided to see how far I could go, hoping that I could go all the way. I unbuttoned her shirt. She didn't say shit, so I started kissing her breasts. They weren't really big, but they were nice sized. A little over a handful, and I had a nice sized hand. They smelled good too. Like strawberries.

As I kissed her breasts, we ended up horizontal on the bed, me on top. I was enjoying myself, and I could tell that she was enjoying herself because she was moaning her ass off. I liked it though, because it made me feel like I was doing something. Like I was the man! Now I was having a good time kissing her breasts, but after a few minutes, it was time to go to the next step—the panties.

I moved my hand down to her belt buckle and unfastened it. That is when all the tonguing and breast-kissing stopped. She pushed me off of her, stood up, and started putting her bra and blouse back on. It caught me totally by surprise. I thought everything was going great. In fact, I thought I was about to get some sexual healing.

"What happened?" I asked. "Did I do something wrong?"

She didn't say anything. She just shook her head. I looked closely at her facial expression to see if she was about to cry or something. I really couldn't tell because she had her face down. I sure as hell hoped not. Of course, I didn't know why she would be crying. It's not like I had forced myself on her. She seemed like she was enjoying it and she certainly never told me to stop.

"Shannon," I said. "Shannon! Look at me."

She gradually looked up. When I saw her face, I was surprised to see that she was smiling.

"Shannon, what's the matter, and why are you smiling?"

She fastened the last button on her blouse and sat down next to me on the bed. "Nothing's wrong, Horne," she said, smiling. She put her hand on top of mine and continued. "We were going too fast. That's all."

"So why didn't you just say stop or something instead of pushing me up and jumping up like you were a crazy woman?" I asked her.

"It was feeling so good that if I hadn't stopped at that instant, we would have had to go all the way," she said, and rubbed my hand.

Damn! One more instant and we would have gone all the way. Why couldn't it have gone one more instant? The more I thought about that one more instant and what possibly could have happened, the hornier I was starting to get. I damn near had blue balls anyway, but now I was really going to have them unless she changed her mind.

"What would be so wrong with us going all the way?" I asked.

"A lot of things. For one, we have never even shown this kind of affection toward each other before, and then suddenly in one night, we do it. I'm not that type of girl. I have to get to know a person very, very well before I do something like that."

"Well, why did you do what you did tonight?"

She smiled and put her hands on her face for a second. Then she looked at me. "I don't know. To be honest, I really don't know."

"I know," I said, and I stood up and walked across the room to the mirror.

"You do?" she said. "Well, please fill me in, since you know so much."

I didn't say anything right away. I brushed my hair a little and then groomed my mustache.

"Horne, excuse me. I'm waiting for your answer since you know everything."

I turned around, walked to her, and motioned for her to stand up. She stood up and looked at me. I looked down at her since I was quite a bit taller than she was. "The reason you did what you did, Shannon, is because you want me."

She started laughing a little bit and then said that it was time for her to go. I kept telling her that it was the truth, and she kept giggling like she was in the fifth grade or something. We exchanged numbers and she said that she was going to call me tomorrow because we needed to seriously talk about what happened. I walked her back to her side of the dorm where she lived. I gave her a hug and a kiss on the cheek and then left.

It was now about one o'clock. I had a good buzz, but I wasn't quite sleepy yet, so I went back over to see if anybody was in the lobby playing cards. Everybody was gone except for one guy and one girl, and they were all over each other. They needed to go get a room or something.

Since no one was playing cards, I went back to my room. When I got there, I turned on the television. I had it on BET, and they were showing some videos. I wasn't really paying attention to the videos because I was sort of in pain. I had blue balls like a motherfucker. It was like my whole lower body area was tightening up on me. Man, for a minute there, I had thought Shannon was going to give up the panties. I had gotten all excited and happy, and now because of the over-anticipation, I had the dreaded blue balls. I started trying to pay attention to the videos on TV, hoping that it would help get my mind off my problem, but it didn't. I was just going to have to suffer until my balls calmed down.

A half hour passed by, and I was finally feeling better. My blue balls had gone away, and now I was ready for bed when the phone rang. I figured that it was probably Tim calling to let me know when he was coming up here, but I was wrong. It wasn't Tim. It was a girl. In fact, it wasn't just any girl, it was a really fine girl. It was Kim. I was very surprised. She had never called me before, and when I called her, she hadn't seemed interested. She said that she needed a favor from me.

I knew it was too good to be true. She was just calling me to ask for something. She said that her car wasn't running and that she needed to take it to the shop. She was stranded over a friend's house and needed a ride home. I asked her why couldn't her friend give her a ride home. She said that her friend's car was also in the shop and that ordinarily, she would have just spent the night, but she needed to go somewhere in the morning, so she needed to get home. I asked her how she had gotten over there, and she said that her mom had brought her over there. She told me that her mom wasn't home, so she couldn't ask her mom to come and get her.

I told her that I was happy that she had called, but I wasn't quite sure why she had called. I told her that she had never even seemed interested in me and now she wanted me to come and get her because she was stranded. I told her that she must be real desperate to be calling me. She said that it wasn't like that at all, but she really would appreciate it if I would come over and pick her up. I really didn't feel like going to get her because I was sleepy, buzzing, and recovering from the treacherous blue balls. But she kept begging, and she sounded so good when she begged that I gave in like a sucker and told her that I would come and get her. She gave me directions and then I hung up the phone and freshened up a little.

I didn't have any problem finding the house. When I got there, she was standing outside waiting on me. She ran to the car because it was very cold outside. When she got in the car, she leaned over and kissed me on the cheek.

"Thank you, Horne," she said. "You're a doll."

I immediately started blushing. "You're welcome," I said, and smiled from cheek to cheek.

This was the first time I had seen Kim since the party. She looked exactly as I had remembered. This was good and unusual because I usually over-rated girls when I was drunk, but I most definitely hadn't over-rated Kim. She was as fine as I had remembered. Her skin was a pretty brown color, and her hair was long and pretty. Man, she was looking good!

While I was driving her home, we talked about a lot of things. This was the best conversation we had ever had. Maybe things were turning around with Kim and me. I sure as hell hoped so. The whole time we were in the car, I kept trying to get a peep of her body, but I couldn't because she was wrapped up in this big ass coat.

It only took about fifteen minutes before we got to her house, and believe me, those few minutes flew by. In fact, the fifteen minutes had seemed more like one or two minutes. It was late, and I was very tired, but I didn't want to end our conversation, so I asked her if she would like to get a bite to eat or something. She said that going to get something to eat sounded good, but she was very tired and since she was already home, she would pass on the offer.

As soon as I heard the word pass come out of her mouth, I remembered that she had told me she would be busy tonight when I had asked her out before. She didn't seem busy to me. Unless you call going to see a friend that you see almost every day busy. I didn't say anything to her about it, though. She said bye and thanks and then ran into the house.

If she wasn't so damn fine and I wasn't so tired, I probably would have asked her about it, but I was too tired and she was too damn fine. I really had the blue balls now.

When I got back home, I soaked my balls in the bathtub in some cold water for about thirty minutes. It relaxed me and helped control the pain. After I got out of the tub, I went to bed.

The next day, Tim came by and got his stuff. He stayed for a little while, and we tripped about old times. We talked about everything from our schoolwork to our hoes. I wanted to tell him about Shannon, but I still wasn't sure if they had ever had something going on. I sure as hell hoped not. Because if Tim had knocked her boots, then I would have had to leave her alone. Not only was Tim my boy, but I wouldn't want to get into a piece that he had been in. The reason was that Tim was known for having unprotected sex with straight up super freaks. I hoped he didn't have any diseases, but there was no telling.

Man, I knew that I wanted to get with Shannon, so maybe it would have been best if I found out if they had ever done anything. Well, Shannon had said that they hadn't, so I would just take her word for now. Maybe I would call and ask Tim later. If Shannon and I did anything, I would just be sure to wear a condom. That's what I needed to do anyway. Start practicing safe sex all the time, but first I would have to start having sex again. Hopefully, things were starting to turn around for me. I didn't want to be a player or anything, but I did want to find one special girl. A girl that I could call my own.

Chapter Twenty-Five

The next two weeks were busy as well as interesting. They were busy because my class work really started kicking in and I started a part-time job. It was a pretty cool job. All I did was walk girls from a particular school building to their cars or to another building. I had a walkie-talkie so I could call security just in case something went wrong. It was called Safety Patrol, and I was a Safety Patrol officer.

So my schoolwork and my new job were the reasons why the two weeks were busy, but they were interesting because of a couple of interesting developments in my personal life. One of them was Shannon. Ever since the night when things had gotten hot and heated, we had been seeing each other almost every day. Things between us were great. We had a lot of fun together and she was very easy to talk to. We had fooled around a couple more times, and each time, I left with the blue balls because she had refused to let me hit it. That was okay, though. I was beginning to really care about Shannon., and I didn't mind waiting. I could tell that she really liked me also.

The other interesting development involved Shirl and Eric. Eric had been waiting for Shirl outside our classroom every day, but last week, I had not seen him waiting for her even once. It was like she was expecting him to be there because she would be looking around and checking her watch. That wasn't really the interesting part though. The real interesting part was that I had seen Eric twice last week walking with some girl other than Shirl. And even more interesting than that, I had seen him kissing the girl.

I was walking with an older lady who had called Safety Patrol when I noticed this girl and guy walking. As I got closer, I saw the guy bend over and kiss the girl on the lips. As I got even closer, I saw that it was Eric. He acted like he didn't see me, but I knew he did. It was Friday night, and I had seen Eric and the mystery woman on the night before.

At first, the incident made me happy because I was going to go tell Shirl and hope that she would break up with him. Then maybe we would hook up again, but the more I started thinking about it, I came to the conclusion that she probably wouldn't believe me anyway. And if she did, I don't think I would want her to be with me just because Eric had cheated on her. If we were to end up together, I wanted her to want me because she really loved me. That's why it didn't work between us the last time. She was with me just because Eric wasn't acting right. She hadn't really wanted to be with me.

On the other hand, I didn't like the fact that he was playing on her. Even though she didn't treat me too good, she didn't deserve to be dogged out by him. She was so dumb though. Hell, he had cheated on her the last time. Why didn't she think he would do it again? Hell, he must have thought he was Billy Dee Williams or somebody anyway. I decided that I wouldn't say anything to her. She would just have to find out on her own that Eric was up to his old tricks again.

Nothing too interesting had happened between Kim and me in the last two weeks. I had been calling her ever other day, and I had only talked to her once. I kept telling myself that I was going to stop calling her, but she was so damn fine. I would start thinking about how sexy she was and I would end up picking up the phone and calling her. Naturally, she wouldn't be there or she just didn't want to talk to me because whoever answered the phone would ask who it was and then say that she wasn't at home. If I continued to call and never got a chance to talk to her, I would sooner or later stop calling her, even if she was one of the finest girls this side of the Smokey Mountains.

Well, anyway, it was Friday, and Stevall was going to be here tonight. I was supposed to be picking him up from the bus station at around six o'clock. He was going to stay for about a week and I was really looking forward to it. We would get to trip out like we did back in the day.

Six o'clock rolled around and I was at the bus station waiting for Stevall. The bus had not arrived when I got there, so I sat down inside and waited for him. And believe me, there were some crazy ass looking people in there. There was one person, though, that bugged the hell out of me. As soon as I sat down, I noticed this old bald-headed black man with no teeth. He kept staring at my shoes and sucking on his gums. After about a minute, he started asking me about my shoes.

"What kind of shoes you got there, son?"

"Uh, they're just some tennis shoes," I said.

"I know they be some tennis shoes, son. What kind? I wanna know," he said, as he continued to suck on his gums.

"They are Nikes."

"Uh, Nikes, that's what that kid Air Russell wears, ain't it?"

"Who is Air Russell?" I asked him.

He then stood up, walked toward me, and sat down right next to me. The smell was unbearable. He smelled like toes and ass. It was terrible. He continued talking, and all I could do was put my hand over my nose and mouth. Well, I could have gotten up and left, but I didn't want to be rude. The man smelled like shit and everything, but he was trying to be nice, I guess.

"You know," he said, "the guy that dunks on everybody in Chicago."

"You mean Air Jordan."

"Yeah, that's the kid."

"Why did you call him Air Russell?"

"You know he Bill Russell's kid, don't you?"

"What? He ain't no Bill Russell's kid," I said.

"The hell he ain't," the man said loudly, and at that point the man started talking crazy and making no sense. The worst part was that he kept moving around in his seat, and every time he moved, the smell got worse. Luckily, Stevall's bus finally arrived, so I got up and walked over to the gate that he had to come through. It was good to get away from the old man and that hellified smell.

The people began coming through the doors and Stevall finally came through. He looked like his usual self, and the good thing was that he was smiling. He spotted me immediately and started walking toward me. He was carrying a gym bag over his shoulder and it looked like this funny-looking white girl was walking with him. I immediately began to wonder what Stevall had done this time.

"What's up, Stevall?" I said, and gave him a brotherly hug.

"What up, Horne, man?" he said.

After we said our hellos, I started looking at this funny-looking ass white girl standing next to him. She just stood there smiling at me. Stevall told me that he had to go and pick up his suitcase, so we walked over to the luggage area. The whole time we were walking, the white girl was right beside him. When we got to the luggage area, I looked at her again. She still had a crazy looking smile on her face.

"Stevall, who in the hell is this?" I asked, pointing at the girl.

"Oh, uh, this is Samantha," he said, and looked at her and smiled.

"Samantha? And why is she following us?"

"Well, I told her we could give her a ride up the street."

"You what?" I said. "When did you meet this girl?"

"On the bus about thirty minutes ago."

I looked at the girl and faked a smile. "Will you please excuse us?" I said to her, and she just smiled harder and nodded her head, yes. I grabbed Stevall by his arm and pulled him to the side.

"Stevall, man, why are we giving this funny ass looking white girl a ride down the street?"

"Well, she said that she was going to have to get a cab to take her to her apartment and that she didn't live too far from here, so I told her that we could give her a ride."

"If she lives down the street, it wouldn't cost her that much to ride in a cab," I said.

"I really don't know if she lives down this street. I just know that she lives close around here. I just said down the street."

I wanted to yell at him, but I didn't. I stood there, nodding my head. Stevall was always doing something stupid. I looked at him and then at the girl. She had long, tangly red hair. Her skin was very pale and she had on some dark purple lipstick. She had a good body for a white girl, but that purple lipstick and tangly hair made her look crazy as hell.

I kept looking at her, trying to decide if we should give her a ride. I know that you aren't supposed to give rides to strangers, but she looked harmless. I was about to say yes, but she did something that changed my mind. While I was looking at her, she started picking boogers out of her nose and eating them. She didn't eat just one or two either. It seemed like she ate about ten of them. It was down right nasty. Her nose must have been clogged up like a motherfucker. I stopped looking at her and turned to Stevall.

"Did you see that nasty shit?" I asked him.

"See what?"

"I know you saw that shit."

"What?"

"You saw that girl eating those boogers!"

"Nah, man," he said, "she was just playing with her nose."

"Hell, naw! That trick was eating boogers like popcorn."

"No, she wasn't."

"She ain't riding with us, Stevall. I'm sorry."

"Come on, Horne."

I grabbed Stevall's bag and started walking. "Come on, Stevall. Let's go."

"Man, what am I going to tell her?" he asked.

"Don't tell that trick shit. Let's go."

Stevall looked at the girl. She was staring at the wall like she was in a daze or something. He walked over to her and started saying something. He was beginning to piss me off, but I was remaining fairly calm. After a minute or two, he turned around and started walking toward me. The girl was still standing there looking crazy.

"What did you tell her, man?" I asked.

"I told her that you weren't going to give her a ride."

"Good! Let's go."

"I still say we could have given her a ride. She seemed like a nice person."

"Yeah, yeah, yeah."

We were almost out the door when somebody tapped me on my shoulder. When I turned around, the smell almost knocked my ass down. It was the old man.

"Hey, son, you ain't leaving, are you?" he asked.

"Yeah, I'm out of here."

"Well, how about giving me a couple dollars so I can get some ripple?"

"Man, you don't need no damn ripple," I said. "You need a bath."

The old man looked at me with a crazy expression. "What?" he said. "What you say, son?"

"I didn't say nothing man and I don't have any money for you," I said, and Stevall and I were still trying to get to the door.

"Naw, son, what up? You trying to say I smell or something?" the old man said, and I started to curse his ass out, but I just ignored him and kept walking. I don't mind helping folks out, but he needed a bath and a new attitude. Stevall and I finally got out of the bus station and to the car. I had a headache by now from having to deal with the old man and the funny-looking white girl. The bus station was most definitely full of crazy folks.

Stevall and I tripped on the way back to school. We talked briefly about a lot of things. I filled him in on my situation with the ladies and other things that were happening around school. When we got back to my dorm room, we just sat around for a while, tripping and watching TV. The night was still very young, so we had plenty of time to find something to do.

Stevall kept asking about Shirl, wanting to know what she was up to. I told him that I hadn't really talked to her lately and that she seemed to be okay. I also told him that I had seen her boyfriend with another girl. He wanted to know if I had told her. I said no and that I was going to leave it alone because she probably wouldn't believe me anyway. He didn't agree. He kept telling me that I needed to tell her. I listened to him and then changed the subject. Hell, telling her would just be a waste of time. She was straight up sprung. He would lie, they would make love, and she would probably never mention it again. Naw, I was just going to let her find out on her own. If she was smart, she would never have gone back to him anyway.

When ten o'clock rolled around, Stevall and I decided to go to a party. This fraternity called Alpha Phi Alpha was having a party on Mud Island. I didn't want to go at first, because we would have had to dress up, but the Alphas' parties were always live as hell. So we decided to go ahead and dress up and fall up in there.

I put on my multi-purpose suit, which I wore to all social and business events. It was the only suit that I owned, but it was pretty sharp. I combed my hair and threw on some Obsession cologne, and I was ready to go. Stevall had put his suit on, and he was looking sharp.

On our way down to the car, we saw Corey and Fred. They were dressed up, so I asked them if they were going to the party. Corey said yeah. Fred just gave me a crazy look. I felt like pimp-slapping his fat ass, but I ignored him. I told Corey that we would meet up with them at the party. He said okay and grinned. It was one of those 'yeah, whatever, I'm drunk as hell right now and really don't care' looks. While you're bullshitting, I needed that look, and I knew I wanted that feeling, so I asked Stevall if he wanted to stop at the liquor store on the way to the party. Naturally, he said yeah. They would probably be selling liquor at the party, but it would probably be so damn expensive that if we bought drinks there, we wouldn't have enough money after the party to go to Krystal.

We went by the liquor store and bought a couple of things. I bought a pint of Jim Bean, and Stevall got a half-pint of gin. After we left the liquor store, we stopped by Lenny's five and dime store to get some soda to mix with our booze. Also, we had to pick up some candy and gum to keep the smell of liquor off our breath so we could get our mack on. College girls seemed to diss you if you had a lot of liquor on your breath. It must make your breath hot and funky. Whatever it was, I had to get my mack on, so I had to go with the flow.

We mixed our drinks in the car and guzzled them down. Once again, I was drinking and driving, something that I really needed to stop doing. By the time we got to the party, I was buzzing pretty good, and Stevall was drunk. He had drunk all of his gin. Since I wasn't through, we hung outside in the parking lot guzzling on what I had left. While we were drinking, we were also checking out the honeys that were going into the party. They were looking good as hell. It was pretty cold outside, so they all had coats on, but you could see legs, legs, and more legs. Big legs, little legs, bruised legs, hairy legs, and just right legs.

"Man, damn, y'all got some hoes up here," Stevall said in a drunken manner.

"Yeah, it's some hoes up here, that's for sure," I replied, staring at some stout girl. It wasn't long before we finished the liquor and started walking up to the party.

Chapter Twenty-Six

As I walked into the party, all I saw were people standing around. It wasn't that no one was dancing. I just couldn't see the dance floor because there were so many people at the party.

"You see anybody you want to step to?" I asked Stevall.

"Hell, yeah," he said. "I'm gonna get me some trim before this night is over."

I looked over at him in disbelief. "You gonna do what?" I asked.

"Well, maybe not tonight, but I'm going to hook some up for later this week."

"Do that, man. Hell, I'm going to set me up some too."

Stevall and I gave each other some dap and then we proceeded to mingle with the rest of the party-goers. We had been standing there for a few minutes, casing the joint out, when they played my jam—"Planet Rock". I had to dance off of that. I began looking around the room for a dance partner. I saw about ten girls standing around, and they were all bobbing their heads and looking good, so I made my way over to where they were standing. While I was walking, I was bobbing my head, trying to decide which one of the girls I would ask to dance.

I had almost narrowed my choice down to this thick ass redhead, but as I zoomed in on her, I noticed that she was dissing brothers left and right. Suave brothers, at that, so I decided to leave her alone. Instead, I decided to ask another brick house to dance. She was about 5'11, and built like an hourglass. I pimped over to her in my best player stroll.

"Excuse me," I said to her in my best Barry White impersonation. She must not have heard me because she kept bobbing her head. So I said it again. "Excuse me." She still didn't respond, so I said it one more time, but much louder this time. "Excuse me!"

She heard me this time because she looked at me.

"Would you like to dance?" I asked, and she didn't say shit. She just looked at me and rolled her eyes. Needless to say, this pissed me off. I mean, really pissed me off. This girl was fine and everything, but she didn't have to treat me like a geek. Shit, she wasn't all that anyway.

"Listen, Miss Thang!" I said to her ass. "I only asked you to dance. I didn't ask you to have my baby."

She rolled her eyes and turned to say something to one of her friends. She still wasn't even recognizing me.

"Go to hell, you damn amazon looking ass bitch! Your breath probably stinks anyway," I said, and walked away laughing. I bet her ass heard that. I wasn't mad that she didn't want to dance. It just pissed me off that she didn't even acknowledge that I was there. I had asked her nicely. The least she could have done was to say no nicely.

Well anyway, the song was almost over, and I still hadn't gotten my groove on. I scanned the room for my next victim. As I was scanning, I saw Stevall out on the floor dancing. He was dancing with some fine ass girl. Shit, she was cutting up, too. She was throwing that ass on him and everything. I needed to get on the floor. I kept on scanning, and then I saw Shannon. I didn't know she was going to be here, but I was glad that she was because she was looking fine as hell. I stepped to her.

"What up, Shannon?"

"Hey, Horne. You didn't tell me you were going to be here," she said to me.

"You didn't tell me you were going to be here either."

"I wasn't going to come, but my friend Angela kept begging me to come with her."

"I'm glad she begged hard enough to make you decide to come."

"Did your friend from your hometown ever come?" she asked.

"Yeah, he's here." I looked toward the dance floor so I could point him out. "That's him dancing over there," I said.

"He's jamming, ain't he?" she said, smiling and bobbing her head.

"Hell, what you expect, baby? We both from the same hometown."

"Oh, really?" she said, looking me up and down.

"Yes, really," I said, while I was dancing and giving her a little taste of my moves. I grabbed her hand and pulled her on the dance floor. By this time, "Planet Rock" had gone off, but the D.J. was still cutting it up though.

"Yeah, baby! Shake what you mama gave you," I said, and she was definitely working it out. She was all up on me, just shaking that ass. I was hanging with her though. We danced for about five songs. Not only was she dancing all up on me, but she was turning around and throwing all that ass on me. I was hard as hell. I know she had to feel it because I didn't back up or nothing. I just kept on jamming.

After we got through dancing, we walked to the bar area and sat down. I wasn't really tired, probably because I was full. It was like when I drunk a lot, I could dance all night.

"You tired?" she asked me.

"Nah, baby. I don't get tired," I said, glancing around looking for Stevall.

"Well, you sure are sweating a lot for someone who's not tired," she said, and I turned and looked at her.

"Baby, that's just from getting my groove on. We can get back on the floor and groove some more if you want to."

"Yeah, yeah. You know you're tired," she said smiling.

We talked for several minutes. We were both flirting with each other. I didn't know what she was thinking, but I was thinking about me and her knocking the boots. I was about to ask her what she was doing after the party when I saw Kim. Shannon was looking good, but Kim was looking GOOD! I know that I should have just concentrated on Shannon since she was the one giving me play and Kim was basically treating me like a taxi that didn't charge. But damn, she was looking good. She had on a tight red dress that was cut very low. Also, the way it was cut, you could see all of her tits except for the nipples, and believe me, she had tits and ass for days. Shannon was still talking, but I wasn't hearing anything she was saying.

"Horne! Horne!" I heard Shannon saying as she waved her hand in my face. I knew she was trying to get my attention, but I couldn't seem to stop looking at Kim. "Horne! Over here. I'm over here," I heard her saying. I eventually managed to turn my head away from the Lady in Red and back to Shannon.

"Who is that?" she asked me.

"Who are you talking about?" I asked, trying to play it off.

"That girl over there in the red dress," she said, and I looked over at Kim and tried to act like I didn't know what she was talking about.

"Which girl in the red dress. There are a lot of girls with red dresses on."

"Whatever, Horne. You can do whatever you want. We don't go together, but don't try to play me like a dumb ass because I'm not," she said, and stood up and walked off.

I started to stop her, but I figured that she would get over it. Anyway, I had some business to take care of. I went to the bathroom to take a piss. Also, I had to check myself out in the mirror to make sure I was looking sharp. I threw some candy in my mouth and went looking for Kim. It took me a while to spot her because she had moved. I finally found her. She was standing, talking to some other fine girl. I pimped over and stood next to her.

"Excuse me," I said. "Do I know you?"

She turned around and smiled. "Hey, Horne. How are you doing?"

"I'm fine. How are you?" I asked, trying not to stare at her breasts.

"I'm fine," she said, and she had a cute ass smile on her face.

"I can see that you're fine. In fact very fine, but how are you doing?"

"Horne, you are so crazy," she said, and I was just warming up. I was about to get my Billy Dee mack on when I felt someone tap me on the shoulder. I turned around to see who it was. It was Eric. What a surprise.

"What up, Eric?" I said.

"Horne, what did you tell Shirl?" he asked, looking mad as hell.

"I didn't tell Shirl nothing. I don't know what you are talking about," I said, in a casual 'get out of my damn face' way.

"You know damn well what I'm talking about. I saw you the other night spying on me," he said, and raised his voice loud as hell.

"Spying on you?" I said loudly. "I could care less what your punk ass did."

"Punk ass? You the punk ass. Shirl told me about you wanting to get with her and how she didn't want your ass," he said, and came closer to me.

That shit that he just said made me mad as hell. Not only was I mad at him, but I was also mad at Shirl. I looked around for a second to see who was looking because I was really considering stealing on this fool. It was like everybody had stopped dancing and was looking at us. Kim and her friend had moved away from us and Stevall was making his way over toward us. He must have drunk some more because he couldn't even walk straight. I turned back and looked Eric in the eyes.

"Fool, I didn't say shit to your girl. You best get the hell out of my face," I said, and tried to calm myself down.

"Fool? You the stupid ass fool! You think by telling Shirl that you saw me kissing another girl, you can make her want you? You damn crazy. You're a loser, and she'll always love me anyway. You deal with that, FOOL!" he said, and walked up so close to me that I could feel his breath.

That was enough. That was all I could take. I turned as if I was going to walk away. Then I turned back around quick as hell with my right fist leading the way. I hit him hard as hell on the jaw. His face turned and spit flew everywhere. He didn't fall down, but he was bent over.

The next thing I knew, I felt a fist hit the side of my head. I fell down on the floor and looked up. I was sort of in a daze. I knew it couldn't have been Eric because he was still bent over. It must have been one of his boys. I looked around to see who had sprung on me. It was this guy named Deno. He was one of Eric's boys, and he was big as hell.

I managed to stand up. By this time, Eric was no longer bent over. He and Deno were advancing. They were almost within a swing's reach when out of nowhere, Stevall hit Eric over the head with a sixteen-ounce long neck beer bottle. Eric grabbed his head and Deno turned toward him to see what had happened. This was the perfect opportunity for me to get Deno back for the cheap shot that he laid on me. Without hesitating, I reared back and stole on his ass right in the side of the head. I hit him with all my might, and it didn't even knock him down. In fact, it didn't even seem to affect him. He put his hand on his head and started coming toward me. Luckily, security reached him before he reached me. Unluckily, they reached me and Stevall too.

The party had completely stopped. The music was turned off and everybody in the club was staring at us. The scrape had only lasted about one minute, but I guess that was long enough to mess the party up. Security escorted us to the back of the club where this old Italian man with a fat ass belly was standing.

"What seems to be the problem?" he asked us.

"Nothing," I said. "We just had a misunderstanding, but everything is straight now." Stevall and Deno agreed with me.

"It doesn't look like everything is straight. You guys fucked up the party and could have tore up my damn club," the Italian man said.

"Everything is straight," I said to the man. "We are sorry for causing problems."

"I'm not sorry, and everything is not straight," Eric said, and walked in with a towel on his head. He was bleeding from the head.

"Who are you?" the Italian man asked Eric.

"Who in the hell are you?" Eric asked him back. Man, he was a straight up ass. Here I was trying to talk calmly, so we could get out of this without going to jail, and here he was talking crazy.

"I'm the owner of this damn club, that's who I am. And who in the hell are you?"

"I'm the guy that got sprung on and got a bottle smashed on my damn head, that's who I am."

"Oh, so you're one of the troublemakers, too," the Italian man said.

"Troublemaker? Look! I'm bleeding. I'm the damn victim," Eric said. Then he pointed at Stevall and me. "Those are the damn troublemakers."

I didn't even say anything. Eric was such a damn punk. All I could do was shake my head and look at him.

"I'm not sure who caused the trouble," the Italian man said. "The police are on the way, and I will let them figure it out."

Damn. This was just great. The night had begun good. I had danced with Shannon and she was looking good. I was about to get my crazy mack on with Kim and she was looking GOOD! Why did this shit have to happen? Eric kept trying to convince the owner of the club that he was the victim while Stevall, Deno, and I stood there looking like future jailbirds.

All of a sudden, one of the security guards burst through the door. He told the Italian man and the other security guards that another fight had started. They all ran out the door to check it out. It must have been a big fight because it sounded like they were straight tearing up the place. There must have been a full moon out because some crazy things had been happening all night. People were just straight up tripping.

I walked over to the door and peeked out. Damn. The police had arrived, but they were currently trying to break up the fight. It looked like some football players, but I didn't have time to worry about all of that. I looked around some more and noticed that there were no security guards around the door. I turned to Stevall.

"Let's get the hell out of here," I said, and began to walk out the door.

"I'm right behind you," Stevall said.

As we were walking, I looked around one more time and then we walked rapidly out the door. As soon as we got outside, we started running to my car. We hopped in the car and I cranked it up. As I was backing up,

I saw Eric and Deno running across the parking lot. I guess they were trying to get the hell out of there too.

After we left the party, we went to Krystal to get a bite to eat. We decided to go in and sit down because it was still relatively early and we didn't have anything to do. While we were eating, Stevall and I tripped about all the crazy ass things that had happened at the club. Even though we had been in a fight, it turned out that we both had a good time. It was all funny to me. There was just one thing I didn't understand, though. How did Shirl find out about Eric kissing that girl. I sure as hell hadn't told her.

"Man, I wonder how Shirl found out about Eric," I said out loud, basically talking to myself.

"I don't know, but she was looking mad as hell at the party," Stevall said.

"At the party? Shirl was at the party?"

"Yes, she was."

"I didn't see her," I said to Stevall, wondering to myself why in the hell he hadn't told me this earlier.

"You probably didn't see her because she didn't stay long."

"Did you go talk to her?" I asked him.

"Yeah. She saw me and wanted to know what I was doing up here. I could tell that she was upset, so I asked her what was wrong."

"What did she say?"

"Something about Eric."

"What about Eric," I asked him.

"I don't remember."

"You don't remember? Well, you need to try to remember. Hell, I want to know why Eric was tripping on me," I said in a serious manner.

"Oh yeah, now I remember something," he said.

"What?" I asked.

"You're going to be pissed at me, but…"

I cut him off. "What?" I said, raising my voice. "Tell me!"

"Well, I sort of told her about Eric kissing that girl," he said, and moved back away from me.

My first instinct was to reach over and choke his ass, but I tried to remain calm. I counted to ten before saying anything. When I got through, I asked him why in the hell he had told her.

"Well, it sort of slipped," he said.

"How in the hell did that slip?" I asked, still trying to stay calm.

"She was complaining about something to Eric and he just walked off. I just figured that she had found out. So I said to her 'you must know about Eric and that girl.'"

I interrupted him. "OK, hold up. You told her that she must know about Eric and that girl? Why?" I asked him. He tried to answer, but I cut him off. "What in the hell were you thinking about?"

"Man, I told you that I thought she already knew," he said.

"Why did you think she knew! She could have been complaining about anything."

"I don't know, man! I was full. Hell, I'm still full."

I looked at him for a minute before I said another word. It was true that he was full earlier and he still looked full, but still that was no excuse. If he couldn't act sensible when he got full, then his ass didn't need to be getting full.

"What happened after you said something about Eric and the girl?" I asked, and munched down the last of my six cheese Krystals with no onions.

"She seemed like she knew. That's why I kept talking," he said, while munching on a chicken sandwich.

"She seemed like she knew? What did she say?"

"She just said something like 'yeah, I know, but go on so I'll make sure we're talking about the same thing," he said.

"And your dumb ass kept on talking?!!"

"I'm sorry, man."

"You know you fucked up."

"I said I'm sorry."

"You know you fucked up," I said one more time.

Chapter Twenty-Seven

The day after the party was a pretty day. It was a Saturday, the sun was out, and it was a little warmer than usual for the time of year. I slept well all night, but the morning was an entirely different story. The phone had been ringing all morning. Everybody was calling me about the rumble the night before. The first person to call was Shannon. It had to be around eight o'clock. She had seen me fighting and wanted to know what was going on. I told her that some dude was talking crazy, so we had to come to blows. She sounded really worried and she told me that she was going to try to come over to make sure I was okay.

The next person to call was Shirl. We talked for about an hour. She called herself cursing me out for not telling her about Eric. I told her that she wouldn't have believed me anyway, and asked her why she believed me now. She said that she had her reasons. She also wanted to come over later to make sure that Stevall and I were okay. One of her homegirls had told her that we had gotten in a fight with Eric and Deno. I wanted to ask her why in the hell she was coming to see if Stevall and I were okay, but I didn't. I just said okay.

Corey called next, talking crazy. He wanted to know who we had been fighting with. Talking about we ought to go cap those niggers. Shit, Corey didn't even have a gun, and if he did, his ass would probably be scared to pick it up. He was always trying to be hard and shit. I told him everything was squashed. He told me that if they started tripping again to call him and Fred because they had my back.

The next call was from Kim. And she wasn't calling because she needed a ride. She called wanting to hook up. In summary, she basically said that she didn't know that I was so hard, and that she and her friend wanted to hook up with Stevall and me later. Man, I guess that was what turned her on. Well, if she wanted a hard nigger, then from that point on whenever I was around her, I was going to make her think I was a hard nigger. Well, actually, I was hard, but not the kind of hard that makes you fight all the time. But I was going to put on a little acting job to get some of that. Hell, I would damn near win an Oscar to get some of that.

By the time I got off the phone, Stevall was walking up. I was still sleepy, so I went back to sleep. Stevall said he was going to go check out the campus. I'm not sure how long I slept, but I was sure that I was awakened by a girl's voice. It sounded like she was calling my name, so I looked up. To my surprise, it was Shirl.

"Hey," I said, wondering how in the hell she got in the room.

"Hey, Horne," she said.

"How did you get in here?" I asked.

"Stevall let me in."

"Oh, where is he now?"

"He went back down to the lobby. I think he was trying to talk to some girl."

"Oh," I said, and wondered in my mind who he was trying to talk to.

"Come on, get up so we can talk," she said, pushing my shoulder. I raised up and sat on the side of the bed. She sat down on the bed beside me. "You going to sleep all day or something?"

"Nah, but I didn't get any sleep this morning."

"Why is that?"

"Because some people called me early as hell wanting to talk," I said, as I looked into her eyes.

"Some people," she said, smiling.

"Yeah, some people, like you and Corey."

"Corey? Is he still a fool? And what did he want?" she asked.

"Yeah, he's still a fool, and he didn't want nothing, really. Just to keep a nigger from getting his beauty sleep, I guess."

I stood up and walked to the sink to wash my face. As I was washing my face, Shirl walked up behind me. All up on my booty, she started giving me a shoulder massage. It felt good, but something seemed strange. After, I got through washing my face, I turned around and looked at her. She looked at me, smiling, and began to massage the sides of my arms.

"What are you doing, Shirl?" I asked.

"Massaging your arms," she replied.

"I know that, but why are you massaging my arms?"

"Oh, I just felt like it, but if you don't like it, I will stop," she said, and interrupted the massage.

"Nah, I don't want you to stop. I'm just not used to you giving me any kind of massage," I said, and took her hands and placed them on my shoulders.

She smiled and then continued to rub my shoulders. As I looked into her eyes, a thousand thoughts started running through my mind. Thoughts like how we met and how we had hit it off so well. Thoughts like how we had become best friends and how we used to be able to tell each other everything. Thoughts like how I had fallen in love with her while we were friends and how I had wanted more than a friendship. Thoughts like how for a short while, we had been more than friends and how we had made love. And finally, thoughts about how she had dumped me for Eric. That had really hurt me. I tried to act like it was just some shit that had happened, but deep down, it was some shit that had damaged my heart.

Although she had tremendously hurt me, there was just one thing that dominated the rest of my thoughts. And that was how pretty she was and how much I was still in love with her. I kept looking into her eyes. They were so pretty. For a brief moment, it was like I just stopped thinking and started reacting. I very gently put my hands on her face, leaned over, and kissed her on the forehead.

"What was that for?" she asked me.

I didn't say anything. I just kissed her on the forehead again. She must have liked it because she moved closer to me. In fact, we were standing there holding each other. She felt so damn good to me. The next time I leaned down, I bypassed the forehead and went straight for the lips. I gave her a soft, juicy kiss. After I kissed her, I moved back to see how she would react. She stood there, looking at me as if she wanted me to kiss her again. So I did. I kissed her again. And what a kiss it was. It was straight up tongue action. Not only were the tongues roaming, but my hand was moving all over her ass.

We kissed and rubbed each other for a long time. Somehow, we had made our way over to the bed, and I was on top of her. I had opened her bra and pulled her shirt up. Her breasts were so beautiful, and I was enjoying every moment seeing them. The more we kissed and touched, the more anxious I got, so I went for the pants.

"Hold up, Horne," she said, and moved from under me and sat up on the bed. I sat next to her and looked at her. "Horne, I'm sorry, but I don't want to move too fast."

"What are we doing anyway, Shirl?" I asked her. "How did this happen?"

"I don't know Horne. You tell me. It just happened, I guess."

"Just happened? I mean, you dissed me, Shirl, and then you come up here massaging my arms and shit. What's up?"

Shirl stood up and walked across the room as if she was doing some heavy thinking or something. She just kept pacing back and forth, and it was starting to get on my nerves.

"Shirl, I don't know what is going on," I said. "You know I have been wanting to be with you for a long time. Obviously, you don't want to be with me because of Eric. I get in a fight with him last night, and you're over here today kissing me and telling me that it just happened. What the hell is up?" I stood up and walked over to her. I put my hands on her shoulders and looked down at her. She wouldn't look at me. She had her head down toward the floor.

"Shirl, talk to me." I said. "I care about you a lot, but I can't keep getting high hopes about us just to be dumped on my face."

Shirl looked up at me. "Horne, don't say anything else," she said, leaning toward me. "Just kiss me."

"But you just said that we need to slow down and…"

She put her finger on my lips. "I know what I said, but now I'm saying kiss me."

So I said to myself 'to hell with it' and leaned over and kissed her. The kiss was soft, wet, and long. We kissed our way back to the bed. I was laying down on the bed, and she was on top of me. We kissed and kissed and rubbed and rubbed some more. The kissing and rubbing led to more kissing and rubbing, and before we knew what had happened, we were both butt naked. She looked so damn fine. Her skin was soft and smooth. Her breasts were beautiful, and her ass was all that.

She was still on top of me, and we were about to do it. I wasn't wearing a condom. I needed to get up and get one, but I didn't. I just slid it in bare. It felt like I had died and gone to heaven. She was on top of me working it out. I felt like nutting, but I was trying my damnest to hold it back. I tried thinking about everything, but what we were doing. I thought about politics, football, basketball, my schoolwork. It worked for about seven minutes, and then the cat took over. I mean it was like she was straight up showing out and I was loving every second of it.

After we finished the first time, we switched positions and did it again. This time I was on top, and I was trying to wear that cat out. I had her ass calling my name out and everything. It was all good except for the fact that I had nutted inside her twice. Man, I just hoped she didn't have a disease and that she wouldn't get pregnant.

After the second round, we went at it one more time. It was just like that dream I had except we were in my room on a bed instead of on a bus. The last time was the best time and it drained all the energy out of me. All I could do afterward was lay there and enjoy the moment.

We laid there for several minutes, holding each other and probably would have kept laying there, but we were rudely interrupted. Stevall came in the room on us. I had left the door unlocked, but fortunately we were under the covers and we were through. He was in the room and had taken a few steps before he saw us.

"Oh, uh. Oh, uh. I'm sorry," he said, and turned around and walked out.

To my surprise, Shirl didn't even get mad. She just laughed, and so did I. "I think you'd better get up and lock the door," she said.

I got up and locked the door. When I got back to the bed, she was ready for some more loving. It was all good.

Chapter Twenty-Eight

A few days had passed, and it was now Thursday. It had been a very busy week for me, but not because of school. In fact, I had only been to one of my classes all week and that was the one I had with Shirl. I had skipped the other classes mainly to rest, because I had been kicking it all week. It seemed like since the brawl, Stevall and I had become hip or something. I guess once the girls saw us kicking some ass, they got turned on.

I had knocked the boots with Shirl Sunday and Monday. I knew I still loved her, but I just couldn't figure her out. We really didn't discuss anything; we just fucked. Every time I tried to discuss what was up with us, she would find one way or another to change the subject. I just figured that when she was ready to talk, she would let me know. In the meantime, I was enjoying the cat and trying not to become too attached to it or to her because there was no telling what she was thinking.

I kept myself from getting too attached to Shirl by seeing other people. Stevall and I had been out with Kim and her friend Lynette Saturday and Tuesday, and we had plans to go out with them again that night. We had been out to eat the first night and then we went to the drive-in the last time. This time, I wasn't sure what we were going to do, but we were taking separate cars. Lynette was going to drive her car so that she and Stevall could be alone. This was cool because one way or another, I had planned to lose them and bring Kim's fine ass back to the room to see what was up with her.

I had also seen Shannon a couple of times. She had come up to the room. Both times, she had brought one of her friends so Stevall would have somebody to talk to. I was having a ball that week and I could tell that Stevall was enjoying himself too. He hadn't gotten any cat yet, but I could tell that he was close with Lynette. She was fine, and I could tell by the way she acted that she had a little freak in her. Hopefully, he would be able to get some of that.

The day flew by and it was getting close to the time that we were supposed to be going out. I was calling Shirl to talk to her before we left, but she wasn't at home. This wasn't usual because it seemed like she was never home. The only time I talked to her was when she called, came over, or when I saw her in class. From time to time I would wonder where she was, but I would try not to worry about it.

Anyway, I needed to start getting ready for my date. Stevall was already ready. In fact he had been ready for about two hours. He was anxious as hell because he thought that this would be the night that he slid into some skins. He had been talking all day about how he knew that this was going to be the night. Right now he was up in Fred's room chillin'. They had hit it off pretty well and had been kicking it together whenever I was busy with one of my women or something. I had asked Stevall if Fred ever talked about his ex-girlfriend. He said no and that every time he would ask Fred about her, Fred would either start eating something, ignore him, or just straight up change the subject.

I still had to get ready for the night. I took a shower and washed my hair. I then threw on my clothes, combed my hair, and put a couple splashes of cologne on. I was ready to go, so I called up to Fred's room and told Stevall to come on.

When we got to Kim's crib, Lynette was already over there. She and Stevall didn't waste any time. They got in her car and left.

"What are they going to do?" I asked Kim.

"They're going over to Lynette's apartment," she said. "I think she's going to cook him dinner."

"Lynette's got her own apartment?" I asked, in disbelief because she had never mentioned it.

"Yeah, she's got a nice apartment."

"Damn, where did she get the money to have a nice apartment?" I asked, slowly looking Kim over.

"You know her parents got a lot of money."

"Nah, I didn't know that. Matter of fact, I don't know shit about Lynette. Hell, Stevall must not know too much or I would have heard about these things."

"Well, she likes to keep her business on the down low."

"That's straight," I said.

"What are we going to do?" she asked me.

"I don't know. Have you eaten yet?"

"No, I haven't"

"Let's go get a pizza and go back to my room and chill," I said, and hoped that she would agree with my plan.

"A pizza sounds straight, but what are we going to do in your room?"

At first I was alarmed at the question because it sounded like she didn't want to go, but when I looked at her, she had a devilish grin on her face. "Whatever you want to do," I said with a devilish look of my own.

"Whatever?" she said, and looked me over.

"Yeah, whatever. So let's get going."

She smiled and then we left. I flew to the pizza place. It seemed like it took them forever to make the pizza. Probably because I was excited and anxious as hell. You see, Kim was probably the finest and sexiest girl that I had ever had a chance to have sex with and I was very horny. I knew that I was in love with Shirl, but Shirl just didn't have the straight up lust appeal that Kim had.

After we got the pizza, we went back to my room. In the room, we ate and listened to the radio. Kim even ate sexy. I was ready to get to the nitty gritty. We finally finished eating and began talking about a lot of things. Well, actually, we didn't talk about much other than the songs that were playing on the radio. I could tell that she was into music and dancing. We had been talking for about twenty minutes when she decided that she wanted to dance. She stood up and just started moving. She was looking good as hell.

"You working it out, ain't you, girl?" I said, enjoying her every move.

"Yeah, this is my jam," she said, as she broke it down.

The song was the jam. It was some new upbeat rap song. The song went off and I thought Kim was about to sit down, but then this cold ass slow jam came on.

"This is really my jam," she said, and started grinding and moving her body in sexy ways.

"Damn," I said. "You look sexy as hell."

"Mmm, I do?" she said.

"Yeah, you do. You need me to get up and be your partner?"

"You can't handle this," she said, smiling.

"Oh, yeah, I can handle it, all right."

"Boy, don't you know that I'll turn your ass out by just dancing?" she said to me as she did some move where she grinded all the way down to the floor.

I smiled at her and stood up. "Girl, I done danced with you before, remember? I handled it then."

"That was in a public place around lots of folks. I was holding back. This is a private place. Just you and me. I ain't going to hold back."

"Baby, I don't want you to hold back," I said, as I walked up and put my arms around her.

"I warned you," she said. "Don't say nothing when you nut on yourself."

"Nut on myself? Girl, you got me messed up, don't you?"

"Shit, your ass is already on hard," she said, and grabbed my thing. I couldn't believe she did that. I was speechless. "Now what you got to say?" she said, and let my thing go.

I just smiled, trying to think of something to come back with. "Uh, uh, baby, I can stay hard all night," I said in a nervous, unconvincing manner.

"Boy, please. I'll have your ass running around here sprung on this cat."

Man, she was talking a lot of shit, and I was tired of talking and ready for action. "Baby, put your body where your mouth is," I said, and rubbed my hands down on her booty.

"What you say?" she asked.

"I said put your body where your mouth is," I repeated, still rubbing her booty.

"What is that supposed to mean?"

"This," I said, and began kissing her on the neck. She didn't stop me either. She just rubbed the back of my head and moaned. From the tone of her moan, I knew it was on. We kept kissing until we ended up on the bed, and it was all good. I was straight up working it out, but to be straight up honest, she turned me out. She was non-stop action. Believe that.

Three hours flew by and we were on our way out. We were going to stop and get a bite to eat because we were both hungry after all that sex. The pizza we had eaten earlier had burned away long ago. We decided to go to Wendy's and get some burgers and fries. We sat down and ate and talked. We didn't even talk about sex as I had anticipated, but we talked about everything else. It was like she was finally letting her guard down and opening up to me. She really surprised me because she was such an interesting person. It's not that I didn't think she was interesting, but before, I only thought she was interesting in a sexual way. Now, she was interesting in all ways.

We sat there and talked for about an hour and then we left. On our way to the car, I saw Shirl. She was with two girls. At first, I was scared because I was with another girl, but then I thought to myself, Shirl was not my girlfriend. Hell, she was probably still screwing Eric, so what in the hell was I worried about. I kept walking with Kim. I couldn't too much avoid Shirl because she was parked right next to my car.

As I got close to the car, we passed each other and made eye contact. At first she smiled, and then she glanced over at Kim. The smile suddenly disappeared and her eyes turned from pleasant to hateful. I started to speak, but the way she was looking, I was ready to get into the car and get out of there. We got into the car and I backed up and pulled off. As I drove away, I looked in the rear-view mirror and Shirl was still looking at us. Hell, forget her. She had no right to get mad at me the way she had dissed me in the past. She had treated me like straight up nothing, and now she was trying to front. I tried not to think about her while I was talking to Kim, but I couldn't help it. It was like seeing Shirl had messed up the whole night even though I had gotten with Kim.

"What's on your mind?" Kim asked, as we pulled up in her driveway.

"Ah, nothing. I'm just a little tired," I said, and turned to look at her.

She put one of her hands on my face and started rubbing it. "I really had a nice time tonight," she said.

"I did too," I said, smiling as I thought about how she seemed like a completely different person since we had sex. She seemed to be a gentler, kinder person.

We exchanged a few more words and then I leaned over to kiss her and told her goodbye and good night. As I was driving off, I realized that I had forgot to ask her about Lynette and Stevall. I guess they were somewhere having fun. Hopefully, Stevall was somewhere tapping that ass.

When I got back to the room, I went to bed. Stevall was still out with Lynette, and I was really tired. The day had really drained me.

The next day, I was awakened by the sound of the telephone ringing. I glanced over at the clock. It was seven o'clock. I then answered the phone, wondering who in the hell was calling me this damn early.

"Hello," I said in a sleepy, pissed off tone.

"Hey, Horne," the other person said.

"Who's this?"

"So you have so many women now that you don't even know who you are talking to?"

"Hey, Shirl, and it's not like that at all. Hell, it's seven o'clock in the morning and I happen to be sleep."

"Don't you have a class today?" she asked.

"Yeah, a couple of hours from now."

"Well, anyway, I called to ask you who was that girl you were with last night."

"A friend of mine," I answered.

"Yeah, right. The same kind of friend that I am. The kind you sleep with."

"Why are you calling me at seven o'clock sweating me?"

"I'm not sweating you. I just want to know who she was and what is up."

She wants to know what is up. When I heard her say that, I had to laugh a little. "You want to know what is up?" I said, still chuckling.

"Why are you laughing?" she asked. "This is not funny. I know it's not to me."

"It is funny."

"How in the hell is this funny?"

"It just is," I said to her.

"I do not understand, but anyway, you need to tell me what is up or nothing's going to be up."

"Oh, so you call yourself threatening me or something?"

"Nah, it's not a threat. It's just the way it's going to be. I ain't about to let some nigger play me."

"Shiiit, you played me. Hell, you need to be played."

"Oh, so is that what you're trying to do, Horne? Play me? And anyway, I didn't play you."

"Oh, so what do you call it?"

"I don't call it nothing. I still had feelings for you, but I was in love with Eric. Basically, I made a mistake and I'm sorry. I didn't try to hurt you."

"Well, you did. You hurt me bad, and you need to tell me what's up. Are you making another mistake or what?"

"Horne, I don't know what's up. All I know is that when I saw you with another girl, it made me feel bad. Part of me was sorry that we ever became more than friends, and part of me couldn't imagine seeing you with another girl," she said, and her voice began to crack a little.

"Shirl, you know how I feel about you. I just don't want you to hurt me again, and I honestly don't feel like you're over Eric." She didn't say anything. It sounded like she had started crying. "Don't cry, Shirl. Don't cry, please." I said that over and over until she responded.

"Can you come over here, please?" she asked.

"You want me to come now?"

"Yeah, I don't feel like being alone."

"Okay."

I got up, took a shower and walked out the door on my way to Shirl's apartment. It was early as hell. I was tired, and I wasn't quite sure why I was going over there. The only explanation that I could come up with was that I was still in love with her. Very much in love with her.

When I got to her place, she must have been looking for me because she was at the door waiting for me. As I walked in, I looked at her. Her eyes were swollen from crying and she looked very tired. We went to her bedroom and laid on the bed. We didn't talk, kiss, or fool around. We just held each other and went to sleep. It was very nice. Something that I could have gotten used to. We slept until about one o'clock. We had both missed our classes. When we finally got up, we talked for a while.

"Horne, I want you to know that I really care about you, and I think that I want us to be together."

"You think? Do you still love Eric?"

"I still care for him, but Eric ain't shit."

"You didn't answer my question. Do you still love him? And if he told you that he wasn't going to mess up anymore, would you take him back?"

"No and no," she said.

I looked into her eyes. I knew deep in my heart that she was lying, but I really wanted to believe her. So I tried to convince myself that she was telling the truth.

We talked for a couple more hours and then I left. We had come to an understanding that we were going to be together and see how it worked out. She told me that she wasn't going to see other guys and that she didn't want me to see other girls. I agreed, but deep down, I wasn't sure if I was going to give Kim up. It wasn't that I didn't want to be with Shirl, but more or less, I wasn't sure how long Shirl would want to be with me. And besides, Kim could really throw her stuff. I was just going to have to lie to Shirl and keep creeping. I knew that this was wrong, but I was at the point that I had to watch out for my own feelings. I was not going to trust Shirl until she proved to me that she was really over Eric and wanted to be with me.

Chapter Twenty-Nine

When I got back to my dorm room, it was around three o'clock. Stevall was still gone, and it didn't look like he had even been back. I was starting to worry about him, but I figured he was old enough to handle himself. I just hoped she didn't whip him so much that he had a heart attack.

The rest of the day, I just chilled until about eight o'clock. Then I went to work. We were pretty busy, so the night flew by. I walked about twenty girls to their cars. Some were fine and some were not. When I got back to the room, it was about 12:15 and Stevall still wasn't back, so I called Kim to see if she had heard from Lynette.

"Hello," Kim said, as she answered the phone.

"What up, Kim?"

"You know what time it is, Horne?" she asked.

"Uh, about 12:15. Did I wake you up?"

"Nah, I was up, but I just thought for some strange reason that you would have called me earlier."

"Oh, I'm sorry, Kim. I've been really busy today. You know between classes and work."

"Oh, well," she said in a low tone. "I was just wondering what happened to you. You must not have liked it."

"Like it? What are you talking about?"

"You must not have liked it last night."

"Oh, last night. Nah, baby, I loved it. Believe me, I loved every minute of it."

"You did, Horne?"

"Yeah," I said.

We talked about our night of sex for about twenty minutes. She was talking so freaky that I had forgotten all about Stevall.

"Yeah, baby, you were straight up showing out," I said, in my best sexy voice.

"You weren't so bad yourself," she replied.

"Man, I wish you were over here right now," I told her.

"Well, if it's not too late, I'll come over there." She was sounding good as hell.

"Nah, it's not too late. I'll just have to sneak you in. Oh, Damn! I can't do that because of Stevall." I had just remembered what I had called Kim for in the first place.

"Stevall?" she said. "He's not there, is he?"

"Nah. Have you talked to Lynette? He hasn't been back all day."

"Yeah, he's going to spend the night over there. She said that he did go over there to get some clothes, but you were gone."

"Damn. He's spending the night again? They must have got busy last night. What did Lynette say they did?"

"Horne, I ain't going to get all up in Lynette's business. I got my own business to worry about. So do you want me to come over or not?"

"Your moms will let you come here this late?" I asked.

"She don't have to let me do nothing. She's sleep. I'll just creep out and then creep back in and she will never know that I was gone."

"Straight. Come on over," I said, without thinking twice.

"I'm on my way," she said, and hung up the phone.

I got up and started preparing myself for the night. I took a shower and then started straightening up the room. I had just finished when the phone rang. I answered it thinking it was Kim, but to my surprise, it was Shirl.

"Hey, baby," she said, "what you doing?"

Damn, why did she have to call me now? Kim was going to be here any minute and I didn't have call waiting so I needed to get off the phone. I decided to act like I was sleep.

"Oh, I was just sleep," I said, in my sleepiest voice.

"Oh, I'm sorry, baby. I thought you might still be up."

"Well, you know I had to work tonight and I'm a little tired," I continued in an even more convincing sleepy tone.

"I was just thinking about you," she said. "You go back to sleep and I'll talk to you tomorrow."

"Okay, good night," I said, and hung up the phone.

I was starting to feel guilty and then the phone rang. It was Kim. She was downstairs on the girls' side, so I went down there and sneaked her up. When we got to the room, she told me to sit down because she had a surprise for me. I sat down on my bed and waited for her to give me my surprise. I was wondering what it could be. She had a little overnight bag with her, so I figured that she must have gotten me a card or something.

She put the bag down and walked up to me. She had this big coat on because it was very cold outside. She slowly took the coat off, and there was the surprise. She didn't have a damn thing on but a red bow stuck on her tummy.

"Surprise, baby," she said.

"Come here, baby," I said, and wrapped my arms around her waist.

Chapter Thirty

The next morning, I got up early to sneak Kim out. Actually, I didn't have to wake up because we had been up all night anyway. It had been one of the best nights of my life. It was better than the other time we had done it. After I got Kim out, I came back to the room and slept. My ass was straight up drained. I had given her all that I had. I must have slept until about three. I probably would have slept longer, but that was when Stevall came in all loud.

"Horne, wake up, man," he said.

"What up, stranger?" I said, and wiped the sleep out of my eyes.

"Man, I got some shit to tell you."

"What?"

"Man, I got some trim the last two nights and this morning," he said, as he danced across the room.

"Straight up? I figured you had. Hell, your ass been gone forever."

"Man, I didn't want to come back. Shit, that shit was good as hell."

"So how does it feel to not be a virgin anymore."

"Man, you don't know. I feel good as hell. Finally! I mean finally! And the thing about it is that I wore her ass out. She thought I was a pro."

"Did you tell her that she was your first?"

"Yeah, I told her after the first time because I was a little embarrassed."

"Embarrassed? About what?"

"I just nutted so fast."

"You wear a condom?"

"Yeah, but I still nutted like in about ten seconds, but the second time, I wore it out."

"I hear you, man. I'm glad you finally got some. Now at least you won't have to worry about when you are finally going to get some."

"Yeah, but now I got to get some more."

"Well, Lynette will probably give you some more."

"I know she will, but I got to get some back at the crib."

"Listen to your ass," I said. "You're a mack now, ain't you?"

"Man, I'm addicted to the pussy now. No lie."

Stevall and I tripped for about an hour. I filled him in on what had taken place with Kim and also about what had happened with Shirl. He kept telling me that I should leave Kim alone and be good to Shirl, but I told him that I really didn't trust Shirl.

Stevall ended up staying an extra week. He spent most of his time with Lynette. That was cool though, because he seemed happy, and he deserved some happiness. He was happy, but my ass was tired and confused since I was supposedly going with Shirl now. We were spending a lot of time together. And the time I wasn't spending with Shirl, I was either in class, trying to study, working, or creeping with Kim.

I was beginning to feel a little guilty about messing with Kim mainly because I was starting to really like her. She was so sweet and exciting. I really liked her, but the more I started liking her, the more I knew that I loved Shirl. Every time Kim did something that made me really like her, Shirl would do something that would make me feel like I could spend the rest of my life with her. I was really beginning to think that she wanted to be with me because she treated me so damn nice. She would cook for me, give me rub downs, and she just seemed to be understanding about everything.

I was waiting for something to go wrong though, because I knew she wouldn't be like this forever, but to my surprise, she was like that for the next few weeks. In fact, she treated me and Stevall to steak dinners on his last day here. She was just so straight, but for some reason, I kept on creeping with Kim. It was a pretty cool arrangement because Kim didn't require a lot of time. So she never really sweated me about spending quality time with her. Don't get me wrong though, because the time we spent together was real quality time, if you know what I mean.

Valentine's Day was coming up, and I knew I had to do something nice for Shirl because I just knew she was going to get me something good. I also had to get something for Kim. I had already decided what I was going to get Kim. I was going to buy her some lingerie from Frederick's of Hollywood—something freaky.

The days flew by. Valentine's Day had crept upon me and I still hadn't decided what to get Shirl. We were still straight, but she had been acting strange for the past couple of days. I continually asked her what was wrong and she would always say nothing and that she was just real tired from school. So I really wanted to make her Valentine's Day something special.

On the day before Valentine's Day, I went to the mall to purchase my gifts. First, I went to Frederick's of Hollywood and bought Kim's present. It was straight up kinky, and I got on hard every time I thought about all the fun we were going to have when she wore it. Next, I went to Service Merchandise and looked at the jewelry. Everything was real nice, but it was all so expensive. I only had eighty dollars, and all the really nice things cost a hell of a lot more than that. I had a Master Card, but I was almost at my limit, so I couldn't charge anything. There was only one thing left to do. I got a Service Merchandise credit card. It only took me about five minutes to apply, and since I already had a Master Card, I got instant credit with a one thousand dollar limit. I wasn't sure how in the hell I was going to pay the bill, but I would just have to worry about that later.

Once I got the card, I picked out a set of gold earrings that were in the shape of a heart, and a gold necklace with a diamond pendant on it, which was also shaped like a heart. Shit, it cost me three hundred dollars, but Shirl was worth it. She was worth that and a lot more. I just hoped she liked it.

On Valentine's Day, I woke up at about 7:30. The first thing I did was call Shirl and wish her a happy Valentine's Day. We talked for about ten minutes and decided that we were going to have dinner at her place at around 6:00. I told her that I would take her out to eat, but she insisted on cooking. I just hoped that she wouldn't cook that damn rice again.

Well, anyway, the rest of the day, I went to class and then I went over to see Kim. I got there at around 3:00. Her mother was still at work, so we were the only ones there. When I went in, she gave me a big hug and a kiss and then I followed her back to her bedroom. She opened the door and as I walked in I saw balloons all over that said Happy Valentine's Day. I was very surprised. All I could do was smile.

"Happy Valentine's Day, baby," she said.

I looked at her and then I bent over and gave her a big hug and a wet, juicy kiss. "Thank you, baby."

"This is not all. I want to take you out to dinner too. Wherever you want to go, baby."

"Oh, you do? That's sweet," I said to her as I desperately tried to think of a way to get out of this situation because I couldn't go out to eat unless we went now because I had to meet up with Shirl at 6:00.

"My mom will be gone until about 10:00," she said, still hugging me. "So I was thinking that we could chill here for a while and then go later on this evening."

"Damn," I said, loud as hell.

"What?"

"Damn, I got to be at work at 6:00."

"Why didn't you tell me?" she asked. "I was hoping we were going to spend Valentine's Day together."

"We are together," I said.

"I meant most of the day together. Not just a couple of hours."

When she said that, I started thinking to myself that she was about to start tripping and wanting us to start spending more time together and shit. Man, we had a good thing going. Damn near perfect and she was about to mess it up.

"Well, baby, I wish I could stay all night, but I got to be at work at six," I said, straight up lying through my teeth.

"Call in and take off," she said.

"I can't do that."

"Why not?"

"I just can't."

"I'll make it worth your while," she said, and moved back away from me and began to take her clothes off. Damn, she was looking sexy as hell, but still the same, I had to leave by 5:30.

"Baby, I really wish I could stay, but I can't. Oh, yeah, here is your Valentine's Day gift." I handed her the box.

"I'll look at it later," she said, and took off her last piece of clothing— the panties. I just stood there, looking at her with an erection in my pants.

"Nah," I said. "Go ahead and look at it now."

By then, she was rubbing my chest. "Just be quiet," she said, beginning to undress me. Once I was naked, we started bumping and grinding and grinding and bumping. The next thing I knew, it was 5:15 and she was wanting some more. The shit was good as hell, but I didn't want to do it anymore because I needed to get ready to break, and I was also tired as hell. And I needed to save a little energy just in case Shirl wanted some.

"Baby, come on," Kim said, and straddled her self on top of me.

"Kim, baby, I need to get ready to go."

"Just ten more minutes," she said. Man, this girl was straight up fiending for the dick, but I had to go.

"I'm sorry, Kim. I'll make it up to you, baby, but I got to go."

She didn't say anything else. She just got up and started putting her clothes on.

"Now don't be that way," I said, and got up and began to get dressed. "Go ahead and open your gift, baby."

"You can keep your gift," she said.

"What?"

"You can keep your stinking gift."

"What's up with you? I told you I had to work."

"I don't know. You know?"

"I don't know?" I asked. "What don't you know?"

"I don't like the way things are going. It seems like all you want from me is my stuff."

"Hold up, now. You're flat tripping. You're the one that acts like that is all you want to do. Hell, I've tried to expand our relationship, but you didn't seem to want to do that at the time."

"I want to expand it," she said. "I'm tired of this 'wham, bam, thank you, ma'am' bullshit."

"Baby, okay, we'll talk about it later. I really hope you open up and like your gift."

She said a few more things. I said a few more things. Then I left. By then, it was around 5:30. I was running real late because I had to go back to my dorm room, take a shower, and change clothes. I certainly couldn't go over there smelling like perfume and cat. When I got to my room, I washed up as fast as possible and then went over to Shirl's apartment.

I was in such a rush to get to Shirl's place, that I had left the balloons that Kim gave me in the car when I went to wash up. Well, since they were still in the car, I just took the card off of them and added it to the rest of my gift for Shirl. I knew it was low down, but hell, I wasn't going to be able to keep them in my room anyway. Shirl came to my room at least every other day and she would have seen them, so I had to get rid of them.

I got to Shirl's apartment promptly at 6:00. I rang the bell and waited for her to come to the door. When she got there, she didn't look at all like she was in a Valentine's Day mood. Here I was rushing, trying to look my best and she was looking like she had been through a straight up thunderstorm or something.

"Hey, baby," I said, smiling.

"Hey," she said, sounding like a sick goat.

"What's the matter, baby? You sick or something?"

"Nah, not really. I just got something on my mind right now."

"Oh, so what's on your mind?" I asked, and walked in and sat down on the couch.

"Well," she started. I interrupted her before she could say another word.

"Before you tell me, I want to give you your present. These balloons are for you. I'm sure you already guessed that. Here is your other gift," I said, and handed her the box with the necklace and the earrings in it.

"Thanks," she said, and smiled at the balloons and proceeded to open the box. When she opened the box and looked at her gift, her eyes lit up and the smile on her face widened. "Oh, this is too much," she said, holding the necklace and earrings in her hand.

"Nothing's too much for you, baby," I said.

"But I didn't get you anything this expensive. Nah, this is too much."

"Baby, it doesn't matter to me what you got me. I love you, and I wanted to get that for you."

"But…" she said.

I cut her off. "But nothing. Give me a kiss." I leaned over, and we kissed each other.

"Let me go get your gift," she said, and walked to the back. She came back with a big box. I smiled and then opened it up. I was pleasantly surprised. It was a very nice shirt, some nice dress pants, and on top, there was a Valentines' Day card.

"Thanks, baby," I said, and leaned over to kiss her.

"You not going to open the card?" she asked.

"Yeah, I'm going to open it." I started to open the card when she suddenly stopped me.

"Wait!" she said. "Don't open it now."

"Why not?"

"Just don't."

"What? Is there something in this card you don't want me to see or something?"

"Well…"

"Baby, let me open the card," I said.

"Okay," she said, and then she took a deep breath, stood up, and turned away.

Suddenly, I didn't want to open the card. If she was doing all that, it had to be some bad news or something. The first thing that popped into my head was that she was dumping me or something, so I just asked her.

"Shirl, are you breaking up with me in this card?" I asked, and she didn't respond, so I asked her again. "Are you breaking up with me in this card, and if you are, just go ahead and say it. Hell, don't make it worse by letting me know in a Valentine's Day card. Damn."

She turned around and took another deep breath. "Just open the card," she said.

I looked at her as I thought to myself that this was really messed up if she was breaking up with me this way. I then went ahead and opened the card. I didn't even look at the words printed in it. I skipped all the way to the bottom to see what she had written in it. At the bottom, she had written, 'Happy Valentine's Day, baby. I really care about you.' I thought to myself that was sweet and nice, but before I could dwell on it, I saw what had been causing her to act so crazy. She had also written, 'P.S. I am pregnant.'

"What?" I said, as my heart pounded like it had never pounded before. "You're pregnant? But how? When?"

"What?" she said. "I think you know how. As for when? All those times we had sex and you weren't wearing any protection and I'm not on the pill. Hell, it was bound to happen. I don't know what we were thinking," she said, and started crying.

"Come here, baby," I said, and pulled her next to me. I hugged her and rubbed her back. My heart was pounding even harder now. I was trying to think what in the hell we were going to do, but I was so shocked I couldn't even think straight.

"Baby, everything's going to be all right," I said, wondering to myself if everything would actually be all right.

Damn! What in the hell was I thinking about when I was nutting all up in her? Shit. I know what I was thinking about, but why wasn't I thinking straight? We sat there I know for an hour without saying a word. I wanted to ask her if she was positive, but I figured that she would have said 'hell yeah' and started crying again. Finally, I decided to break the silence.

"So what are we going to do, baby?" I asked.

"I don't know," she said, and her eyes were swollen from all of the crying. She looked like she could burst into tears again at any moment.

"We will work something out, baby. Everything's going to be all right. Everything is going to be all right," I said, and I think I was trying to convince myself of that more than I was trying to convince her.

The rest of the night, we managed to have somewhat of a good time. We went ahead and ate, and then we cuddled and watched TV until very late. I spent the night holding her in my arms.

Chapter Thirty-One

The day after we woke up, Shirl and I still really didn't discuss what we were going to do. I guess we weren't ready to talk about it or something. Anyway, I ate breakfast there and then went home. The entire day, my thoughts were solely on what in the hell we were going to do. The way I saw it, we had three options. First, she could get an abortion. Second, she could have the baby. Third, we could get married and then she could have the baby. I most definitely would have been willing to marry her because I really loved her, but I didn't think she would marry me. Even though we were a couple, I knew that she wasn't completely over Eric, but I suppose that was natural. It takes time to get over things.

As for the first and second options, I wasn't sure of her opinion on abortion. We would just have to discuss it. I really wasn't against abortion, but the more I thought about the situation, I sort of wanted to have the baby. I loved Shirl so much. I knew I would love our kid to death. I would be a good father, and I was sure that she would be a good mother. The only thing that put some doubt in my mind was our financial situation. I really didn't have any money. I didn't really make shit with the little job I had. I would just have to get another job. Hell, I would have to do whatever I had to do.

That evening, I decided that the stress was starting to get to me, so I decided to go get a forty-ounce to relax my mind a little. On the way to the car, I ran into Corey.

"What up, my nig?" Corey said to me.

"Shit, man, just trying to make it," I replied.

"Straight? You look like something's wrong with your ass."

"Nah, I just got a lot of shit on my mind. I was about to roll out and get a forty-ounce."

"Straight? I'll roll with your ass, because I got some shit on my mind too. A forty will hit the spot."

Corey and I rolled out to the little Quickie Mart up the street. I got a forty of Bull, and he got a forty of Cool Mint Colt 45. As soon as we got in the car, Corey opened his up and started guzzling that shit.

"Man, I don't see how you drink that shit," I said, watching him kill his drink like it was Kool-Aid or something. "That shit is nasty."

"Shit, this is some good ass stuff. And it leaves your breath minty fresh."

"Minty fresh, my ass. Your breath will be just as sour."

"Shiiit, the hoes love it when you be macking up on their asses after you drink this. Your breath be all minty and shit."

"Whatever," I said, and we argued about that shit all the way back to the dorm. When we got back to the dorm, we went up to my room to drink our forties.

"So what's on your mind, player?" Corey asked.

"Man, just shit."

"What kind of shit?"

"Basically, I'm just having woman problems."

"Man, you too? All three of my hoes are tripping," Corey said, and took another swallow of that nasty ass shit he was drinking.

"Why are they tripping, Corey?"

"Man, these hoes want some more quality time and shit, but I can't do nothing for their ass. That just ain't my style. I leave that shit for weak niggers like you and Fred."

"You tripping now," I said, with a smile on my face. "Man, I still don't know the low-down on what happened between Fred and old girl."

"Shit, basically, she just took that nigger for his money and fucked off on his ass."

"Straight? I thought she was real religious."

"Man, her ass was too religious. Shit, she was fucking the preacher."

"You lying!"

"If I'm lying, I ain't a player, and you know I'm the king player."

"Damn. How did Fred find out?"

"Man, this nigger had went over to see her, right?"

"Right, right," I said.

"And nobody answered the door when he knocked and shit, but he saw a car in the driveway, so he knew somebody was there. So he walked over to the window to see if he could see if somebody was in there and shit. Man, when he looked in the window, he saw her and the preacher boning on the damn living room floor."

"Damn, that's some crazy shit. What Fred do?"

"Man, he started crying like a little girl. You know his weak ass."

"You know he probably was in love wither her," I said.

"Exactly, and you can't love these hoes."

"Damn, she did that nigger wrong, but he be acting like he mad at every damn body."

"He mad at your ass because you didn't think he could get a girl, and when he finally did, that shit didn't work. So I guess that shit just made him madder and shit."

"Nah, it wasn't that I didn't think he could get a girl."

"Yeah, it was," Corey said.

"Nay, it just seemed like she was running his ass and shit. And for what ended up happening, that could have happened to anybody. Even you."

"Yeah, but I don't love these hoes, so I wouldn't give a damn," Corey said, and we talked about Fred a little more, and then we started talking about Shirl and me.

"So what up with you and Shirl?" he asked. "Have you had to kick Eric's punk ass again?"

"Nah, I haven't even seen that fool. But me and Shirl, we straight."

"You said that like you ain't straight."

"We're just going through a little crisis right now," I told him.

"What up? Talk to your boy."

"Man, this is some serious shit. You got to keep this to yourself."

"Horne, man, you're talking to your boy. What up?"

"Okay, man, but I'm serious. This is between me and you," I said reluctantly. I was thinking that maybe I shouldn't tell him, but I needed to talk to somebody, so I went ahead. "Check this out, Corey."

"Yeah?"

"Shirl is pregnant."

"Is it yours?" he asked.

"What do you mean, is it mine? Hell yeah, it's mine."

"Okay, I just wanted to know if you were sure because you know how these hoes be trying to trap a brother and shit."

"Man, you're always thinking crazy."

"That's not crazy. It's logical. What are you two going to do?"

"I don't know, man. We really haven't discussed it."

"Well, that sounds like something y'all need to do. Hell, the longer you wait, the more expensive an abortion is. And believe me, I know."

"I sort of want to have it, but I don't know what Shirl is thinking."

"Why in the hell do you want to have a kid? Your ass ain't got no money."

"I know, man, but I don't know. I just sort of do."

"I know you're in love with Shirl and all, but man, your ass ain't ready to be a daddy."

"You're right, but I just sort of want to be one for some reason," I said, and we were back in my dorm room now. The phone rang and it was Shannon. I had damn near forgotten about her. We talked for a minute, then I told her that Corey was in the room and that I would call her back.

"Who was that?" Corey asked me.

"This girl named Shannon. You know Shannon, don't you?"

"Yeah, she's straight. You hitting that?"

"Nah, man."

"Why not? I know I would hit that shit."

"It's just that ever since Shirl and I got back together, I haven't been interested in her. Also, it's another girl that I'm seeing."

"Who's that?" he asked.

"You remember that girl I met at that house party we went to a while back?"

"House party?"

"Yeah, don't you remember?" I said. "Everybody was downstairs and I think you saw her first, and then I went over to holler at her."

"Yeah, I think I do remember her. She was dark-skinned and fine as a motherfucker."

"Yeah, and she was with another girl that was pretty straight, too."

"Yeah, what was her name?"

"Kim."

"Yeah. Was she at the party that night you got in a fight?"

"Yeah."

"I know who you talking about. You hitting that?"

"Yeah," I said.

"Man, I bet she can work it out."

"Yeah, she can, but I'm fixing to leave her alone."

"Why?"

"I'm going to treat Shirl right. And plus, I really don't need anybody else. Shirl is all I need."

"Do you think she's treating you right?"

"Yeah, I really do."

"Eric?" he said.

"Man, I told you she ain't messing with him anymore."

"That shit happened all of a sudden. I don't know. All I'm saying is, don't get rid of your girls on the side, because you can't trust no bitch."

"Man, you need to chill with that shit because she ain't no bitch," I said, and he was beginning to seriously piss me off.

"Man, you know what I mean. We say that shit all the time, and now all of a sudden, you're Mr. Sensitive."

"My bad, man," I said. "You're right. I don't know. I just got a lot of shit on my mind."

"Man, you need to go over to Shirl's crib tonight. Y'all need to decide what y'all are going to do or something."

"Yeah, you're right. Let me call her up."

I picked up the phone and called Shirl. She was at the crib, so I told her that I was about to come over so we could discuss the situation. She told me to come on over. We said a few more things and then we hung up.

"What she say?" Corey asked as he finished his forty.

"She told me to come on over."

"That's straight. Man, just really think about what would be best. You can't afford no kid."

"Yeah, but if we do decide to go the abortion route, I hope she got some money, because I don't."

"If you need some money, I'll hook you up."

"You ain't got the amount of money that I need," I said.

"Man, I told you I'll let you borrow the money, so I must have the money."

"Well, shit, if I really need it, I may come to you, man. So I hope you ain't bullshitting. I'll pay you back too."

"I know, man, and I'm not bullshitting. I can round up three to four hundred dollars from my hoes in no time."

"From your hoes?" I said.

"Man, trust me."

"Well, all right. I'm fixing to break," I said, and got up and finished my last swallow of beer. I then proceeded out the door with Corey behind me.

The whole way over to Shirl's crib, I thought about what might take place when I got there. The more I thought about it, the more I decided that I needed another forty because this was going to be a long night. I stopped by the store and bought a forty, some Tic Tacs, and a bag of Doritos. After I left the store, I went directly over to Shirl's apartment. Shirl seemed to be down and out when I got there.

"Hey, baby," I said, and she said hey back in a mumbled, groaning way. I then followed her back to her bedroom. She laid down on the bed, and I sat on the edge. "You want some beer?"

"I can't drink beer," she said, sarcastically. "I'm pregnant, remember?"

"Okay, Shirl, let's talk. Come on and sit up here with me."

"I can't. I'm pregnant, remember?"

"Okay, if you're not going to come down here, I'll come up there." I moved up on the bed and laid down next to her. "What are we going to do?" I asked.

"I didn't know we had a choice," she replied, still sounding sarcastic.

"Get serious, Shirl. I came over here so we could seriously discuss what we are going to do."

"Seriously, huh?" she said. "If you're so damn serious, why in the hell are you drinking a forty?"

"What does me drinking a forty have to do with what we need to discuss?"

"Your ass is a drunk."

"Okay, I'm a drunk now. Can we discuss what we need to discuss—you being pregnant?" I said, trying to ignore the little comment about being a drunk. Maybe I was a drunk, but hell, she had known that for a long time. This wasn't the time to discuss it. She was just being a smart ass since she was in a shitty mood. "Do you want to have the baby?" I asked her.

"I don't know. What do you want to do?"

"To be honest, I sort of want to have it."

"I don't," she said.

"You don't? Why did you say you didn't know if you don't?"

"I didn't know. I just decided this minute."

"You just decided this second?"

"Yeah, I'm just not ready," she said.

"So you want to have an abortion?"

"I don't know."

"I mean, you don't want to have it, but you don't know about an abortion. What do you want to do, put it up for adoption or something?"

"Shit, I don't know. I guess I want an abortion. Why in the hell did this shit happen anyway?" she asked, in her sarcastic tone. It seemed like she would have been crying or something, but she wasn't. I guess she was all cried out.

"That's it," she continued. "That's the only way. I've got to get an abortion. I can't have a baby now. That's what we're going to have to do."

I was about to say okay, but before I did, I paused for a minute because, honestly, I sort of wanted to have the baby.

"Is that what you want to do?" she asked me.

Without thinking, I grabbed her hand and said something that I had no business saying. "Will you marry me?"

"What?" she asked.

"Will you marry me?" I repeated.

She looked at me and then started smiling. "You're tripping, right?"

"Nah, I'm serious. I want you to marry me, and I want us to have the baby."

"That's crazy," she said.

"Why is it crazy?" I asked. "I love you, and I know you love me."

"Horne, I do love you, but I'm not in love with you. At least not yet."

"Well, you will be, and I can see myself spending the rest of my life with you. We have been the best of friends for over two years. I know over the past seven months, we haven't been as close at times, but that's because we have been trying to move our relationship to another level. And it's natural that we have had problems, but look. We're together now, and in time, we're just going to become closer."

"This all may be true, Horne, but I'm not ready for marriage, and I'm not ready to have a baby. Besides, if we are meant to be together for the rest of our lives, it will happen. There is no need for us to rush into any-thing. Okay?"

I just laid there as my eyes began to water up. I don't know why I was getting so emotional. I wasn't sure why I had asked Shirl to marry me. I guess I just really loved her, and I knew that I would love our kid. I would be a great dad, and we would be a great family.

"Horne, baby, I appreciate that you want to do the right thing," she said. "You really mean so much to me." She kissed me on the cheek, wrapped her arms around me, and continued. "I just feel that the best thing for us to do at this time is to get an abortion. It's really the best choice, Horne. I know it is going to be hard for you. Just think about it."

I still didn't say anything. By this time, the water that had collected in my eyes was running down my face.

"Baby, don't cry," she said, and held me. "Please don't cry. Everything is going to be all right."

Those were the last words spoken that night. I ended up crying myself to sleep and spending the night.

Chapter Thirty-Two

The next morning, I woke up very early. I tried to go back to sleep, but I couldn't. I had so much on my mind. I sat in the bed, staring at Shirl, thinking about the whole situation. I guess she was right about the abortion. We definitely were not ready, and I guess trying to rush things would just make it harder on us. I just couldn't deal with the idea of an abortion. Every time I thought about it, I thought about us killing a baby that I knew I would love to death. Every time I thought about that, my eyes would start watering up again. So basically, I sat there thinking and crying all morning. I think I laid there for about three hours before Shirl woke up.

"Hey, baby," she said. "You feeling better this morning?"

"Yeah, a little."

"Good. Come over here and give me a kiss." I leaned over and kissed her. Her breath was funky as hell, but I'm sure mine was too since it was morning and everything.

I ended up spending the majority of the morning there. We discussed the issue again. It still wasn't easy to accept, but we agreed on an abortion. I even asked her to marry me again and tried to convince her that it would work, but that idea was quickly shot down.

Now that we had agreed to an abortion—or rather, now that she had insisted on an abortion—we had to come up with the money. We had called around to find a place where they did abortions and to get an estimate on the cost. We basically only had two choices. There was a place in Midtown and a place in Mississippi, just outside Memphis. The place in Midtown was always being picketed and receiving bomb threats, so we decided not to go there. That left us with our only other option—the place in Mississippi.

The abortion was going to cost three hundred fifty dollars. I think I had about forty dollars, and Shirl only had sixty, so this left us short by two hundred fifty dollars. The only place I knew where we could get that kind of money was from our parents, and that certainly was not an option. Then I thought about Corey. He had told me that he could let me borrow the money. I guess I would have to ask him.

After I left Shirl's apartment, I went back to the dorm and up to Corey's room. As I was walking to the room, I saw Fred sitting outside the room. He was reading a Jet magazine and eating some Twinkies.

"What up, Fred?" I said. "Is Corey in there?"

"Yeah. He got a girl in there though."

"Straight? Tell him, I came by."

"Nah," he said, "I'll get him because it's time for that girl to go anyway. They been in there all damn morning." He stood up and started banging on the door.

It was a couple minutes before Corey finally came to the door. He cracked the door a little and stuck his head out. "What's up?" he said.

"That girl was supposed to be gone an hour ago," Fred said, mumbling because he was trying to talk with a twinkie in his mouth.

"All right, man. Give me a minute to wrap things up, okay?"

"All right, a minute," Fred said, " and Horne is out here. He needs to talk to you about something."

Corey stuck his head out the door and looked at me. "What up, Horne?"

"Man, I need to talk to you about what we were talking about yesterday," I said.

"Bet. I'll come up to your room after I get through handling this business right here."

"All right," I said, and Corey closed the door.

"So what you been up to, Fred?" I asked, hoping that he wasn't still holding a grudge.

"Shit," he said.

"Man, we need to get together one day and drink some beers and trip."

Fred didn't say anything. He just nodded his head.

"All right, man. I'll be hollering at you soon so we can do that."

He still didn't say anything, so I said goodbye to him and went back to my room. Fred was still tripping, but I figured it was nothing that a few beers couldn't handle. Hell, guys aren't like women. Women stay mad at each other forever. Guys get drunk together and forget what in the hell they were mad about in the first place.

While I was in my room, I just laid in the bed and watched TV. I really wasn't paying attention to what was on because I kept thinking about Shirl, Kim, my schoolwork, and basically a bunch of other stuff. I would think about Kim and what I was going to do about her. I really liked her, but I loved Shirl, and I was not about to mess that up. I guess there was only one thing to do, and that was to cut things off with Kim. The only question was how. Should I be up front with her, or should I just play her off? I thought about it for a while and decided that I was going to be straight up with her. She was too straight for me to be playing games with her. Just as I decided to do that, the phone rang. It was Kim.

"Hey, baby," she said.

"Hey," I said in a low tone.

"What's wrong with you?"

"I just got a lot on my mind."

"You want me to come over? I bet I can make you forget about what's on your mind."

"I bet you can, but nah, you ain't got to come over."

"I know I don't have to, but I will anyway," she said.

"That's all right. Listen, Kim, we need to talk."

"What's up?"

"Well, uh, uh," I said.

"What's up with all the 'uh, uh'? Tell me what you're trying to say."

"Okay. Basically, Kim, I think we ought to stop seeing each other."

"You what?" she said.

"I think we ought to stop seeing each other."

"What in the hell is that shit? You don't think we ought to see each other again? What the hell?"

"I just don't think that we should," I said.

"Well, you need to tell me more than that."

"Actually, to be honest with you, I've been seeing someone else, and now we are getting serious, and I don't think I should see you anymore."

"What the hell? Your ass bold, ain't you? You been seeing someone else and y'all about to become serious. What kind of shit is that?"

"Like you haven't been seeing someone else," I said.

"I haven't, nigger. I don't know what kind of girl you think I am. I ain't no motherfucking ho like you."

"Calm down, Kim. It ain't like that at all."

"I can't tell."

"Kim, I really like you, but I've been…Well, you wouldn't understand."

"Try me, bitch," she said.

"Hey, I ain't going to be too many bitches, okay? I'm trying to be honest and straight with you."

"Oh, so I'm supposed to thank your punk ass for that?"

"Kim, are you going to let me explain? I'm hoping that we can still be friends."

"Friends this shit!" she said, and I heard a click and a dial tone.

I started to call her back, but I figured that I would give her some time to calm down. I felt bad because I really did like her. But I had to cut her off. I wasn't about to mess things up with Shirl. I only hoped that I wouldn't regret this later. I was still thinking about my conversation with Kim when I heard a knock at the door.

"Who is it?" I asked.

"Corey," he said, and I got up and opened the door.

"What up, dog?" Corey said.

"What up, man? You finished handling your business?"

"Yeah, dog. I had to get my sex on this morning, player. You know how pimps like me do it."

"I hear you."

"So what up?" he asked. "What happened with you and Shirl?"

"We decided that we are going to have an abortion, and I wanted to hit you up on that favor you said you would do for me."

"How much you need?"

"Anything will help," I said.

"Man, I asked you how much you need."

"Fifty, hundred, anything, man. It will help."

"Well, let me see what I can do. Where is your phone?"

I handed him the phone and watched him start dialing some numbers. I sat there and watched in amazement. He would dial a number and ask to speak to a girl. Then he would just tell the girl that he needed some money and ask her to hook him up. He would then say that he needed the money by this evening. He must have called about six girls.

"Okay, man," he said, when he had finished his last call. "I got everything hooked up. The money ought to be rolling in by this evening."

"Man, what you be saying to these girls to get money from them?"

"I don't say anything," he said. "I let my dick do the talking for me."

"So you're boning all of those girls?"

"I have boned all of them, but I'm not currently boning two of them. They are just stand-by's. Just in case I can't hook up with one of the others or I need some money or something."

"I'm going to pay you back as soon as I can so you can pay these girls back," I said.

"What?" he said, in amusement. "Pay these girls back? Man, I ain't paying shit back, and you don't have to pay me shit."

"I'll pay you back."

"Nah, I don't want you to. If I can't help my boys out, who can I help out? God has blessed me with this gift with the women, so why not share the wealth with my boy in his time of need?"

"Won't they get mad?" I asked.

"As long as I keep supplying them with the dick, they won't say a word. Just come and holler at me around six. I should have the cheese by then."

"All right."

"Well, I got to go get a little rest. Holler at you later," Corey said, as he walked out the door. Corey really turned out to be a good friend even though he may have looked at things a little differently than I did.

For the rest of the afternoon, I tried to catch up on a little homework because I had really gotten behind. I had been skipping classes and everything. I had also missed a couple of days of work. I basically had not been on top of my shit. I had been so caught up with Shirl and Kim. I tried to call Kim a couple of times, and she hung up on me both times. I could understand why she would be mad, but if she couldn't appreciate my honesty, forget her.

The time flew by, and it was six o'clock before I knew it, so I went down to Corey's room. I knocked on the door, and he answered.

"What up, man?" he said.

"Nothing, man."

"I got your cheese. Come on in."

I walked in the room and sat down in a chair beside his desk. The room looked as if it had been hit by a tornado. There were clothes and empty food cartons and wrappers everywhere.

"Excuse the mess, player," he said. "As you can see, Fred and I have been lounging all day. We ain't had a chance to clean up yet, but I got your cheese." Corey reached down under his bed and pulled out a roll of money. "Here you go, player," he said, counting out a hundred fifty dollars.

"Thanks, man," I said. "I really appreciate it."

"Anything to help my boy out, but you know I had to get me a little cheese for myself," he said, counting out about a hundred more as he smiled.

"You in there, ain't you?" I asked.

"Best believe it, and I'm about to go to the store and buy me some of those new Air Penny's."

"Straight up?"

"Straight up. So the next time we hoop, I'm going to be dunking on your ass like Penny Hardaway."

"You ain't going to do shit," I said.

We talked bull for about ten more minutes and then I left to go over to Shirl's to tell her that I had the money—well, some of the money. We were still a hundred dollars short. When I arrived at her apartment, she was at the front door, about to go in.

"Shirl!" I shouted, and she turned around and waited for me to walk up.

"Hey, baby. I got a little good news," I said, and walked up and kissed her on the cheek.

"What's your news, baby?" she asked.

"I got a hundred and fifty dollars."

"You did? That's great, but where did you get it from? You didn't tell your parents, did you?"

"Nah, Corey loaned me the money."

"Where did he get it from?"

"Don't ask," I said.

"He ain't selling drugs, is he?"

"Nah, he got another gig."

"Another gig?"

"Yeah. Just trust me, you don't want to know."

"I'm glad you got that money because now we have enough. I got the last one hundred dollars."

"Straight. Where did you get the money from?" I asked.

"Some of my girlfriends."

"Who?"

"Tracey and Alicia."

"Straight. They know what you need it for?"

"Nah, I just told them I really needed to borrow the money for an emergency. You didn't tell Corey what you needed the money for, did you?"

"Nah, I made up some lie," I said to her, making up some lie. We walked inside and went back to the bedroom where she laid on the bed and I sat on the edge of the bed. "So when are we going to do this?"

"As soon as possible. I'm going to call the place tomorrow morning and find out the earliest time we can be seen."

"Okay," I said, and we spent the rest of the evening cooking, watching television, and talking. I ended up spending the night.

The next morning, I was awakened by Shirl's voice. She was on the telephone. At first I didn't know who she was talking to, but then I could tell it was someone at the abortion clinic. She sure as hell didn't lie when she said she was going to call them in the morning. I looked over at the clock. It was 8:15. I laid there half listening and half nodding off. When she got off the phone, she turned to me and started shaking me.

"Wake up. Wake up," she said.

"I'm up, baby. I've been up ever since you've been on the phone."

"Not only wake up, but get up. We have to be down there at one o'clock."

"One o'clock? Today?" I said in disbelief.

"Yeah, one o'clock today. So get up."

"It is only 8:15 now. Why are we going so soon?" I asked.

"The sooner the better. Less time to second guess. I just want to get it over with. The sooner we get there, the less time we have to think about it."

"Well, can they do it in one day?"

"Yeah. The lady I talked to said it would only take a couple of hours and then I could go home."

"Will you have to stay in the bed for a few days or something?"

"Nah, I'll just need to rest that day and take it easy for a few days after that."

She continued to tell me about the process. After we finished talking about that, I got up so I could go to my dorm room, take a shower, and change clothes. My initial thoughts of going back to sleep had long been erased from my mind. I was too worried, nervous and excited to go back to sleep. I mean, I was really, really nervous. I was so nervous that I stopped by the store and bought a beer and some pork skins. True enough, it was only about 9:30, but I really needed a forty to calm my nerves.

When I got to the room, I drank my forty and ate my skins. Then I went up to Corey's room. As I was walking down the hall, I saw Fred's fat ass laid out in front of the door, asleep with an open bag of Cheetos beside him. Corey must have been entertaining again. I started to wake Fred up and tell him that he could come to my room and lay down on Tim's old bed, but I didn't even feel like having company. I just wanted to talk to Corey for a few minutes to ask him what I should expect because I knew he had been to a few of these things. I would just check back with him before I left.

I went back up to my room, took a shower, and got dressed. Then I sat around listening to music and thinking. I thought about a lot of things. How Shirl and I had been best friends for two years and how I had fallen in love with her. I admit that I sort of missed the way things were when we were friends because we used to constantly trip, but I guessed that we would get all that back once we got adjusted to our new roles. Then it would be even better because we would be best friends and lovers. The more I thought about it, the more I knew that I could spend the rest of my life with Shirl. The more I thought about how I could spend the rest of my life with her, the more I thought about how we may have been making a mistake by having the abortion.

It was about eleven o'clock, so I decided to go ahead and head over to Shirl's place. First, I was going to check up on Corey again. I looked down the hall to see if I saw Fred's fat ass, and I did. He was still on the floor asleep, looking like a wounded whale. So I didn't bother to go up to the room. I got back on the elevator and went downstairs. I was walking to my car when I heard somebody calling my name. I turned around and it was Shannon.

"What up, girl?" I said, checking her out.

"Nothing, stranger."

"Stranger? It ain't like that, is it?"

"Yeah, I'm afraid so, stranger. It's like that. You can't call nobody and you ain't never at home, so I can't get in contact with you."

"Well, I've been busy with school and everything."

"Oh, so you can't make no time to even call?" she said. "I bet if I had gave up the ass those times, your ass would be making the time."

"It's not even like that," I said, wondering to myself why I had to see her at that time of all times.

"Well, I really can't tell that it is not like that."

"Shannon, I'm going to call you so we can get together and talk, okay? But I'm sort of in a hurry right now."

"Don't do me no favors, Friend!" she said, and turned away and walked off.

I watched her walk away, and then I got into my car. I really felt terrible about Shannon and Kim. It seemed like when I didn't have any one, I couldn't find anyone to be with, but as soon as I found someone that I really liked, women started popping up everywhere. I never could figure that out, but it always proved to be true.

While I was driving over to Shirl's apartment, I did a lot of soul searching, and I decided that I was going to try one more time to talk Shirl out of the abortion. I loved her, and I wanted us to have the baby. I would just have to get a better job or maybe two jobs and go to school part-time. As long as I was with Shirl and our baby, I would be happy.

I must have knocked on Shirl's door for at least ten minutes before she answered. I was about to leave when she finally came to the door.

"Hey, Horne," she said.

"Hey, what were you doing? I know you heard me at the door."

"I was in the bathroom. I'm sorry. I came as fast as I could."

"Well, that's okay, baby," I said, and kissed her on her soft lips. I then grabbed her hands and we walked to the front room and sat down on the couch.

"Let's not go today or any other day," I said. "Let's have the baby." I had a serious, but loving look on my face.

Shirl looked at me and rolled her eyes. She then stood up and walked toward the bedroom. "We've already made our decision," she said, with her back to me.

"But we can change our decision. It's not too late."

She stopped at the doorway and turned around. "Exactly, Horne. It's not too late, after this, for me to have another baby, but it is too early. I wouldn't be able to handle it. Maybe you would, but I wouldn't. We are doing the right thing, Horne."

"Baby, you would be able to handle it. You would be a great mother, and I'll be here for you every step of the way."

"Horne, forget it!" she said. "I've made my mind up. I hope you will support me and come with me. If not, I will go by myself. Listen, Horne, it's hard enough as it is. Don't make things harder."

She turned around and walked through the bedroom door. I just sat there, thinking. I guess there was not too much I could do. There were less than two hours before the appointment, and even if I had kept her from going then, she would have gone another day on her own. I just sat there for the remaining time, thinking about how dramatic things had been lately. I really hated it, too. Some people like drama, but I was the type that shied away from it. It was all a bunch of shit to me. I decided that since her mind was made up, I was going to make it as undramatic as I possibly could.

Shirl finally came out of her bedroom at around 12:15. She was ready to go. The clinic was right outside Memphis, in Mississippi. It would take us about thirty-five minutes to get there. During the ride, we talked a little. We didn't talk about anything serious. I was tired of being serious, and I was sure she was too. We just tripped a little and tried to make the situation as normal and calm as we could.

The lady had given Shirl very good directions. We found the place very easily. The clinic looked like a typical family doctor's office. It didn't look like a hospital or anything. There were a few people in the waiting room sitting down. The nurses seemed very nice. We signed in and sat down.

We sat there, holding hands for about twenty minutes before they called Shirl to the back. I got up with her to see if I could go back with her. They said that I could come with her, but when it was time to do the actual procedure, they would prefer it if I remained in another room. Of course, that was cool with me because I didn't want to see it anyway.

We sat back in one of the rooms, filling out a lot of paperwork. After we finished that, a nurse came in and told us how the process was going to work. She then gave Shirl this little blue gown to put on and told her that she would be back in a minute. When she returned, she started giving Shirl a little test, and then it was on. Before I knew it, they had laid her down on this rolling bed and rolled her out to begin the process. I squeezed her hand and kissed her on the forehead on her way out, then I went back out front to the waiting room.

While I sat there waiting, I started thinking about everything from Shirl to how I was messing up in school this semester. I had been skipping a lot of classes. I had also been missing days at work. It wasn't too late for me to wake up and get back on the right track. Maybe this had happened for a reason. Maybe this would be a reality check for me to start studying, going to work, going to class, going to church, and practicing safe sex.

The time seemed to fly by, probably because I was constantly thinking, but before I knew it, the nurse was calling me to the front. She told me that I could go in and see Shirl. As I walked to the back, I prayed that everything had gone all right. When I walked into the room, Shirl had her clothes on and she looked very tired. I guess she was probably still under the influence of the medication. I asked the nurse if she was okay. She said yes and told me that everything had gone well. She told me a few do's and don'ts that Shirl would need to follow. Afterward, I paid for the abortion and Shirl and I left. She made it to the car all right, but when she got in the car, she began to act like she was about to die.

"What's wrong, baby?" I asked, and cranked up the car.

"I don't know. I feel nauseated. I think I just need to lay down."

"Let the seat all the way back."

She reclined the seat and didn't say another word. I reached over and took her hand, then I pulled out of the parking lot. On the way back to her apartment, we didn't say anything. The music was very low, and I was driving with one hand, holding her hand with the other. When we got to her place, we went in and she got into the bed. I straightened her room up some and made sure she was comfortable. Then I sat in a chair and watched her sleep.

At that moment, I had mixed emotions. Half of me was sad because of what we had done, and the other half was somewhat relieved. Even though I had decided that I wanted us to keep the baby, I was sort of glad that we had done what Shirl wanted. We really weren't ready, and maybe now we could get our acts together and do it the right way when we were ready.

Chapter Thirty-Three

The next day, Shirl was feeling a lot better, but she didn't seem to be happy. It was as if she was trying to be happy, but it all seemed like a front to me. I could tell that the ordeal had really upset her. We spent the day lounging around in bed. I waited on her hand and foot and tried to make her feel loved. The funny thing, though, is that we didn't talk about the abortion once. I didn't ask her how she felt and she didn't ask me. I guess we were trying to forget it and move on. I stayed there until about five o'clock and then I left. Shirl said that she was feeling better and that I didn't have to stay if I didn't want to. I wanted to stay, but I got the feeling, by her constant reassurances that it would be okay for me to leave, that she must have wanted to be alone.

On the way to the dorm, I stopped by the corner store and bought a twelve-pack and some hot fries. Then I drove back to the dorm and went up to Corey's room. I knocked on the door, and he answered it.

"What up, player?" he said.

"It's done," I said, and walked in and sat down.

"Straight?"

"Yeah. We went up there at one o'clock yesterday."

"Damn, y'all didn't waste no time, did you?"

"Nah. She wanted to get it over with, so we got it over with."

"How is she?" he asked.

"She's straight."

"How are you?"

"I really don't know. Half of me is sad, and the other half is relieved."

"You did the right thing," Corey assured me.

"Yeah, I suppose. You want a beer?"

"You know I do." I passed him a brew and got one for myself. "Fred and I are going to a little party tonight. You ought to roll with us."

"I don't know. You know Shirl may need me for something."

"Man, are you supposed to go over there tonight?"

"Nah, but…"

"But nothing, man," he interrupted. "You need to be out to get rid of some stress. Hell, we ain't kicked it anywhere in ages anyway."

"Well, I might go. Where is Fred?"

"I don't know? He will be back a little later. So what's up with you besides the abortion deal?"

"Everything, man," I said. "I'm messing up in school. Kim and Shannon are tripping. Everything is just crazy. I'm missing days at work. Everything is just crazy."

"Just straighten that shit out. Especially those hoes, man. They got to understand that they come last and accept that shit."

"Well, now, it ain't like that. I don't want them to be last. I just want to be with Shirl and only Shirl. I'll be friends with them."

"You need to keep those hoes around. Just in case Shirl starts tripping. You'll have some back up."

"Man, I ain't going to do that."

"You need to do it, man," he said. "I'm telling you. You never know, and plus, Shirl just broke up with Eric, so you really need to watch your back."

"Man, I ain't even worried about that. If we work out, we work out. If not, then it wasn't meant to be, but I think it is."

"Well, I'm glad you think it's meant to be, but I'm telling you that you can't trust no hoes."

"Man, let's just talk about something else," I said.

"All right, your ass is just sprung now, but one day, you'll realize that I'm kicking knowledge."

"Whatever."

We sat there drinking for a couple of minutes in silence, and then we started talking about something else. Actually, Corey was talking about all of his women as usual, and I was thinking about what he had just said. Maybe he was right. Then again, maybe he was wrong. I would just have to take the risk. If things were not going to work out between Shirl and me, it was going to be because of Shirl, not because I got caught cheating. I loved her, and I wanted to be with her for the rest of my life. We had so much fun together and we got along so well. We had to be meant for each other.

I sat there thinking and acting like I was listening to Corey for about thirty minutes, and then Fred came in. I asked him if he wanted a beer. He said yeah and came over to drink with us. Not only did he start drinking, but he started talking too. It was like old times. Corey was talking about his women, and Fred was lying about some women. There was only one thing missing. Tim wasn't there talking trash. If he had been there, things really would have been just like the old days. I was going to have to call Tim to see how he was doing. Hopefully he would be back next year.

Thirty more minutes passed and the beer was gone. So that meant that it was time to go back to the store. So that is exactly what we did. We went to the store, got another twelve-pack, came back to the room, and drank that up. After we finished the second twelve-pack, we were straight up buzzing. Corey and Fred convinced me to go to the party. When we first got there, it really looked dull. It was at this hotel downtown in some room you could rent out. There was hardly anybody there. Corey said that we were early and that it would probably pick up, so we just chilled.

I would have been ready to go, but they had a nice little food table. They had some chips, finger sandwiches, chicken wings, and cookies. So you know where we were hanging out. Exactly, right next to the food table. We were straight up getting our grub on. Two hours passed by quickly. I think Corey and I had spent one of those hours eating. Fred was still at the table eating. I was standing on the wall, and Corey was macking up on some thick ass cutie.

The party had picked up like he said it would, but I was ready to go. All I could think about was Shirl. I was feeling bad that I was actually at a party the day after she had gotten the abortion. I should have been with her instead of being at the party. I decided that I was going to leave. The only problem was that I hadn't driven and I knew Corey and Fred weren't ready to go. I didn't care. One of them was going to have to take me back to the dorm so I could get my car. I walked over to Fred at the food table.

"Fred, man, see if you can get Corey's keys so you can take me back to the dorm," I said.

"You ready to go?"

"I really need to go. It's sort of an emergency."

"Emergency? Well, go ask him for the keys. He'll probably listen to you before he'll listen to me," he said, spitting food crumbs everywhere.

"All right," I said, and walked over to Corey and motioned for him to excuse himself from the thick honey for a second. He whispered something in her ear. She giggled, and then he came over.

"What up, man?" he said.

"Let me see your keys so Fred can take me back to the dorm," I said.

"What? Why do you want to go back to the dorm?"

"I need to get my car so I can go over Shirl's."

"Why do you need to go over Shirl's?"

"She needs me, man."

"You must have called her or something," he said.

"Nah, I just know that she needs me."

"Man, your ass is sprung. You can't kick it one night with your boys."

"I have been kicking it with you."

"I mean tonight at this party," he said.

"Not tonight, man. I can't get her out of my mind. I'm sure she needs me."

"Man, you are a trip," he said, as he smiled and handed me the keys. "There you go, man. Go handle your business and tell Fred to come straight back after he drops you off."

"Thanks, man."

I gave Corey some dap and then I went and told Fred that I had the keys and was ready to go. Fred grabbed one more chicken wing and then we left. On the way back to the dorm, Fred and I tripped and caught up on a few things. When we got to the dorm, I went up to my room, brushed my teeth, used the bathroom, and then headed back down to the car. I started to call Shirl and tell her that I was on my way over there, but I decided to surprise her. Even though she had been acting like she wanted to be alone, I knew she would be happy to see me.

When I got over to her apartment, I hurried to the door because it had started to get cold. The hawk was most definitely out. I was at the door, about to knock when the door opened, and I'll be damn what I saw. Eric was standing right in front of me. I just stood there, dumbfounded, looking at him. What in the hell was he doing there. I didn't know, but I sure as hell was going to find out.

"What in the hell are you doing over here?" I asked, as the rage inside of me kept building up. He looked me up and down with an evil smirk on his face, but he didn't say anything, so I asked his punk ass again.

"What in the hell are you doing over here?" I repeated, trying to keep myself from knocking his head off.

"Man, I ain't even in the mood for your shit," he said.

"Like I give a damn."

"Punk, I said I ain't even in the mood for your shit."

I don't know why he said that, but when he did, I totally snapped. I went straight for his throat and started choking the hell out of him.

"Stop! Horne, stop!" I heard Shirl yelling. I didn't stop though. I kept choking his ass until he fell to the floor. I got on top of him and kept choking. He was trying to pull my arms away, but I had a tight grip.

"Let him go, Horne! You're choking him to death. Let him go!" Shirl kept saying, and she ran over to me and began trying to pull me off.

I felt like I was in trance. I was trying to let go, but all of my built-up frustrations had taken control of me. All of a sudden, I felt a thud on my head, and I fell sideways to the floor. I wasn't sure what had hit me, but it had damn near knocked me out. It took a few minutes for me to gather myself and look around. I saw glass everywhere, and blood was running down my face. As if that wasn't enough, Shirl was on the floor, holding Eric as he held his throat, still gasping for air.

"What in the hell you hit me for?" I said to Shirl.

"You could have killed him!" she said, and started to cry.

"Why in the hell is he over here! Hell, you could have killed me!"

"What you going to do, kill everybody that comes over here?" she asked.

"Nah, but what is he doing over here?"

"I'll tell you why I'm over here," Eric said, in a raspy voice, still holding his throat.

"You shut the hell up," I said to him. "You had your chance to talk."

"No, you shut up," he said, and stood up.

"What's up, fool?" I said. "You want some more?"

"Stop, both of you, before I call the police," Shirl screamed, and I started to say something, but the blood was still trickling down my head and I was beginning to feel lightheaded, so I walked over to the couch and sat down.

"You'd better sit down, punk," Eric said.

I didn't even say anything. I just looked at him and shot him a bird. Shirl was standing by him while I was bleeding, and this was pissing me off. "So why is he over here, Shirl?" I asked.

"Man, my ass can talk for my damn self!" Eric said. "I came over here to check on my baby!"

"That's where you're wrong," I said. "Shirl ain't your baby no more."

"Shirl will always be my baby. Won't you, Shirl?" He looked at Shirl, and she didn't say anything. "Won't you, Shirl?" he asked again.

"You see she ain't saying nothing," I said, "so leave her alone."

"I don't know why she tripping because she called me over here, and besides, punk, Shirl is carrying my baby."

"Shirl is what?" I said, and my heart started beating about a hundred times faster.

"You heard me the first time, fool. Shirl is carrying my baby."

I heard him, but I didn't believe he had said what he had said. My head was hurting and my heart was hurting now, but I managed to say something. Actually, it was nothing that I hadn't already said. "Shirl is what?"

"Man, I'm going to say this one more time. Shirl is carrying my baby."

I looked at Shirl. She looked like she was about to shit on herself. "What is this shit he's talking about?" I asked her, trying to stay calm.

"Uh, uh," she said, and immediately started crying hard as hell as if she was a two-month-old baby.

"Baby, it's all right," Eric said, and put his arms around her. "It's about time that Horne knew the truth."

By this time, I was totally tripping. I couldn't believe Eric even knew that she had been pregnant. Also, she must have told him that it was his. Furthermore, he didn't even know that she had an abortion. Shirl was still crying, and this was really pissing me off. She had obviously been lying to both of us, and she's up here crying. Instead of crying, her ass needed to be explaining.

"Baby, it's all right," Eric repeated. "This nigger needs to hear the truth."

"You dumb ass fool!" I said to him, and stood up, walked toward Shirl, and continued. "Fool, Shirl ain't pregnant. Her ass got an abortion yesterday."

Eric looked at me crazy, then looked at Shirl, and then looked back at me.

"Yeah, that's right. She got an abortion yesterday morning, and I was there with her when she got it."

Eric's jaw dropped, and he turned to Shirl. By this time, she was sitting on the floor, still crying. "You killed our baby, Shirl?" he asked her.

"Our baby?" I said. "She told me it was my baby, and I paid for half of the abortion."

Eric looked at me. He looked like he was about to throw up. He bent down over Shirl and tried to make her look at him. "Look at me. Shirl, look at me," he kept saying, as he grabbed her arms.

She wouldn't look, though. She kept looking down.

"Shirl! Shirl! Look at me, dammit! Did you tell that nigger it was his baby?" he said, in a loud, violent manner.

"Hell yeah, she told me it was my baby. Whose baby did we kill, Shirl? Mine or his?" I asked her, and I was standing directly in front of them. The bleeding had slowed a lot, but it was hurting really bad. It was like I was living in a soap opera or something. I couldn't believe Shirl had told both of us that we had gotten her pregnant. This was some straight up bullshit.

"Shirl! Answer me, dammit," Eric said, and Shirl was still looking down, crying. Eric asked her one more time and then he straight up lost it. He reached back and pimp slapped her ass. I couldn't believe it. Her head went to the side and hit the floor. Eric stood up and tried to head for the door, but I stood in his way.

"What is your damn problem?" I asked him.

"You can have the bitch," he said, and shoved me to the floor.

I was about to get up and whip his ass when I saw Shirl stand up and run toward him. I thought she was going to hit that nigger like she had hit me, but to my surprise, she started begging that punk. I couldn't believe it. She was on her knees begging him to forgive her.

"Get away from me, Shirl," he said.

"Eric, I'm sorry," Shirl said, still crying. "I'm sorry. I couldn't have a baby now. I just couldn't."

"Whose baby was it anyway, Shirl? Tell me that," Eric said. He had turned around and was now facing her. She was still on her knees and she was holding on to his knees. She looked pathetic. "Whose baby was it, Shirl?" he repeated, grabbing her around her elbows.

She didn't say anything. She just kept holding on to him. I was standing there, looking in disbelief. He kept asking her over and over and she wouldn't say anything. As I stood there, my eyes started watering. I was really hurt because it was obvious who Shirl wanted, and it was not me. She had damn near knocked me out. Eric had damn near knocked her out, and she was in here begging him to stay. I had seen about all I could take, so I headed out the door. They didn't even notice that I was leaving. On my way out, I heard Shirl say the words.

"It was yours, Eric. I'm so sorry, baby. I didn't know what to do. You wouldn't talk to me, and…"

I heard that and kept walking. The water that was in my eyes had become tears and was running down my face. I wanted to turn around and curse her out, but I didn't even think she would have cared.

Chapter Thirty-Four

The next week was hell. All I did was drink, curse, sleep, and cry. I didn't go to class or work. I barely ate anything. I didn't even take a shower. I was straight up in a state of depression. The only person I talked to was Shannon. She had really turned out to be a good friend.

The night I left Shirl's crib, I felt like I was going to die. My head was pounding and for some reason, it seemed like I was suffocating. I was so hurt at times, I felt like I couldn't even breathe. I had to talk to somebody, so I had called Shannon. She was tripping at first, but when she realized that I was upset, she stopped tripping and just listened. I explained what had happened. After she had heard the whole story, she came over and comforted me. I sneaked her up, and she was there for me all night. She was there for me all week. She tried to make me feel better, but it still hurt like hell. I loved Shirl so bad, and I was trying to give my best to her. I guess that was why I couldn't get over what she had done. What made it so bad was that she hadn't even tried to call me or see me or anything. She hadn't once told me she was sorry.

The second, third, and fourth weeks were just as painful. By the third week, I was attending class regularly, and I saw Shirl every other day in class. Not once did she say anything to me. She would just look at me like I was supposed to say something. I wanted to say something. I wanted to curse her ass out, but I didn't. I would just look the other way and try not to get too emotional.

I only went back to work once and only once because they fired me for missing all those days. This was really one of the low points of my life. I was doing badly in school because I was so far behind. I was broke because I was unemployed, and I was very depressed. I avoided everybody but Shannon. Every time I saw Corey or Fred, I would go the other way. I just didn't feel like talking to anybody.

I acted that way for the rest of the semester. I went to class, and I came home. I didn't go anywhere. Not to church. Not even to the barber shop. I had a straight up fro. I went the rest of the semester without saying anything to Shirl. I know that this sounds crazy, but I didn't have anything to say to her ass, and she never said anything to me.

Chapter Thirty-Five

The summer finally came, and I was back home for summer vacation. When my family saw me, they straight up tripped because I had a nappy afro and a beard. My dad told me that I had better get a shave and a haircut by the end of the week or else. I had to admit that I had let myself go, and I guess it was time to straighten up. Like I had said earlier how everybody thought only niggers in the hood had problems, I had problems too. They were different problems, but they were problems all the same, and they were serious to me. I suppose everyone had problems, but it was time for me to get over mine and get on with my life.

The next day, I went to the barber shop and got all of my hair cut off and got a clean shave. It was a symbol of my new birth per se. My getting my life together and making a fresh start.

I spent the rest of the summer kicking it with my boys and spending time with my family. Also, I started a vigorous exercise program. By mid-summer, I was happy again, and I rarely thought about Shirl. I was finally getting over her.

Chapter Thirty-Six

The summer was over and it was time to go back to school. Summer had been fun, but I was ready to go back. I was determined to make the Dean's List. I really needed to because I had barely made passing grades in the spring. I knew that if I worked hard enough, I could make the Dean's List. My hair had grown back. I had a nice fade now. I was in good shape—both body and mind. I had a feeling that I was going to have a great semester.

When I got back to school, everything was basically the same. Fred and Corey were back. Tim had even come back to school. However, he wasn't my roommate because I had declared my room single so I could focus on my schoolwork. The first thing I did when I got back was to find myself a job so I wouldn't be broke during the semester. I found one after about a week of looking. It was at a warehouse. I worked twenty hours a week and made nine dollars an hour, so it wasn't that bad.

When I wasn't working, I was either studying, in class, exercising, or kicking it with my boys or Shannon. Shannon and I were still very close friends, but that was all we were. At times, I had thought about us being more than friends because we had fooled around a few times, but I never pursued it because I didn't want to damage our friendship. I had definitely learned my lesson from my ordeal with Shirl. As for dating other girls, at first, I didn't even consider it because Shirl had left a bad taste in my mouth, but by mid-semester, the taste had begun to wear off, and I was ready to start dating again.

The first couple of girls I dated were okay, but there were no sparks. They were basically someone to pass the time with. I didn't date any of them long because I never saw the point. The third girl I dated was more than okay. At least at first, I thought she was, but she turned out to be too unreliable. She was constantly standing me up. Well, I wouldn't say constantly. She stood me up twice, but that was two times too many, so I stopped dating her.

I tried to get back with Kim, but she wasn't even trying to hear that. I had come to the conclusion that I wasn't going to look hard for anybody else to date. I was just going to lay back and enjoy life and whatever was to happen would happen naturally. This was my new attitude.

That attitude only lasted three days. That was when I saw her. And when I saw her, I knew I had to have her. She was 5'4", and lightly complected. She had long hair, a nice figure, and the most luscious lips that I had ever seen. I didn't know who she was, but I was determined to find out. I was afraid that if I didn't say anything to her, I may never have seen her again, so I walked over to her and started a conversation. To my disappointment, she told me that she had a boyfriend. I asked for her phone number anyway. She said no, and that it was nice meeting me.

The funny thing about this girl is that before seeing her then, I had never seen her before, but afterward, it seemed like I saw her every other day. Her name was Asia, and every time I saw her, I had to try again. I would always smile and say hello. She would do the same. Though she had a boyfriend, and we never said anything significant to each other, for some reason, I just felt that she might be the one. I had promised myself, however, that I wasn't going to set myself up for heartache. Talking to a girl with a boyfriend would have basically done just that. So I tried to talk myself out of trying to pursue Asia. But Asia had an air about her. It was in the way she carried herself. She just captivated me. So I said 'whatever' to all my preset rules and went after her.

I started by advancing our conversations from the usual 'hello' to a little more chit chat. I would start a little conversation with her every time I saw her. Eventually I asked her for her number again. This time she gave it to me. I wasn't too surprised because she seemed to like me. I started calling her, and we began talking and spending time together, but it was in a buddy type of way. It was not the way I wanted, but I wanted her to feel comfortable around me before I made any big moves.

The semester had been flying by, and it was almost over, so I finally told her how I felt. It didn't go as well as I had expected. I got dissed. She told me that she liked me, but she loved her boyfriend and wasn't going to do anything to hurt him. I probably should have left well enough alone, but her boyfriend wasn't even in town. He was back in her home-town of Nashville, Tennessee. I just figured that maybe since he wasn't in town, I might have had a chance to move in on him. It was just going to take a little longer than expected.

Asia and I remained friends for the rest of the semester. Every day, I just hoped that she would tell me that they had broken up, but when the semester ended, she was still with him. This was disappointing, but I had managed to have a good semester anyway.

I didn't make the Dean's List, but I came awfully close. I was happy that I had done well in school, but as I reflected on the school year, I got upset with myself for going after a girl with a boyfriend. Sometimes I guess I was just too much of a romantic. That is, I expected things to be the way they were in the movies, where a guy sees a girl, falls in love at first sight, pursues the girl, and gets the girl. Things just didn't go that smoothly in the real world, and I was too good a guy to be going after somebody that didn't want me. Shit, the girl should be chasing me, and if she didn't want me, it was definitely her loss. Yes, and this was going to be my new attitude, and I was determined to make it last for more than three days this time. So I decided to stop pursuing Asia. I figured if we were meant to be then we would be.

Chapter Thirty-Seven

The holidays were here again and once again, I was at home with my family and friends. I did the usual holiday thing—that is, I kicked it with my boys and spent quality time with my family.

I didn't really kick it with Stevall much because he had a new girl-friend. Over time, he had lost touch with Kim's friend and met some girl named Anna. They had been talking for the last four months and seemed to be getting serious. He was always asking me about Kim's friend, though, wondering if I had ever seen her or anything. I would always tell him no because I never saw her.

Stevall would also ask about Shirl, Fred, Tim, and Corey. I told him that I hadn't seen Shirl all semester or during the summer. He seemed to find this hard to believe, but it was true. I hadn't seen her since last spring. I don't even know if she was in school because it seemed like I would have seen her at least once. I saw her punk ass man all the time though. I wouldn't say anything to him. I just ignored him. As for Corey and Fred, they were still the same. Corey was still playing the field, and Fred was still being Fred.

Stevall had never met Tim, but I used to always talk about him, so I guess that is why Stevall always asked about him. Tim was basically the same. At first, he seemed to be more serious about his schoolwork, but by mid-semester he was just as foolish as he had always been.

Christmas finally came, and what a glorious day it was. I got gifts for all of my loved ones and I got everything that I needed and wanted. I spent most of the day just visiting people and calling my friends from school. I called Fred, Corey, Tim, Shannon, and Asia. I talked to all of them except Asia. She wasn't at home, so I left a message with her father. I wasn't surprised that she wasn't home because I had called her several times before over the break, and she hadn't been home once. I had left my number three times, but she had never bothered to call back. I guess she was with her boyfriend. It wasn't like I was still trying to sweat her or anything like that. I was just wanting to talk to her and wish her happy holidays, but I sure as hell wasn't going to call her again.

That night, there was a big Christmas party downtown. The local radio station was throwing a Christmas bash, and Stevall, Anna, and I were going. I really didn't feel like a third wheel because Anna was cool as hell.

We arrived at the party at around eleven o'clock, and it was definitely bumping. I could tell that it was going to be a good night. I was looking sharp in my Christmas outfit, and there were fine women everywhere. I must have started dancing as soon as I walked in. Some pretty, young tenderoni was eyeing me down, so I asked her to dance. We must have danced for over an hour. We were straight up getting our groove on. She kept turning around and throwing her ass on me, and I was all up on it. Straight up grooving. When we got through dancing, I walked around looking for Stevall and Anna. It didn't take me long to find them. They were standing in line, waiting to take a picture.

"Stevall," I called to him. "Stevall!"

"Yeah, what up?" he said, and turned around. He had his arm around Anna, and he was straight up cheesing.

"You finally through dancing?" Anna asked me.

"Yeah, for now," I said. "Old girl couldn't hang."

"Oh, she couldn't hang?" Anna said, smiling.

I was about to say something else when somebody tapped me on my back. I turned around to see who it was. It was Shirl. She didn't say anything at first, and neither did I. I was so surprised. I guess I was nervous because my legs began to shake. She must have been nervous because she must have stood there playing with her hands for about fifteen seconds before she ever said anything. When she finally did speak, she asked a question so stupid that I felt like cursing her out. She asked me what was up.

"What's up?" I said, looking at her as if she was crazy.

"Yeah, how have you been doing?" she asked, still playing with her hands.

"I haven't talked to you in damn near ten months. Better yet, you haven't called me or said shit to me in ten months, and your ass has the nerve to ask me what's up? To hell with you," I said, and turned around and started walking away. Then she grabbed my arm.

"Horne, wait! I'm sorry, Horne. Please don't do this. I'm so sorry."

"You're damn right, you're sorry. Your ass is sorry and good for nothing. Now get your hands off me!"

"Horne, just listen to me!"

"I don't want to hear shit you got to say."

"Well, you're going to hear it if I have to chase your ass all around this party."

"Shirl, go to hell!"

"Horne, you can curse me all you want. I deserve it, but you are going to hear me out. I'm sorry, okay. I haven't said anything to you because I was so ashamed. I couldn't believe I had done what I had done, especially to you."

"Well, you did, and it's over. Just stay away from me and stay out of my life."

"I'm not going to stay away from you, and I want to be a part of your life."

I looked at her again, as if she had lost her damn mind. I turned around and started walking. She grabbed me again.

"I told you not to touch me. You must want me to slap your ass like Eric did. You did seem to like it."

"Forget Eric. He was an ass, I know."

"Oh, so that is it. You and him must be broke up now, so you want to come running back to good old stupid ass gullible Horne. Is that it?"

"I'm not trying to run back to you. I know I did you wrong and I just want you to forgive me. I love you, Horne. You are the best friend I ever had, and I want you back in my life as my friend."

"You what? You're actually dumb enough to think we can be friends again?"

"We are going to be friends again. I know we are."

"Not in this lifetime. Bye, and don't touch me again," I said, and turned around and walked off.

"Walk away, Horne," she shouted. "It doesn't matter. We will be friends again! You'll see!"

That girl had completely lost her mind. She hadn't talked to me in ten months, and now on Christmas day, she wanted to try and apologize. She had completely lost her mind, and once again, she had ruined my night. Stevall and Anna had witnessed the whole thing and they were really cool about it. They knew that she had upset me, so they were okay with my decision to leave the party early. We left the party and went to the Waffle House. There, we sat around and tripped. Tripping with Stevall and Anna really took my mind off the incident with Shirl.

Chapter Thirty-Eight

The next day, I woke up around eight o'clock in the morning. It wasn't by choice, though. It was because some fool was calling our house and the phone had rung about twenty times. I guess everybody in my house was asleep, and it didn't seem like the phone was ever going to stop ringing, so I got up and answered it.

"Hello," I said in my deep, just waking up voice.

"May I speak to Horne?" the person asked.

"This is he."

"Hey, Horne, how are you doing?"

"Fine," I said, wondering who in the hell it was. It was some girl, but I didn't recognize her voice.

"You know who this is?" she asked.

"No, who is this?"

"Asia."

"Hey, Asia, what's up?"

"Nothing. I just wanted to call you to see how your Christmas was."

"It was straight," I said. "I called you yesterday, but you weren't home."

"I'm sorry. I was gone all day."

"Actually, I've called you several times. Do you ever get the messages?"

"Yeah, but things have been so crazy around here, I honestly haven't had the time."

"Things have been crazy?" I asked.

"Yeah, me and my boyfriend broke up."

When I heard her say that, a big smile appeared on my face. "Oh really," I said, trying to sound sensitive. "Sorry to hear that. Are you okay?"

"Yeah, I guess."

"When did y'all break up?"

"Two days ago."

"On Christmas Eve?"

"Yeah," she said. "Hold on a minute." I heard her scream 'what' and mumble something. Then she came back to the phone. "Horne, I'm going to have to call you back. My dad needs to use the phone."

"All right," I said.

"I miss you, Horne, and even though I haven't called you before now, I think about you every day."

"I miss you too, Asia."

"Well, I'll talk to you later, then," she said. "Bye."

"Bye," I said, and hung up the phone and went back to bed. I must have been one of the happiest guys in the world at that moment. She had broken up with her boyfriend and called me early as hell. I must have been on her mind all night or something. I still wasn't going to get my hopes up, though, because you can never tell about these girls that just broke up with their boyfriends. They are usually quick to go back. I was just going to expect nothing and let things happen the way they would happen.

I got up at around eleven o'clock. I spent the majority of the day hanging out with my dad. He had taken off work, so we basically just kicked it. It was very warm for a winter day. It was about fifty-five degrees outside, so we went to the neighborhood park and shot ball and jogged. After that, we went back home and watched some western movie on television. While we were watching the movie, my little sister came in and told me I had a phone call. I asked her who it was and she said some girl. I figured it was Asia calling me back, so I got up and rushed to the phone.

"Hello," I said, sounding all happy.

"Hey, Horne." It was Shirl.

My tone and attitude suddenly changed. "What do you want?"

"I just want to talk to you."

"We talked last night, and that was enough," I said.

"No, it wasn't enough, Horne. We need to get together and talk this out so we can be friends."

"Shirl, your ass should have been woman enough to get together with me that night or at least sometime in the next ten months so we could have talked, but now, I don't want to talk about shit."

"Horne, I'm really trying."

"And?" I said. "You should have tried not to lie in the first damn place."

"Just hear me out. You don't know what I've been going through. I wasn't even in school last semester. My ass damn near had a nervous breakdown. I sat out all last semester seeing a psychiatrist," she said, and started crying on the phone.

I really hated hearing her cry. Even though I was mad as hell at her, I couldn't help but feel a little something for her. I'm not sure what it was I was feeling. I knew it wasn't sympathy because she deserved whatever she got for that shit she pulled, but I felt something.

"Stop crying, Shirl," I said.

"You hate me. I don't blame you. I hate myself," she said, still crying.

"Don't say that, Shirl."

"You going to be my friend again?"

"I don't know."

"See, you do hate me," she said, and really started crying. She was straight up hollering.

"Okay, Shirl, please calm down. We can get together and talk, but I'm not guaranteeing you anything."

"When?" she asked. "When can we get together?"

"You calm down, and I'll call you back in a couple of hours and we'll talk. Okay?"

She said okay and then we hung up. I didn't know why I had told her
that I was going to get together with her. Well, I could always tell her I
changed my mind. I got up and started heading back to the TV to finish watching the movie with my dad when the phone rang. I turned
around and answered it.

"Hello."

"May I speak to Horne, please?"

"This is he."

"Hey, Horne, what are you doing?"

It was Asia. This time I recognized her voice. I was happy that she had
called back. I was also relieved that it wasn't Shirl because I sort of
thought it was her calling right back.

"Nothing," I said. "What are you doing?"

"Sitting here, thinking about you."

"Really? What are you thinking?"

"Just some stuff," she said.

"What stuff? Tell me."

"Just some stuff about you, Horne."

"Like what? Don't try to be shy now."

"Well, how I wish me and you had got together earlier this semester."

"Oh, really?" I said.

"Yes, really, and I hope that we can get together when we get back
to school."

"That's what you say now. You'll be back with your boyfriend by then."

"No, I won't."

"Yeah, you probably will. Y'all only been broke up for two days."

"I guarantee that I won't be back with him, and I promise you that I
want us to be together," she said.

"Oh, really?" I said.

"Yes, really," she said.

"Well, Asia, one thing I have learned is that when it comes to life, love, and relationships, there are no guarantees. None.

But now, let's talk about you and me…"

About the Author

S. Easley lives in Memphis, Tennessee with his wife. He was born and raised in Chattanooga, Tennessee and moved to Memphis to attend The University Of Memphis. He graduated from the university with a manufacturing engineering technology degree and an MBA. He is a member of Alpha Phi Alpha Fraternity, Inc.

Notes

This is a work of fiction. Any references to actual events, real people, living or dead, or to real locales are intended only to give the novel a sense of authencity and reality. Other names, characters, places, and incidents are either the product of the author's imagination or are used fictitiously and their resemblance, if any, to real-life counter parts, is entirely coincidental.